Praise for
Shelly Fredman's
Brandy Alexander Mysteries

Fredman expands Brandy's collection of entertaining, exotic and eccentric friends in this installment of the Brandy Alexander series, even as she ratchets up the action...*No such Things As A Good Blind Date* is a rip-roaring good time.

--Midwest Book Review

Brandy Alexander could hold her own as the third member of an urban Northeast detecting triangle, anchored by Janet Evanovich's Stephanie Plum and Sarah Stromeyer's Bubbles Yablonski... Fans of those sleuths will find a new set of books to read with this series.

--Rambles.NET

Author Shelly Fredman continues her Brandy Alexander series with a topnotch sophomore effort. Fast paced fun, in-your-face Philly attitude and mayhem ensue.

--Mid Columbia Library System

An excellent fast-paced entertaining book you'll find a challenge to stop reading until the last page is finished.

--Skye Lindborg - *Mystery Lovers Corner*

Other books in the
Brandy Alexander Mystery Series

No Such Thing as a Secret
No Such Thing as a Good Blind Date

No Such Thing As A Free Lunch

A Brandy Alexander Mystery

Shelly Fredman

AK

Aquinas & Krone Publishing, LLC

First published by Aquinas & Krone Publishing, LLC 5/27/2008

ISBN: 0-9800448-1-2

Printed in the United States of America

This book is printed on acid-free paper.

Cover design by Louis Castelli, Ph. D. with Tim Litostansky.

Part of the proceeds from this book will be donated to charity.

Acknowledgments

I would like to thank the following people for their infinite patience, creative input, technical help and emotional support: Dudley Fetzer, Corey Fetzer, Franny Fredman, Kris Zuercher, Judith Kristen, Andrew West, Bruce Gram, Bill Fordes, Renee Greidinger, Jerry Fest, Julie Dolcemaschio, Nancy Kenyon, Marty Schatz, Susan Jaye, Cherise Everhard, Christina Grecco, Sharon Ayers, Jan Felton, Gail England, Dawn Freeman and Debbie Schwartz. Special thanks to Aquinas & Krone Publishing and to the creative genius of Dr. Louis Castelli for his brilliant cover design. And to Johnny Depp and Ringo Starr… just because.

For Kris Zuercher

Prologue

Whoever said, "The truth will set you free" obviously has never met my mother.

My first instincts were to lie. Lie, lie, lie. As soon as my mom told me that she and my dad were coming in from Florida, where they now reside, to South Philadelphia, to see my thirty-year-old, Italian-Jewish, born-and-bred-Roman-Catholic brother get "Bar Mitzvah," and they'd "naturally" be staying with me, I should have told them that the house had, unfortunately, burned down. Or was being fumigated for rats. Or that I have a psychotic roommate who hears voices and talks to his hands (which is actually true, but kind of endearing.)

The one thing I definitely should *not* have done is tell them the truth—that being, I love my parents dearly, but they drive me up a wall. (Okay, to be fair, it's just my mom, but they're sort of a package deal.) Then when you add the fact that said house used to be the family home, until I moved back from Los Angeles and they sold it to me at "well below market value," well, you can see where they might take a weensy bit of offense.

Okay, so I was wrong. I should have bit the bullet and told them how great it would be to have us all under one

1

roof again. After all, it was only for a few weeks. How bad could it be? And then I remembered, how, when I was eighteen, my mom cancelled my subscription to Vanity Fair, because she thought the ads were "too risqué," and my stomach did the "Acid Reflux Rumba" and before I knew it, I was telling them I thought they'd be much more comfortable at Paulie's.

"Your brother lives in a 'one bedroom', over a garage."

"Yeah. It's so convenient. You could get the rental car tuned up for the ride back to Florida."

"Don't be ridiculous, Brandy. Paul has enough to worry about, what with his becoming a man." *Unhhh!* She made it sound like he was undergoing a sex-change operation. "And you have plenty of room at the house," she continued, oblivious to the knot that was forming in my stomach. "Is that Ventura boy still staying with you?" Toodie Ventura is thirty. Two years older than I am, but to my mother, we are eternally twelve.

"No," I sighed. Toodie had recently moved back to his Granny's house, at her request. Seems she missed his shadow puppet shows.

"Good. It's settled then. Oh, and don't forget we're having people over on Sunday, after church. It'll be good to see Father Vincenzio again."

Father Vincenzio is a senile, old goat. If I *never* saw him again it would be too soon.

"Sounds like a blast."

She couldn't decide if I was being sarcastic or not so I decided not to press my luck.

"I'll see you on Thursday, Mom. Give Daddy a kiss for me."

I guess if I were being totally honest, I'd have to admit that a part of me was relieved to have the company. About a month ago, I'd been involved in a series of pretty scary events, which left me with a two-inch scar on my side, courtesy of a gunshot wound. Since then, I've been afraid to go to sleep, spend time alone, be in a crowd or pass a mime on the street. (But that has nothing to do with my "ordeal." Mimes are annoying.) My friend, Franny DiAngelo told me she thought I should "talk to a professional" about everything I'd been through, lately. I told her I was fine—if night sweats and facial tics constitute a healthy psyche.

The thing is I'm not all that good at expressing my feelings. I believe it's best to keep them bottled up until they can't breathe and die a natural death. Besides, if I dwelled on every Tom, Dick or Harry who's tried to kill me, I'd never get anything done, and as it was I was late for work.

I am an investigative reporter for a local cable TV news station. Okay, so maybe the title is a slight exaggeration. Technically, I'm their puff piece reporter (a lateral move from my job in L.A.) but it's just a matter of time before they see my full worth and promote me to hard news.

It's only my third week there, and I've already made some inroads. The station manager knows my name now—but that's only because I keep parking in her spot—or did until she had the car booted. The important thing is I'm getting to know people in high places—which is good, because all my co-workers seem to hate me.

It's not my fault the last person to hold the job was fired. Her name was Wendy and she was beloved for her sunny disposition and home baked sticky buns.

Unfortunately, Wendy became enamored with her own culinary skills, gained about seventy-five pounds and was no longer able to perform the sometimes-rigorous physical requirements of the job. A lawsuit is pending, but the show must go on, so they hired me to take her place. It would not have been my first choice, but I had mortgage payments and home-improvement bills to pay. Plus, I like to eat. (But apparently, not as much as Wendy.)

Chapter One

I knew it was going to be a crappy day the minute I crossed Ridge Avenue at five-thirty a.m. and nearly got mowed down by some idiot running a red light. I'd just dashed across the street from work to the Seven-Eleven to buy some baked goodies for my co-workers. I figured I could win them over if I could just make them forget about those damn sticky buns.

I walked into the store and perused the bakery case. There were some cinnamon rolls in there that looked about a month old. I tried one just to be sure and thought I felt a tooth crack. "Do you have any fresh ones?" I asked, ever hopeful.

The guy behind the counter gave me a sour look. "Those *are* fresh."

I looked around some more. Everything was pre-packaged and I didn't have time to rewrap them to make them appear homemade. It was a little discouraging. In the end I bought a Hershey bar and fifteen corn dogs. I just couldn't go back to work empty handed.

The light changed and I stepped off the curb. In the next instant, a dark green sedan careened past me, nearly taking out the traffic light. The bag of corn dogs flew out of my hand as I dove back to the curb. "You suck," I yelled to no one in particular, as the car was already long gone.

Only a handful of the corndogs had actually fallen out, and they didn't look too damaged. I glanced around and when I didn't see anyone from the office lurking about, I picked them up and stuffed them back into the bag. I even mixed them up a little so that everyone would have a fair chance of getting one that hadn't been scraped off the sidewalk.

I'd ripped a huge hole in my brand new slacks and my knee was dripping blood. The elbow of the new winter coat I'd bought on sale at Urban Outfitters was laced with street grime from my fall. That's what happens when I try and look nice. I should've worn my dad's old pea coat like I usually do, but Franny had talked me into a new wardrobe.

"New job, new attitude," she'd said. She'd also told me to cut down on the chocolate. Said I was hyper enough without the sugar rush. I opened the Hershey bar and ate it on the way back to the studio.

I was headed for the bathroom to clean myself up when I heard footsteps behind me.

"There you are. I've been looking all over for you."

Wow. Someone around here is finally speaking to me. I turned around, flashing a big, friendly grin. It was Craig, one of the reporters' assistants. "Well, you found me. What can I do for you?"

Craig looked confused. "Oh, sorry, Randi, I thought you were Tamra. You look a lot like her from the back."

Oh, great. He only spoke to me on accident, plus he got my name wrong. That settles it. No corn dog for Craig.

I sighed. "If I see her I'll tell her you're looking for her."

"Thanks." He started to walk away and then turned back to me. "Uh, you've got a glob of chocolate stuck to the corner of your mouth."

"I do?" He nodded and smiled shyly as I swiped at the smudge.

"Did I get it?"

"Yep. Well, catch you later, Randi."

Oh boy, my first friend! "Hey Craig, you want a corn dog?"

Encouraged by my encounter with Craig, I walked into the newsroom and scoped out my co-workers. Lynne Schaffer, line producer and well-known bitch was leaning against her desk, deep in conversation with the station's political pundit, Art Metropolis. Art is a right wing bigot with the personality of a sewer rat and the IQ of a ball of lint—and hopefully, my next best friend.

They glanced up when I approached, making a big point of looking interrupted.

"Hi, guys," I said, giving it my perkiest shot. "Would you like a corn dog? They're fresh from the oven."

Art's eyes lit up like I'd just offered him a sip from the Holy Grail. He reached for the bag but was stopped cold by a withered glance from Lynne. "How thoughtful," she sneered. "Breaded nitrates on a stick. What are you trying to do, kill us?"

Actually, Lynne, the thought hadn't occurred to me—until now.

Art grunted, disappointment oozing from his pores. He lumbered past me, but when Lynne turned back to her work he pressed his thick chapped lips against my ear. "Save me one for later."

By the end of the morning, I still had thirteen corn dogs left. I'd eaten two on my coffee break, along with another Hershey bar. Making friends is really stressful.

In the afternoon, my boss, Eric, came by my desk with an idea about Honey Farms. Eric is twenty-six and was hired to capture the "youth market." Eric thought it would make a hilarious visual to see me dressed up in one of those caged, veiled helmets, with hundreds of bees swarming all over my body.

"That's swell, Eric. And then we can do a piece on anaphylactic shock. I'm allergic to bee stings."

"That's what Benydril is for, Alexander. Don't be such a wuss."

I couldn't protest too vehemently, since I'd made up that stuff about being allergic.

"Eric," I said, instead, "I was thinking. Homelessness is up twenty percent this winter. I could get some good interviews with some of the people living out on the street."

He cut me off with an exaggerated sigh. "And where are the laughs in that? I hate to break it to you sweetheart, but you're not Katie Couric. People tune in to your segments to be entertained, not enlightened."

"Couldn't I do both?" I asked. "I'm multi-talented."

There was a sympathetic groan from the next desk over, as Tamra Rhineholt labored at her computer. She waited for Eric to wander back down the hall and then she swiveled her chair in my direction. "Don't be discouraged by the Erics of the world, Brandy. You're smart and you genuinely want to make a difference. You're not going to be stuck covering honey farms and Junior Miss Beauty Pageants forever."

"Hey, that was a step up from the wet-noodle wrestling I covered the day before."

Tamra laughed. "You should hear some of the stories they foisted on me, when I first started out. Just hang in there."

Despite a ten-year age difference, I could see why Craig had mistaken me for Tamra.

We're both slight of stature—I measure five-feet-two inches (*if* I adhere to my mother's admonitions not to slouch), with shoulder length brown hair and identical winter coats—although I doubt Tamra had to wait for the 70% off sale.

Tamra has been at WINN for about a year, as a hard news investigator, having worked previously at a cable news station in Des Moines. She's married to Jeff Rhineholt, a Biology professor at U of P. They have no children. I found all of this out online, while reading the publicity department's bios for the on-air talent. Mine says I'm a "fun-lovin' Philly native with an extensive stuffed animal collection." I could seriously kill someone.

Talking to Tamra made me feel better. I admired her work, especially her story on toxic dumping along the Schuylkill River. She'd made a few enemies on that one, but she didn't back down. I guess that's another thing we have in common. My whole life, everyone from my parents to my high school principal has told me I go looking for trouble. Only I don't think they meant it as a compliment.

"How about we knock off for lunch," Tamra said an hour later. "My treat. I've got a story that's about to break and I feel like celebrating."

The Walnut Street Inn is an old-world, luxury hotel, located about half a block from work. We'd walked over and were now seated at a window table in a cream-colored room with dark paneling and polished wood floors. Tamra picked up the wine list and ordered half a carafe. It cost more than I spend on groceries for the week.

"Tamra," I gulped, "when you said you wanted to go out to eat, I thought you meant McDonald's. I can't let you pay for me." Actually, my conscience told me I couldn't let her pay, but my pocketbook was screaming, "Oh boy, free lunch!" I'd spent my last dime on the corn dogs and I was nearly max-ed out on credit, so I hoped she'd argue the point. She did.

"Look, I wanted your company. I could use some intelligent conversation after spending half the morning listening to that blow-hard Metropolis."

"One lousy meal and you think you're entitled to intelligent conversation? What kind of girl do you think I am?"

Tamra smiled. "A smart one. Brave, too, from what I've read about you in the papers. That was some stunt you pulled off last month."

Tamra was referring to a little situation I'd gotten myself into, involving a crooked lawyer, a psycho-meth freak and the fate of the free world.

"Dumb luck," I said, making a mental note to learn how to accept a compliment. I pulled some fresh sour dough out of the breadbasket and took a bite.

Tamra ordered the "special"—grilled swordfish with a lemon-butter sauce, baked potato and asparagus. She insisted I get a big lunch too—"and save room for dessert, they have homemade cherry pie." She didn't have to tell me twice.

In the middle of lunch, Tamra's cell phone rang. She looked at the caller ID and tensed. Instead of answering, she slipped it into her bag and continued eating, although her whole demeanor had changed. "Are you married, Brandy?" she asked, suddenly.

I was surprised by the question. "No. I guess I never felt ready for that kind of commitment." Just a small white lie. In actuality, I'd practically been left at the altar.

"Smart girl," Tamra said. "If I had it to do over—" She let the thought hang in the air and went back to her asparagus.

Wow. I wonder what that was all about. I didn't have time to dwell on her remark, because at that moment Yankees' shortstop, (and my vote for "freebie" if I'm ever in a serious relationship with someone, but we each get to pick one famous person to fulfill our deepest fantasies, should the occasion ever arise), Derek Jeter, walked past our table and winked at me. Without thinking I winked back, only to discover he'd squirted lemon juice in his eye and was actually in a good deal of pain. *Damn, now he thinks I'm making fun of him and he'll never agree to sleep with me.* Reluctantly, I turned my attention back to Tamra, but she didn't seem inclined to elaborate on her comment.

Before the waiter brought dessert, I excused myself to go to the bathroom. When I returned, there was a guy standing by our table. He looked to be in his early forties, with sandy brown hair and wire-rimmed glasses. He was wearing a sport's coat and khaki pants. As I approached the table I heard Tamra's voice, shrill with anger. "You're making a spectacle of yourself, Jeff. I'll talk to you when I get home."

"I'm not leaving until you tell me the truth."

I did an about-face and began walking toward the rest room when Tamra called me back to the table.

"Here's my *date*, Jeff."

Well, this is awkward. "Nice to meet you," I said, extending my hand. "I'm Brandy Alexander. I work with Tamra."

Jeff loomed over Tamra, ignoring my outstretched hand. "You're lying to me, Tamra. You've been lying for months."

Tamra stood up, pushing her chair back with surprising force. She threw her napkin on the table, the words spewing from her mouth like acid rain.

"I will not stand here and have this conversation with you. I'm leaving!"

She grabbed her coat and made a furious exit, stranding me with her husband. Jeff reached into his coat pocket and for a brief, hopeful moment I thought he was going to pull out his credit card and say, "Sorry for the interruption, Brandy, lunch is on me." He didn't.

The waiter came by with the bill. Oh my God, it was over a hundred dollars. That woman sure could pack it away. I wondered what the chances were of making it out the door before Jeff did—you know—last one out is a rotten egg and has to pay the check.

While I was pondering this, he left.

I didn't get back to work for another hour and a half. That's how long it took for Paul to get to the restaurant and pay the bill. I passed the time by helping the staff set up the tables for the dinner crowd.

I didn't see Tamra again until late afternoon. She walked into the bathroom when I was heading out. She looked upset, her eyes wet and smeared with mascara.

"Are you all right?"

"Yeah, sure, fine," she said. She went into one of the stalls and closed the door.

I felt bad leaving her when she was obviously upset, but I didn't want to intrude, so I walked out of the bathroom, only to return a minute later to retrieve my coat from the lounge. Tamra was still inside the stall and she was crying.

"Can we please talk about this later?" I heard her say. There was a pause, then, "Richard, I'm at work for God's sake."

Richard? Who the hell is Richard?

I heard the door unlatch so I grabbed my coat and tiptoed out of the lounge.

By the time we finished shooting promos for the station, it was after seven p.m. and pitch dark outside. I ran to my car, looking over my shoulder every step of the way, convincing myself it was just a necessary precaution in this day and age, rather than the paranoid antics of a woman in dire need of therapy.

I drive a 1972 metallic-blue, classic Mercedes sports car. Technically, it's on loan from my brother, but I remind him that possession is nine-tenths! of the law. The funny thing is Paul would hand over the pink slip in a second if I really wanted him to. He's the sweetest guy ever.

I reached the car and fumbled for my keys, cursing the enormous satchel I cart around with me. (I figure you never know when you're going to need a band-aid or a screwdriver or a can of creamed corn.) As I rooted through my bag, a shadow passed in the dim light of the parking lot and I froze. Beads of sweat popped out on my forehead as I willed myself to stay calm. The shadow moved closer, and instinctively, I spun around, swinging my pocketbook for all its worth. It met with something hard, and a hand reached out to grab me. "Help!" I screamed, panic overtaking me.

"Jesus, Brandy, what'd you do that for?"

I looked up to see a six-foot-one, Irish-Italian God in a leather motorcycle jacket and jeans, holding the side of his head where I'd clipped him with the creamed corn. Oh great. I'd just decked Robert Anthony DiCarlo, Philadelphia homicide detective and former love of my life. My panic receded, replaced by a wave of pleasure in the pit of my stomach and a touch of remorse over his injury. I decided to go on the offense.

"What's the big idea sneaking up on me like that, Bobby?"

"Ya think you might've overreacted just a little?" he asked, rubbing his temple.

"A girl can't be too careful. Hey, what are you doing here? I thought you were in Disney World."

About a month ago, Bobby's wife, Marie, went off the deep end and was deported back to her homeland of Guatemala, leaving him with full custody of their two-year-old daughter, Sophia. Marie's exit was no big loss; he was never all that attached to her in the first place, (apparently her homicidal tendencies were a bit of a turn-off) but he would do anything in the world for his little girl. After Marie was sent packing, Bobby took a leave of absence from work so that he could concentrate on helping Sophia cope with the loss of her mother. I guess he thought a couple of weeks in Florida, in the company of a big rodent and a little mermaid would help take her mind off things—and if all else failed, there were always the 'gator farms.

"Got back yesterday afternoon." Bobby looked me up and down, his gaze resting on my torn pant leg and battered coat. He leaned over me, grinning as he swept my bangs out of my eyes. "Have you been getting into fights with the other kids at work? How many times do I gotta tell you to play nice?"

I gave his hand a half-hearted slap. "Very funny. And don't change the subject. Why are you lurking around in the parking lot of my place of employment? Oh no," I said, suddenly panicked. "Nobody's hurt, are they?" My ability to leap to the worst possible conclusion is world class.

"No. Everything's fine. I was on my way home and I saw Paul's car in the lot. Sophia's staying with Eddie's mom tonight, so I thought I'd see what you were up to." Eddie is Bobby's friend and my best friend, Franny's new husband. He is an extraordinarily nice guy with a really big mouth.

"Okay, I see what's going on here. Franny told Eddie I'm afraid to be alone and Eddie told you. And now you think you have to baby-sit me. Well, I've got a newsflash, DiCarlo. I'm fine!"

Bobby puffed out his cheeks, expelling a breath of air. "You really need to get more sleep. You're cranky."

Unhhh! It's not like the idea of spending time alone with Bobby didn't appeal to me. The truth was it appealed to me way too much. Bobby and I had a ten-year history together. It's been four years since we'd broken up, but the physical and emotional ties run deep. They'd been buried by a lot of anger on my part, but we'd made peace

15

with that, and now with Marie out of the picture, it would be so easy to fall back into old patterns. I'd told him I thought we needed time to be friends again, without the complications of sex. Sensibly, Bobby had agreed with me. Only the predatory look in his eye begged to differ.

I heard voices in the parking lot and noticed Tamra a few lanes over, walking toward her car. She was being escorted by Nelson, one of the night security guards. I called out to her and she waved, but she seemed distracted and tense. She looked about as happy to be going home to Jeff as I was, going home to an empty house.

"Well?" Bobby said. You want company or not?"

"Not," I lied.

"Suit yourself." He pulled open the driver's side door and watched me slide into the seat. "You're really missing out," he said, the grin on his face telling me he knew I wanted him bad.

"Get over yourself, hotshot." I threw the car in reverse and peeled out of there before I had a chance to change my mind.

Traffic was backed up on Broad Street. I turned on the radio and caught the tail end of the news. A murder in the Bella Vista district, a robbery at gun point at an ATM on Rising Sun Avenue. City Hall is bracing for a protest next month over the scheduled execution of some guy convicted of murdering a co-ed, gas prices are up and the Flyers won in overtime.

At the next red light I dug in my bag, pulled out my phone and punched speed dial for my friend Johnny Marchiano. John is in-between boyfriends, so I was hoping he'd be free for dinner and a movie at my house.

"Yo, Sunshine, what's up?"

I ran the plan by him, enticing him with promises of take-out from Woo Chin's.

"Sorry, dollface. I've got plans for tonight."

"What kind of plans?"

John hesitated a beat. "A party."

"Can I come?"

"No."

"Oh, *fine*."

Next, I called Franny, who, according to Eddie, was in the middle of a major hormonal meltdown and was refusing to come out of the bathroom. Franny is pregnant and her mood swings are legendary. I then called Janine, Fran's twin sister and alter ego.

"Chinese gives me a rash."

"Since when?"

"I've got a headache."

"God, Janine, if you don't want to come over, just say so."

"I'm washing my hair."

My uncle Frankie didn't get off from work until nine. He's the hunky manager of the South Street Boxing Gym and the reason half the female population in town has signed up for private boxing lessons. His girlfriend, Carla, who manages a beauty shop, was busy too; she was giving herself a bikini wax.

As I pulled up in front of my house, I thought about asking my geriatric next door neighbor, Mrs. Gentile, in for a couple of brewskis, but she keeps calling Animal Control on me because my dog pees on her azalea bush, and anyway she's not all that much fun.

My neighborhood is made up of predominantly working-class Italian families with some Irish and a few other ethnic groups thrown in for good measure. My

17

house is at the end of a row of small, attached homes, which made it handy for me when I was a teenager, to sneak out my bedroom window and climb down the trellis to meet Bobby.

I could hear my dog, Adrian, barking on the other side of the door. Adrian is a twenty-pound fur ball with a water fountain tail and an appetite for basically anything that's not nailed down. I recently bought a new couch, which started out with four legs and now has three and a half. Ah, the joys of motherhood.

John had come by earlier in the afternoon to walk and feed Adrian, but it's still a long day for the little guy. He pounced on me the second I opened the door. In his mouth was a half-chewed oven mitt. The other half was under the dining room table. "Looks like you've already had your dinner," I told him.

Adrian padded after me as I turned on all the lights and put the television on for comfort. I have a theory that nothing awful can happen when one is watching Nick at Nite. The Cosby Show was on. Rudy watched a scary movie and now she's afraid of the dark. Welcome to my world, kid.

I was trying to decide between mac n cheese and a grilled hotdog for dinner, when the phone rang. I ran to the kitchen to answer it, but the caller had already hung up. A sick feeling surged in the pit of my stomach. The last time that happened, someone left a severed goat's head on my doorstep. Well, what are the odds of that happening again?

Two seconds later the doorbell rang. I fought the urge to throw up and inched over to the hallway. "Who is it?" I asked, standing on tiptoe to peer out the spyglass.

"Surprise!"

Relief and gratitude flooded through me as I yanked open the door. Standing on the top step was John, all five feet, three inches of him. Crowded in next to him were Franny, Janine and Carla. Carla held a casserole dish in her manicured hands. Her lacquered beehive shot straight up from her head, rivaling Marge Simpson's for world's tallest protein-based structure. Uncle Frankie stood on the next step down and lagging a few feet behind him was Bobby, carrying a couple of six- packs of Rolling Rock and a bottle of black cherry soda. Janine was toting a large shopping bag filled with brightly wrapped packages.

"What's all this?" I asked, stepping aside as everyone trooped in. Adrian began to bark and run around in delighted circles, while my gray and white kitten, Rocky, hid behind the china cabinet, licking the paste off the peeling wallpaper.

"Consider it a housewarming party," Franny announced.

"Oh, goody. What's the theme?" I was thinking I could really use a new can opener. The other one broke when I tried to open a quart of paint with it. Actually, it had done the trick, but now everything tastes like enamel.

"Home security," Bobby said, sitting down on the couch. He popped a beer and stuck his boot-clad feet up on the coffee table, settling in.

"Yeah," Carla added. "Since you won't admit you've been afraid to stay here alone, we decided to get you things to make you feel safer."

I rolled my eyes in a big show of denial, but it was really to keep from crying. These were the people who loved me and they showed me on a daily basis.

"Paul says he's sorry to miss the party, but he had to go see the rabbi tonight," Frankie said. "I think he's really

19

nervous about getting up in front of all those people." My brother has a little problem with stuttering. He's usually okay, but once he gets rolling, he sounds like an AK-47.

Carla wrestled the half-an-oven-mitt away from Adrian and headed for the kitchen with the casserole dish, while I set about trying to find enough forks and plates. John came up behind me, throwing a skinny arm around my shoulder. "You okay?" he asked quietly.

I looked around at my house filled with friends. "I am now."

The phone rang in the middle of dinner and I let the answering machine pick it up. There's not a whole lot that can separate me from a plate of my uncle's homemade lasagna.

After we ate, everyone settled on the couch to watch me open up my gifts. Janine bought me some pepper spray and Franny got me a stun gun that was shaped like a cell phone. Then Uncle Frankie started playing with it and almost zapped himself, so Carla made him put it away. Johnny got me a subscription to "Guns and Ammo," but judging by the male models on the cover, I think it was more of a present for him than for me.

"Mind if I borrow that when you're done?" he asked, confirming my suspicions.

Paul, Carla and Frankie chipped in for an alarm system for the house and Bobby arranged for some target practice over at the police station. "I'm not advocating that you get a gun," he said. "I know they freak you out, and frankly, I don't think it's a great idea for the general public to be armed. But I want you to know what to do, in case you're ever in a situation where you need to use one." I nodded, painfully aware that the situation had already come up more than once.

At around eleven p.m. everyone began shuffling toward the door. Bobby remained rooted to the couch, legs still stretched out on the coffee table, draining his beer. His smoky-blue eyes were closed, his head resting against the back cushions.

"You coming, DiCarlo?" There was a faint warning tone in my uncle's voice, and it made me smile inwardly. As a kid, Bobby DiCarlo was trouble. Orphaned at sixteen, with no outlet for his rage and sadness, he'd found his way to the South Street Gym, where Frankie took him under his wing. He taught him how to box, gave him focus. With all of his pent up anger, Bobby easily could have chosen the wrong side of the law. But Frankie's guidance helped keep him on track. He loved Bobby like a little brother—but he loved me more. My uncle knew our history and he wasn't sure I was emotionally ready for a repeat performance. And to be honest, neither was I.

Bobby opened his eyes, looking slightly amused. "Thought I'd help Brandy clean up." Getting off the couch, he gathered up the remaining bottles and glasses and took them to the kitchen.

"Yo, midget brat," my uncle said, looking down at me fondly, "try and get some rest tonight. You're gonna need your strength when your mother arrives." Oy.

Bobby was pressed up against the sink, washing some plates. He'd rolled up his sleeves, exposing strong forearms, the right one newly tattooed. I walked over and touched his arm lightly, turning it over to read the inscription inside a small red heart. *Sophia*.

"How's she doing?" I asked. Stupid question, considering she's two and just lost her mother a little over a month ago.

21

Bobby frowned and turned off the water. "She hasn't asked about Marie lately. I don't know if that's a good thing or a bad thing. I'm taking her to counseling. I think it's important for a person to deal with their problems," he added pointedly. "Don't you?"

"Couldn't agree more," I said, being purposely obtuse.

Bobby studied me, concern written all over his face. "Bran, Franny says you're—"

I cut him off. "Franny says she's going to divorce Eddie and run off to Tahiti with a Colin Farrel look-alike she met at the Acme the other day. You can't believe everything Fran says right now. It's the hormones talking."

He gave me an exaggerated eye roll. "Anyone ever tell you that you have a real stubborn streak?"

Yes. Constantly. "No. Never. You're the only one."

Bobby snorted, but he let it drop and we finished up the dishes in companionable silence.

"Thanks for helping out," I said a little while later as I walked him to the door.

"I'll call you about target practice," he said, shrugging into his jacket. He bent down and grazed my cheek with his lips. "Sleep tight."

I nodded, ignoring the rising skitter in my stomach as his skin brushed against mine. *Damn hormones!*

I closed and double-locked the door and then headed back into the kitchen to turn off the light, when I remembered the message on the answer machine. I walked over to the phone and hit play.

"Brandy, it's Tamra." Her voice was steady, but there was a quality I couldn't quite put my finger on. "I'm sorry about what happened at lunch today. I owe you one. Listen, I really need to talk to you. Call me in the morning." I hit play again, listening, this time, for what she *didn't* say. I recognized that quality in her voice now. I knew it only too well. It was fear.

Damn. I really didn't need something new to obsess over just before going to bed. I grabbed a pack of TastyKakes out of the cupboard and popped one in my mouth while I listened to the message again. Yep, fear. Well, she'd had that fight with her husband today. Maybe he'd threatened her somehow. Or—ooh—Nelson, the security guard was looking at her kinda weird. Maybe he came on to her and she needs me as a witness for the sexual harassment suit she planned to file. Okay, if it were really something bad, she wouldn't be calling me. I barely know the woman. The thought calmed me a little.

I took the rest of the pack of chocolate cupcakes upstairs with me and got ready for bed. Adrian followed me into the bathroom while I brushed and flossed my teeth. As I stood before the mirror, I did a quick appraisal of the face staring back at me. A month of nightmares had really taken its toll. If the circles under my eyes got any darker, I'd have to hire a special effects artist to cover them. No wonder my friends were worried about me.

Back in my bedroom, I turned on the overhead light and crawled into bed. Adrian climbed on top and began rooting around for TastyKake crumbs. Rocky crawled out from under the chair, dragging what looked like the ear off my Winnie the Pooh bear in her mouth. She leaped up onto the bed and snuggled in next to me. I closed my eyes and thought about Bobby. He looked good tonight. Hah. Who am I kidding? He always looks good. This wasn't helping.

My thoughts drifted back to Tamra. *I'm probably jumping to ridiculous conclusions, and everything is fine between her and her husband. So they'd had a little fight. I'm sure it's all forgotten by now. In the mean time, I'm laying here worried sick about her, with an earless Winnie the Pooh and a cat that eats wallpaper for company, while she's no doubt having wild, passionate make-up sex with Jeff. Boy, I'm really beginning to resent ol' Tamra.* I rolled over on my side and fell into a fitful sleep.

Chapter Two

I woke up at five a.m. feeling tired and anxious, which was a step up from my usual state of "exhausted and terror-stricken." I was scheduled to do some voiceover and I didn't have to be at the studio until late afternoon, so I forced myself to stay in bed, at least until the sun came up. I passed the time thinking of clever retorts I could have said to Lynne Schaffer over the corndog debacle. I'm always brilliant well after the fact.

At seven, I turned on the news and saw Tamra sitting behind the desk, exchanging some lighthearted bantering with Art Metropolis. She looked to be her perfectly poised self, which both relieved me and ticked me off. I'd spent a lot of good worrying time focused on her when I could have been obsessing about myself.

An hour later I climbed out of bed, determined to get a jump-start on cleaning up the house. My parents would be here in about a week, so by rights I should have started a month ago. My mother ascribes to the adage that cleanliness is next to Godliness, and she cleans as if God is moving in next door—which actually would be a nice change of pace from Mrs. Gentile. He's probably less judgmental. I figured it would be hard enough on my mom to accept that her beloved shag carpeting (a staple in the house since 1970) had been replaced with hardwood floors, without the added stress of seeing a month-old, dried out Christmas tree still prominently displayed in the living room. I would have gotten rid of it weeks ago, but Rocky likes to play in the branches. She doesn't understand about fire hazards.

I shoved the tree through the front door and dragged it down to the sidewalk, trailing petrified pine needles along the way. The trash had already been picked up, which meant it would be another week until the truck came around again. Mrs. Gentile would have a fit if I just left it there, which made the idea all the more appealing.

I was debating whether to hoist it onto my neighbor's porch and make a break for it, when Heather Koslowski from across the street stuck her head out the front door. She had hair rollers the size of orange juice cans clamped to her head, and she was wearing frosted lipstick. Either that or she was in the critical stages of rabies. Heather is three years older than I am and still lives at home with her parents. She works at City Hall in the Department of Records.

"Yo, Brandy."

"Yo, Heather."

Heather's dog, an asthmatic pug named Mr. Wiggles, followed her down the front steps on four squat legs. His bug eyes stared as he inched closer to the tree, which was propped up against my knee.

"Bran," Heather said, licking her frosted lips, "I saw your mechanic this morning. He is *really* cute! I was wondering if you could introduce me—that is if *you're* not interested in him."

My mechanic is a sixty-two year old ex-biker named Snake, with a face full of tattoos and no front teeth. But hey, there's no accounting for taste.

"No, sure—I guess so." Mr. Wiggles began rooting around at the base of the tree, making little grunting sounds. I turned slightly, angling the tree away from him. "So when did you see my mechanic?"

"Early this morning. I was out walking the dog and— oh! Mr. Wiggles. No! Bad dog!" Mr. Wiggles lifted one fat leg and squirted the side of the tree. Only he missed the tree.

"Brandy, I'm so sorry."

I looked down at my leg, which was now saturated by Mr. Wiggles. "I've gotta go, Heather." I handed her the tree. Just in case Mr. Wiggles wasn't finished yet.

I jumped into the shower and hosed myself down. Then I changed into fresh jeans and a sweatshirt and headed downstairs to make breakfast. Adrian was in the kitchen, gnawing a hole through the bag of cat crunchies he'd somehow managed to drag out from under the sink. Rocky sat close by, waiting for the fallout. I grabbed a bowl of Cheerios and was just about to sit down when the phone rang. It was Paul.

"B-Brandy," he said. "Ya-ya gotta h-help me."

My adrenalin shot up four notches. "Paulie, what's wrong?"

"It's M-Mom. She's d-d-driving m-me crazy."

"Oh." I stifled a laugh.

"It's n-not funny."

"I'm sorry, Paul. Okay, take a deep breath and tell me what happened."

Paul took a deep breath, only I'm not sure of what. When he got back on the line he was a lot calmer.

"I just got off the phone with her," Paul began. "She said when she comes in she's taking me shopping for a Bar Mitzvah suit. She's already spoken to Uncle Manny and he's got a good deal on woolens—whatever the hell that means. Uncle Manny is a pervert, by the way. I'm not letting him anywhere near my inseams." Uncle Manny is my mother's uncle. We used to avoid him like the plague when we were kids. "Brandy, I'm a grown man. I can pick out my own suit."

"Have you gone to get one yet?"

"No, I was planning on wearing the blue one." Paul has had the blue suit since his high school graduation. It's so shiny you can see yourself in it.

"Would it kill you to give the woman a little pleasure, Paulie? Let her pick you out a nice suit." I could feel another laugh coming on so I bit down hard on my lip.

"You're enjoying this way too much," he growled.

I had to admit that I was. Growing up, Paul was the "good child," while I—well, let's just say I kept a lot of people busy praying over my immortal soul.

"Look, Paul," I said, gazing down at my rapidly wilting Cheerios, "it's just Mom's way of letting you know she's accepted your decision to get Bar Mitzvahed. I think she'd always hoped you'd come back to the church. And anyway, once Mom gets here she'll be so busy running my life, she'll have forgotten all about your suit."

"You think so?" he asked hopefully.

I sighed. The sad fact was I could guarantee it.

I decided to go into work early. I was really hoping Tamra would ask me to lunch again. I am so broke. As I was leaving the house the phone rang. It was Megan, one of the P.A.'s. Turns out they were scrapping my segment, so they didn't need me to come in after all. Damn. I was really looking forward to showing our viewers "how to turn ordinary dryer lint into works of art for fun and profit."

I left the house at a little after 1:00 p.m. to meet John at "Lucinda's on South," one of a dozen up-scale art galleries that have sprung up on South Street in recent years. John is a portrait photographer, and his work is starting to garner a lot of favorable attention. He was having his first one-man show and he wanted me to check out the gallery space.

It was raining and the roads were slick with grease. I maneuvered my way through the narrow streets, pumping lightly on my brakes as I stopped for a light. They felt loose. I'd have to take them to Snake to get looked at, and while I was there I figured I'd do a little matchmaking for Heather.

I found John bent over a desk in the back room, matting some photographs. He glanced up when he saw me and quickly slipped one of the pictures under the pile.

"Hey, Sunshine."

"What'cha got there, John?" I gestured toward the pile of photos on the desk.

"Oh, those," John said. "Just some new stuff I'm still working on."

"Can I see?" I craned my neck over John's shoulder but he wedged himself between me and the pictures, striking a ridiculously casual pose.

"They're not ready for the general public."

"Since when am I the general public?" He was hiding something. Now I *had* to see them. I sized him up. John is an inch taller than me, but I outweigh him by about five pounds. I could take him. "Come on, John. Let me see."

"No. God, you're a pain."

I decided to go with a diversionary tactic. "Wow," I said, taking a sudden interest in his shoes. "Those are nice. Are they new?"

John slid his eyes downward. "Cole Hahn was having a sale. How do you like them?" In lieu of an answer, I quickly sidestepped him and grabbed the pile off the desk.

"Jesus, Brandy," he yelled, and there was genuine panic in his voice.

"I'm not going to hurt them. I just want to take a look." But I waited, in case there were naked pictures of him in there or something.

"Oh, alright." John heaved a resigned sigh. "But don't get all mad, okay?"

"Why would I get mad?" Carefully, I began perusing the photos. His subjects were shot in black and white, mostly with a zoom lens so that he could get up close without intruding on the moment. Caught unaware, there was no pretense in their faces, only raw, honest, sometimes painfully intimate emotion. I studied a picture of a homeless man, picking a half-eaten soft pretzel out of the trash. "John," I breathed. "These are beautiful." I turned to the next shot and suddenly I understood what he'd been trying to hide. It was a picture of me.

I've been a television personality for over four years. I'm used to seeing my smiling, public persona plastered all over morning T.V. But this was different. The face that stared up at me was so lost, so forlorn, so—so vulnerable I flushed with embarrassment.

30

"Brandy, I—"

"When did you take this?"

"Last month. It was the day after you got out of the hospital. Remember, you dressed up the dog and wanted me to take pictures of him wearing antlers for your Christmas card, only he kept pulling them off and humping them."

I did remember, but I was too mad at John to laugh. It was really funny, though.

"So anyway," John continued. "You got a phone call and you went to talk in your bedroom—as if I'd listen in—and I was fooling around with my camera lens when you came out. You had this expression on your face. I don't know. I'd never seen you look that way before."

"So you thought you'd share it with hundreds of our closest friends and relatives? John, how could you not tell me?"

"I was going to. I was just waiting for the right moment."

I stared down at the picture again, remembering. I'd been terrorized, shot in the gut and almost left for dead. But it was the phone call that had put me over the edge.

"Hello, angel." I didn't think it possible to have such primitive urges two days after major surgery, but if anything could send my libido soaring, it was those words, spoken by that voice.

I shook my head to clear away the memory of the phone call. "John, tell me you weren't planning on using this picture in the exhibit."

John wouldn't make eye contact. That was a bad sign.

"John—"

"Please, Bran, I wouldn't ask, except that Lucinda saw the picture and that's what sold her on showing my work.

31

She thinks it's the lynchpin of the entire collection. If I take it out now she'll say I've reneged on the deal and I'll never get another show in a reputable gallery again. But if you want me to take it out, I will."

"I want you to take it out."

"No way! It's a friggin' masterpiece."

"I look pathetic."

John leaned over me, gently taking the photo out of my hands. "Sunshine, I don't know who or what you were thinking of, but I've never seen you look more beautiful."

"You are so full of shit."

John grinned. "Can I take that as a yes?"

"Yes," I sulked. "But only because I don't want you to end up a penniless wino, living out on the streets because I ruined your one chance at success. Look, just promise me you'll stick it in the corner somewhere—and no back lighting and—and you can't sell it. Not that anyone would want it, but—"

John interrupted me. "Come on. I'll take you to lunch." He knew how to shut me up in a hurry.

John's BMW was parked in a garage so I drove. It was raining harder now, the rain coming down in icy sheets. I blasted the heat and turned onto the Schuylkill Expressway, careful to avoid the merging traffic.

The road is a death trap, but it's fast and I was hungry. I'd just gotten up to speed when a car came out of nowhere and swerved in front of me. Cursing, I slammed on the brakes, but for some reason we kept on moving. *Uh oh.*

"Yo, Sunshine, slow down. I'm gettin' carsick here."

"I'm workin' on it." I tried pumping the brakes but it was no good. Frantically, I tromped on the pedal. It went all the way to the floor.

"What do you mean you're 'workin' on it'?" John screeched, his voice a full octave higher than normal. He was leaning against the door, hanging onto the handle for dear life. "Stop fooling around. Just take your lead foot off the gas and slow the hell down."

I shot my arm out reflexively and whacked him in the arm. "I'm not fooling around," I yelled. "The brakes aren't working." And in a split second I was drenched in sweat and I knew that we were going to crash.

"Oh fuck, John. Hang on." I leaned on the horn, zigzagged across three lanes, said a quick Hail Mary and squeezed between a big rig and a tour bus, narrowing missing an SUV coming up on my right. Suddenly, the road began a downhill slope and the car picked up speed. "Oh God! Oh God! Oh God!" someone screamed, but I honestly couldn't tell if it was Johnny or me.

Vehicles careened past as I jumped into the far right lane. The hill was getting steeper, so I stomped on the clutch and shifted into second, in a desperate attempt to slow the damn thing down. The Mercedes shuddered from the abrupt change and I lost control of the steering. The car pitched sideways and hurtled into the guardrail. The sound of crunching metal was the last thing I remembered before blacking out.

I opened my eyes slowly. I was still sitting in the car, but now there was an unfamiliar hand on my shoulder. It belonged to a chubby, uniformed man named Leon. At least that was the name that was embroidered on his shirt pocket. "Don't try to move," Leon said.

I looked out the shattered windshield and saw a TastyKake delivery truck stopped nearby. I'd always suspected that TastyKakes were heaven-sent. Now I was sure of it.

"How are you feeling?" he asked.

My chest hurt and my head felt like a boulder had just landed on it.

"I'm fine." For some reason the car was facing the wrong direction, and I had the vague feeling I was forgetting something. *Johnny!* The passenger door was ajar and the seat was empty. "My friend—" I stammered, struggling to clear the fog in my brain. *He must have been thrown from the car on impact. Oh my God, I've killed him.*

At that moment, John appeared in front of me, pasty-faced and streaked with blood from a gash on his forehead, but otherwise alive and kicking. He wobbled toward the car, followed by a leather jacketed Philly motorcycle cop and a couple of paramedics.

"You okay, Bran?"

I nodded. "You?"

"I'm good, but the shoes are wrecked. You can't get blood off of leather."

"I guess this means you're not taking me to lunch, huh?" I was only half joking.

The TastyKake man went back to his truck and returned a minute later, carrying a box of chocolate cupcakes. "Here ya go, honey. You earned these. By rights you guys should be dead." He gave me a quick pat on the back. "That was some seriously awesome driving."

With trembling hands I ripped open the box and before the paramedics could stop me, I popped a cupcake into my mouth. The chocolate provided just the rush I needed to keep from passing out again. I turned to thank the TastyKake man, but, like the Lone Ranger, he was gone.

Half an hour later I was sitting alone in a tiny cubicle in the emergency room of Jefferson Memorial. The paramedics had insisted we get checked out at the hospital. Since the car was inoperable, the cops called in for a tow while the paramedics took us to the E.R. John thought it was a great idea. He'd never had the thrill of a ride in an ambulance before, and he all but hung his head out the window like an overgrown puppy.

A large, smiling woman entered the room and took my face in her competent hands. I recognized Dr. Martine Sanchez from another one of my near-death experiences and was comforted by the sight of her. "Dios Mio! It's you again. What have you gotten yourself into now?"

"I missed you. What's it been, a month?"

"I don't like repeat customers," she scolded. "You need to stay out of trouble." It would have been funny if there hadn't been such a hard ring of truth to it. My only consolation was that at least nobody was *trying* to kill me this time. It was an accident, pure and simple.

"Well," Dr. Sanchez announced after examining me, "you've suffered a mild concussion and your chest is going to be sore for a while, but the good news is nothing's broken. All things considered, you're fine."

Johnny and I met out in the lobby. He'd gotten five stitches over his right eyebrow.

"Does it hurt?" I asked.

"I'll let you know after the Vicodin wears off. By the way, I'm telling everyone I was in a bar room brawl and they should see the other guy."

"Speaking of big fat lies," I said, "don't tell Paul about this, okay?"

"You don't think he's going to notice the entire right side of his car has a guardrail attached to it?"

"You're exaggerating."

"Not by much."

"All the more reason not to tell him. Look, John, you know how Paul is. He's going to blame himself for the brakes messing up. He'll say he should have had them checked out before he started letting me use his car. Paul's really happy right now. I don't want anything to take away from that." Miraculously, the car wasn't totaled. All it needed was a new set of brakes and some cosmetic surgery. With any luck, I'd have it back in no time.

"It's your call, toots."

We took a cab back to my house. "Do you want to come in?" I asked. "I could make some grilled cheese sandwiches." Dr. Sanchez made me swear I wouldn't be alone. It was the only way she'd agree to release me.

"Thanks," John said, "but I think I'll take a rain check—unless you need me to stick around for a while." He looked exhausted.

"No, I'm fine." I tried to give him cab money but he swiped my hand away.

"Are you kiddin' me? You saved my life today. I guess all that drag racing we used to do at Front and Delaware when we were kids finally paid off."

Somewhere in my mind, John's words hit home. *We could have died in that crash.* The realization was overwhelming, and I reached out and hugged him to me. We stayed that way for several minutes, until the cabbie interrupted in a thick Russian accent. "Okay, lady, in or out?"

I pushed open the door and climbed out of the cab.

It took me ten minutes to negotiate the three steps up to my front door. The initial adrenalin rush and my natural instinct to fake being brave for Johnny had finally worn off, and I was left with a major headache and rubbery legs. Mrs. Gentile found me kneeling on the top step. She paused on her way out to the trashcans, scrunching her unibrow into half its original size. "Are you drunk?" she demanded.

"Rip roarin', Mrs. Gentile."

"You're going to Hell," she said, with smug satisfaction. She should know. The woman has a direct pipeline to Satan.

While I was gone, one of the animals had gotten into a vicious brawl with my mother's plastic statue of the Virgin Mary. For as long as I can remember, it sat on her bedroom windowsill, overlooking the street below. When I bought the house, I'd left it there. I just sort've liked the idea of someone watching over me when I came home late at night. Now, she lay at the bottom of the stairs, tiny teeth marks embedded in her head.

I picked it up and looked around for the culprit. Adrian was lounging on the couch, eating the TV remote. Rocky sat beside him, clawing at a cushion with her tiny paws.

"Okay, which one of you ate Grandma's statue?"

Adrian wagged his water fountain tail and rolled over onto his back. I sat down between them and rubbed his tummy. Every bone in my body ached, so when the phone rang a few moments later, I let the machine pick it up. It was A-1 Security, confirming my appointment for the next afternoon.

37

Heeding Dr. Sanchez's warning about concussions, to have someone wake me every hour, I set my alarm and lay down on the couch. My head buzzed with anxiety and soon I was floating in and out of restless dreams about car wrecks and a giant man-eating sea turtle that ate Mr. Wiggles. Where *that* came from I have *no* idea.

I awoke to the sound of a barking dog and a ringing bell. I reached over to turn off the alarm, but the bell kept on ringing. In the semi-darkness I could make out Adrian's furry little body scratching at the door. I turned on the light next to the couch and stumbled over to the door, craning my neck to check the spy hole. Bobby peered back at me, rocking back and forth on the balls of his feet, his hands shoved deep into the pockets of his leather jacket. His dark hair, dampened by a light drizzle, hung in soft curls around his face. God he was gorgeous. I remained quiet and took a minute to gaze at him.

"Come on, Alexander, are you going to let me in or what? I'm freezing my ass off out here."

I opened the heavy front door and unlocked the storm door. Bobby pulled it open and sauntered into the living room. He peeled off his jacket, tossed it on the couch and sat down. Adrian hopped up next to him.

"You weren't sleeping were you?" he asked. "Because when you have a concussion you're not supposed to fall asleep if you're alone."

"Of course I wasn't sleeping. I'm not stupid. Hey, how did you know about —"

Bobby grinned. "Cop grapevine. I ran into Mike Mahoe. He'd heard about it from a cop at the scene." Mike is a big, good-natured transplanted Hawaiian who looks more at home surfing the waves of Maui than walking a beat in Philly. "So you weren't sleeping. My mistake."

"You don't believe me," I said hotly. God I hate it when he doesn't believe my lies.

"You fell asleep on the TV remote, sweetheart. The buttons left an impression on your cheek."

My hand flew up to my cheek, massaging away the indentations. "That's why they pay you the big bucks, Detective. Hey, don't you have a missing cat to check out somewhere?"

"Nope. Everyone in the city is behaving tonight. Sophia's asleep and Mrs. Bonaduce is babysitting, so I'm all yours. If you want to go back to sleep be my guest. I'll wake you in an hour."

"I *wasn't* sleeping."

When I woke up an hour later, Bobby was in the kitchen, cooking what smelled suspiciously like real food (as opposed to my usual dinners, which can be found at the checkout stand of the local Seven/Eleven, and while both are delicious, the latter has the nutritional value of plastic).

I snagged a carrot out of the pot he was using as a salad bowl and sat down at the table. Bobby was busy mushing something pink and lumpy around in a bowl. He added some breadcrumbs and scooped them into patties.

"You could use some cooking utensils," he said, expertly flipping the patties into a hot, oiled frying pan.

"I'll get right on it. What's for dinner?"

"Salmon croquettes. It was the only thing in your cupboard that didn't have an expiration date that's older than we are. How're you feeling?" He kept his voice light, but I knew he was concerned.

"Good. Much better. Thanks for making dinner. When did you learn to cook?"

Rocky climbed up on the table and swiped a carrot out of the pot. Before I could stop her, she shot out of the room, the carrot dangling from her mouth like a cigarillo.

"I've got a two-year-old whose favorite show is *The Iron Chef*," Bobby laughed. "We spend quality father-daughter time together learning how to make meals made entirely of sticky mung beans. Hey, do me a favor?" He stuck a well-muscled arm out in my direction. "Could you hike up the sleeve?"

"Sure." I walked over to the stove and began rolling his shirtsleeve up his arm. His skin was warm to the touch, his bicep bulging beneath my hand, and I flushed as a current of electricity shot straight down my arm and veered off south of the border. I guess I kept my hand on his arm a little too long, because Bobby stared down at me, a slow, seductive smile playing about the corners of his mouth.

"Y'know, we could skip dinner, if you have something else in mind you'd rather do."

I yanked my hand away. "*Shut up.* I was just checking to see if your new tattoo was infected. You can never be too careful about these things."

Bobby stayed until after dinner. It was nice to have company, especially company that packs a .38 and is willing to use it to protect me. For all my yelling about being able to take care of myself, it was a relief to not have to for once. He offered to spend the night, but, tempting as the offer was, I told him it wasn't necessary. I was not ready to let Robert Anthony DiCarlo just waltz back into my life. Not yet.

I woke up on the couch on Saturday morning, having fallen asleep watching reruns of Miami Vice. That Sonny Crocket sure was a hottie. My usual bout of anxiety was forming in the pit of my stomach, so I decided to stuff it down beneath a hardy breakfast.

The only thing in the house to eat was a cold, leftover salmon croquet and some dog kibble, so I pulled on some jeans and my dad's old pea coat, filled Adrian's bowl, chopped up the croquet for Rocky and headed for Melrose Diner.

I was driving my dad's 1987 burgundy Buick Le Sabre. The car had only slightly more pickup than one of the pretzel wagons around town, but it beat walking. When my parents moved to Florida, they threw it in with the deal on the house. I figured I could sell it and buy a houseplant with the profit.

I passed Snake's garage on the way there and since it was open, I swung a u-turn into the lot. Paul's car was up on the lift. I was a little worried that Paul would drive past and see it hanging up there, so I thought I'd ask Snake to throw a sheet over the Mercedes when it wasn't being worked on.

Snake was in the back office, eating a Dunkin' Doughnut and drinking out of a large Styrofoam cup. He raised his tattooed head when he saw me and belched loudly by way of greeting. My stomach growled, and I scanned the room to see if there were any more doughnuts floating around. I finally spotted the empty, crumpled up bag in the trashcan next to his desk. Swallowing my disappointment I asked how the car was coming along.

"This don't make no sense, doll." He shook his head and lit a cigarette. I tried not to think about the possible ramifications of lit cigarettes and open tanks of gasoline and asked, "What's wrong?"

Snake stubbed out his cigarette as quickly as he'd lit it. "Paulie brought this car in not two months ago for a tune up. I worked on it personally. The brakes were fine, I'd swear by it."

"So now they're not. Can you fix them?"

Snake cut me a look. It screamed, "I can't believe you're so stupid."

"The brakes wouldn't just all of a sudden give out like that. Not without help."

I was a little slow on the uptake, what with being faint from hunger and all, but then his words registered in my brain and my stomach did a one-eighty. "You mean —" I squeaked.

"Looks to me like your brake line was cut."

Chapter Three

Someone's out to get Paul! I thought hopefully. After all, it was *his* car's brakes that had been tampered with. Even as I reasoned this out, I knew it wasn't true—or very nice. And the truth is I'd rather take a bullet than let anything happen to my brother. But my defense mechanisms are really strong and I just couldn't wrap my brain around the idea that somebody was trying to kill me—again.

I left Snake's and drove around for an hour, alternating between deep sweats and icy chills, my inner thermostat carrying the brunt of my fear. Maybe Snake was mistaken. *Maybe Snake was the one who had cut my brake line in a misguided attempt to boost business.* Didn't Heather say she'd seen him when she was out taking an early morning walk with Mr. Wiggles? Okay, that scenario was unlikely.

I would have called the police, but Snake wasn't even a hundred percent sure the brakes had been tampered with.

"Don't brake lines just wear out sometimes?" I asked.

"Yeah," he conceded. "It happens. See this steel rod?" He pointed at the underbelly of the car. "This isn't a clean break. It's possible that the rod broke from rubbing against the body of the frame." Before I could take a breath of relief, Snake reiterated, "If I hadn't just

43

checked this car out, I'd say it could've happened that way. But I'm telling ya, the brakes were in mint condition when the car left my shop."

Hey, maybe Snake's a little sensitive about his mechanical abilities and he's afraid Paul will blame him for not doing a thorough job on the repairs. But if Snake's theory is right and someone really did screw with the brakes, I was in deep doo-doo.

I needed to talk this over with someone, but who? John would be the logical choice, since he'd almost been killed in the accident too. The thought made me sick and I gave an involuntary shudder. Bobby? Fran? They both think I'm in dire need of counseling. Since there's no real proof, they'd just chalk it up to another paranoid delusion and cart me off to Hall-Mercer for psychiatric evaluation.

I made a left and found myself in the neighborhood of Rittenhouse Square. In the next minute I was sitting in front of a four story, ivy covered brick apartment building, staring up at one of the windows on the top floor. Primal instinct had brought me there. Common sense told me to leave. The occupant was out of town and besides, I'd already far exceeded my lifetime quota of favors. I put the car in drive and headed home.

Heather was just getting into her car when I rounded the corner onto my block. I pulled up in back of her and parked. She had Mr. Wiggles with her. He was sniffing the ground like he really had to go. I jumped out of the car and called out to her.

"Oh, hi Brandy. I'm taking Mr. Wiggles for a walk in the park. Do you and your dog want to come along?"

My dog hates Mr. Wiggles. He can't stand his holier than thou attitude.

"Uh, no thanks, Heather. I'm a little busy right now. Listen—"

"We should get our dogs together for a playdate sometime. Wouldn't that be a blast?"

"Yeah, totally," I agreed.

Mr. Wiggles ventured up to my shoe and gave a long sniff. Then he lifted his leg. I nudged his fat little pug nose with the tip of my boot. "My foot is not a urinal," I growled, moving away.

Heather giggled. "He really likes you, Brandy."

"Yeah, I really like him too. Listen, Heather," I said again, this time with a slight edge of impatience, which of course was lost on Heather. "Remember you said you saw my mechanic early yesterday morning?"

"Yeah, did you talk to him? Do you think he'd go out with me?"

"The thing is I'm not sure we're talking about the same person. Could you describe what the guy looked like?"

"Well, I didn't have my contacts on, so don't ask me to pick him out of a lineup, but he was a white guy, around five-eleven, curly brown hair, muscular build," she finished.

Great. That narrowed it down to about fifty billion people, none of whom even remotely fit Snake's description. "Heather, what made you think he was my mechanic?"

"Well, he was wearing a coverall and he was just climbing out from under your car when I was coming out of the house."

My stomach rolled. "Didn't you think that was a little suspicious?" I asked. "I mean we're talking practically the middle of the night."

Heather shrugged. "No. Should I have?"

It's a good thing Heather still lives with her parents. She'd never survive on her own.

"Did you happen to notice if he was carrying anything? Did he say anything to you?"

"He seemed shy. I guess that's what attracted me to him. When I said hello he bent his head and just kept walking. He did have something in his hand, but I couldn't tell what it was. He walked up the street a little ways and got into a dark colored sedan and drove off."

"Would you recognize the car if you saw it again?" I asked.

Heather shook her head. "Like I said, I wasn't wearing my contacts. I think it was black. It was hard to tell in the dark. Bran," she said, suddenly, her eyes getting wide. "Are you working on some kind of an investigation?"

"Yeah," I said. "Something like that. I'll see you later, Heather." I turned and walked into the house.

Oh goody. Something new to worry about. Heather had seen and could possibly identify the guy who cut my brake line. He doesn't know she's half blind without her contacts. He could end up going after her...on the other hand, what if it was just one big coincidence? Maybe he was just some guy retrieving a ball that had rolled under my car, before going off to his early morning job as— okay, she said he was wearing overalls—a farmer. No, wait, she said, "coveralls," not "overalls."

"Paranoid Brandy" battled it out in my mind with "Denial Brandy." In the end, "Paranoid Brandy" won. I picked up the phone and punched in some numbers.

"Detective DiCarlo."

"Hi. I wanted to see if you were in your office today."

There was an instantaneous shift in Bobby's voice from professional law enforcement officer to sexy guy on the prowl.

"Yo, sweetheart, what's up?"

I ignored the term of endearment and got right to it. "I need to run something by you. Are you going to be there for a while?"

His voice shifted back to intuitive cop. "Should I be worried?"

I hesitated a beat too long.

"Shit."

"You've got to promise me you won't overreact," I told Bobby. "But you can't just blow me off, either. I mean it could really be something…or it could be nothing. I don't know." We were sitting in his cubicle down at the station. Bobby slouched at his desk, a beat up gunmetal gray rectangle with photographs of Sophia adorning the top.

He focused his blue eyes on me, the little pulse on the side of his temple telling me he was running out of patience. "If you're through giving me instructions on how to react, why don't you tell me what's going on?"

So I told him.

Bobby took a pad of paper out of his top drawer and began taking notes, interrupting me for more detail. I knew he was worried, because he was all cop now with none of the joking, flirty manner I'd grown accustomed to.

"You think someone screwed with the brakes, don't you?" I asked, keeping my voice as devoid of emotion as possible. I needed him tell me the truth, and if he thought I was going to fall apart he'd sugar coat it.

"Looks like it, Bran." Not the answer I wanted to hear, but at least it was honest.

Bobby leaned back in his chair and picked up the phone. He punched in some numbers and waited for a response.

"Yeah, Heidi," he said, to a voice on the other end, "could you do me a favor? Check and see if we've gotten any calls in the last couple of weeks—I don't know, anything to do with cars in the neighborhood being tampered with. Maybe suspicious characters being spotted in the area. See if anyone's reported a guy in a mechanic's outfit hanging around. Yeah, I know it's vague, but see what you can do, okay, sweetheart?"

Sweetheart? He called her sweetheart? I always thought that was just what he called me. I didn't realize it was his pet name for every bimbo in the Lehigh Valley.

Bobby hung up the phone just as Mike Mahoe appeared at the door. Mike flashed me a grin. "Hey, Brandy, how's it goin'?"

"Hi, Loverboy." As soon as the words left my mouth I cringed. *Unhh! I'm such a geek.*

Mike turned an interesting shade of red, mumbled something about lunch and left.

Bobby stared at me. "Loverboy?"

"Sweetheart?"

"What?"

"Nothing," I said, trying to salvage what little dignity I had left. "So do you really think other people's cars are being messed with and it's not just mine?" Somehow, it didn't seem so awful if I were just one of a bunch of anonymous souls whose cars were randomly sabotaged in the middle of the night. I could chalk it up to good-natured psychotic hijinks, instead of a personal attack.

"That's what I'm trying to try to determine," Bobby told me. "In the mean time, I'm going to talk to Snake again. He could be wrong about the brake line, and it may end up all being a bizarre coincidence."

"As my mother would say, 'from your mouth to God's ear'."

I went home to make some lunch and wait for the security people to come set up the alarm system. While I was waiting I made a fried egg sandwich on week-old organic wheat bread. There was some mold in the center, but since that was the only bread I had, I punched a hole out of the middle and ate it anyway. That's what I get for trying to eat healthy. I never have this problem with Wonder Bread.

After lunch I turned on the TV to take my mind off things, but Saturday afternoon television sucks, so I spent my time alternating between peering out the window in search of car bombers and working up a list of people who might want me dead, just in case it turned out it *was* personal.

First I went with the obvious; relatives and close friends of Bobby's ex-wife. After all, it wouldn't be the first time one of them tried to kill me. Next, I wrote down the names of people associated with criminal cases I'd inadvertently become involved in. Then, I added anyone I'd had a disagreement with in the past month or so. I stopped when I reached twenty-five names. Turns out, I can't get along with anybody.

"So how's the new job goin', Neenie?" I was seated cross-legged on the bed in Janine's studio apartment, shelling peanuts for her pseudo pet pigeon, Ozzie. Ozzie was hanging out on the ledge outside her windowsill crapping up a winter storm.

After the security guys had left, Janine called. There's a new Greek restaurant that just opened in Center City West, and Janine heard all the waiters looked like a cross between Grecian Gods and Chippendale dancers. Seeing as the only thing I had on my agenda for the evening was trimming Mrs. Gentile's toenails, (there's no end to what I'll do to get someone to like me) I decided instead to accompany Janine on her quest for cultural diversity.

Janine stepped out of the bathroom, wriggling her perfect five-foot nine-inch body into ultra skin-tight hip huggers. "The job didn't work out," she said, pulling a too-small t-shirt out of her closet and yanking it over a pair of size 36C's.

"Oh. But last week you were so sure that 'motivational speaking' was your calling. What happened?"

Janine shuddered. "Too depressing. All those needy rejects with no hope of succeeding. They were draining my essence."

"So you quit?"

"They fired me. *Can you believe it?* They said I 'lacked compassion' and I kept making the clients cry. What babies."

"Hey," I sympathized. "Their loss."

"I hear there's a job opening for a slut goddess down at the Peeping Tom," she said.

"Please tell me you're joking."

"Actually, I'd considered it, but when I mentioned the idea to Franny, she flipped out. She said," Janine continued, slipping her feet into a pair of banana colored Frye Dorado Slouch boots, "that as long as I'm walking around with *her* face I'm not exposing *my* ass to a bunch of slobbering, horny losers. Sheesh. She's so touchy lately. Do you think it has something to do with her being pregnant?"

"Could be. Y'know, I'd hold off on the whole 'slut goddess' thing for a while if I were you. Franny's under a lot of pressure right now."

"I was never serious about it anyway. So, who are you taking to the bar mitzvah?" Janine grabbed a pink lip gloss off the dresser and held it up to the light. "What do you think? Too Britney Spears?"

"Whoa," I said. "Back up." I got off the bed and tossed a few peanuts to Ozzie. He cut me an accusatory look as I held back a few for myself. "What do you mean, 'who am I taking to the bar mitzvah?' I thought we agreed to go together."

Janine hesitated. "There's gonna be dancing."

"So?"

"So I wanna dance—and no offense, but I don't wanna dance with you. Look, the invitation says 'and guest'."

"Oh, fine," I sulked. "So who are you bringing?"

"I don't know. Maybe Tony Tan." Tony Tan is Janine's former boss and the Number One Sleazeball Realtor of the tri-state area.

"Tony? But I thought you couldn't stand him."

"I ran into him at "Ducky's" the other night. He's a good dancer." She shrugged. "And kisser."

My eyes narrowed into slits. "You already asked him, didn't you?"

At least she had the good grace to blush. "Sort've. I can un-ask him if you want."

"No," I sighed. "That's all right." Suddenly I panicked. "Is DiCarlo bringing a date?"

"I don't know. I saw him talking to Tina Delvechione outside the post office the other day. They looked pretty chummy."

"Get out!" Back in junior high, Tina Delvechione was the first girl to "develop" and by the looks of her, there'd been no sign of stopping. Oy. This was not good.

"Hmm," said Janine.

"Hmm, what?"

"I thought you said you just wanted to be friends with Bobby."

"Yeah, so?"

"So then why should you care if he brings a date?"

"I don't care," I said, a little too petulantly to be believable. I was really going to have to work on my delivery. "I just don't want to be the only one there without a date, is all."

"Bran, we are independent women. We don't need men to show us a good time."

"So does that mean you're going to ditch Tony and come with me?"

"Not a chance."

"But, what about all that stuff about being independent women?"

"I lied. Let's go eat."

Janine was right about the waiters. They were all drop dead gorgeous. Turns out, Demitri's was a family owned restaurant, and all the guys who worked there were related. They kept coming over to our table to see us—okay, technically, they came over to see Janine, but I was there too—and filling our glasses with ouzo. I ended up getting really drunk and spent much of the evening making out with a nineteen-year-old busboy named Alex—a cousin who had just arrived from Greece and was looking for an American wife. I found this out from his uncle, the head chef and another Alex, who offered to broker the marriage for me. I think I agreed. I really can't remember.

At closing time, Alex the Younger asked to drive me home.

"Go on," Janine prodded me.

"Janine, he's a baby."

"Who cares? He's legal. You're entitled to have a little fun, and you may wind up with a date for the bar mitzvah after all."

In the end, I decided to let him drive me home. In my altered state of consciousness, Janine's reasoning sounded pretty good. Plus, he'd promised me leftovers from the kitchen.

I waited outside in the parking lot while Alex locked up the restaurant. The cold air sobered me up a bit, and I started to feel the first pangs of regret over my decision. I am not a "one-night-stand-with-a-stranger" kind of girl, no matter how much I'd like to be. It's awkward, at best, and even though I was pretty sure Alex Junior wasn't a serial killer, I didn't think I'd feel too good about myself in the morning. I was just going to have to tell him that the wedding was off and, by the way, I wouldn't be sleeping with him. I really hoped he'd still let me have the leftovers.

The street was dark and empty, so that even the sound of a car door softly closing somewhere nearby put me on edge. I decided to wait for Alex inside. As I began walking toward the door, I got the sudden and distinctly creepy feeling that I wasn't alone. Prickles of sweat broke out on the back of my neck as my imagination raced.

Slowly, I reached into my coat pocket for the set of "Clear Knuckles" I found on the Internet, *"designed to tear flesh and inflict topical pain. Legal in every state!"*

As I reached the building I breathed a sigh of relief, and then a hand came out of nowhere, grabbing me by the back of my head, its fingers fisting in my hair. I tried to scream, but another hand, large and gloved, clamped itself over my mouth and nose. A slightly sweet odor filled my nostrils, making me dizzy. I held my breath and swung my arm backward, blindly reaching for my assailant's face. He growled low in his throat as the Clear Knuckles made contact with soft muscle tissue. The hand over my face tightened and I tore at his arms, struggling to loosen his grip on me. I was suffocating and I gasped for air, sucking the sickly sweet scent into my lungs. It was the last thing I remembered before I passed out.

"Do you think she's dead?" The voice was muffled and seemed to be coming from far away.

"Christ, I hope so. The bitch took a chunk out of my face with her fist."

I was just conscious enough to realize that the person he was calling a bitch was me and to take offense to it. But it was hard to muster up righteous indignation for name-calling when the real offense seemed to be they were plotting to kill me. *Whoever they were.* I was still too groggy from my chloroform and ouzo cocktail to believe any of this was real.

I had been blindfolded and stuffed into a cramped, dark space, my hands and ankles bound with some kind of cloth. The earth seemed to move beneath me, making it hard to get my bearings. I struggled to sit up and bonked my head against something hard, a tire iron, I think. *Shit. I'm in the trunk of a car. What's that thing you're supposed to do if you're ever kidnapped and locked in the trunk of a vehicle? Oh yeah, kick the taillights out. Okay… where are my feet?*

While I pondered this, the car stopped moving. The driver cut the engine and popped the trunk. I thought about jumping out, but then what? Yell, "Surprise!" and hop away on my shackled legs? I could barely lift my head—or remember my own name.

Another car approached and stopped and soon I heard footsteps crunching along the ground. I lay motionless, doing my best impersonation of a dead person, which I would be soon if I didn't get my wits together. I was too out of it to be scared, which was actually a good thing, because if I fully understood how much trouble I was in I would have peed my pants.

"Where is she?" asked a new voice, male and slightly more upscale.

In response, the trunk lid was yanked open, letting in a blast of fresh air.

"Signed, sealed and delivered."

I braced myself for the worst, made the sign of the cross in my head and began to thrash about, shouting my lungs out. "Help! Someone help me! Call 911!"

Mr. Upscale banged his fist against the trunk and the lid slammed shut again. "For Christ's sake, you morons, you got the wrong girl."

His outburst was followed by a moment of stunned silence, which I felt compelled to fill. "Hey, anyone can make a mistake," I yelled through the closed lid. "No harm, no foul."

There was the sound of crunching gravel, as three sets of feet stomped away from the car. More muffled conversation; quiet murmurings punctuated by angry expletives. Then the trunk popped open and the gloved hand pressed itself against my nose once again. I tried to fight the guy off, but there were three of them and one of me and I was just too damn tired. For the second time that evening I was out like the proverbial light.

I woke up, face down in the gutter about three blocks from where I'd been abducted. It was two a.m. by my watch. My pocketbook lay on the curb next to me, my arms and legs freed from the bonds that had constrained them. The Clear Knuckles were gone, but beyond that, everything was as it had been. It was as if it had all been a horrible nightmare, conjured up after eating bad oysters or watching The Fox News Network. *Had I dreamed it?*

I ripped open my bag and fumbled around for my cell phone. When I found it I began to punch in 911 but stopped midway through the call. *What would I even tell the police? And would they even believe me? I could hardly believe it myself.* Nothing was stolen, I wasn't dead, there were no telltale marks on my body. I hadn't seen a thing and I couldn't identify any of those guys if they came up and bit me on the butt. I had nothing to offer the cops and no matter how I sliced it, I'd end up sounding like some nutcase rambling on about UFO's and alien abductions.

The effects of the alcohol and chloroform had, for the most part, worn off, leaving me depressed and vulnerable. I hated feeling so defenseless. I put my phone back in my pocket, willing myself not to cry. It didn't work. Big, fat tears spilled out of my eyes and rolled down my cheeks.

After a few minutes, I wiped my nose on my sleeve and tried to get some perspective on the situation. Okay, the good news was, no one was trying to kill me after all. They'd simply mixed me up with someone else. And when you think about it, they were really quite gentlemanly about the whole thing. Once they realized their mistake, they let me go. I was in the clear. No need to drag this on, what with my parents arriving in town and Paul's big day coming up. To tell the truth, I was happy to put it all behind me. There was just one nagging, little detail. If I was the *wrong* girl, who then, was the right one? Crap. I took out my phone again.

I woke Bobby out of a sound sleep. He was there in less than twenty minutes, dressed in sweat pants and his motorcycle jacket, his hair tousled, the rough stubble of a five o'clock shadow running the length of his jaw line. He picked me up off the curb and opened the passenger door.

"Are you okay?" he asked.

"I'm fine," I said, shivering my brains out as hypothermia set in.

He turned up the heat and pointed the vents in my direction. "What happened?" he said quietly. So I told him.

"I can see where you might not want to mention this down at the station," he said when I was finished.

"But you believe me." It wasn't a question.

"I believe you. So what were you doing making out with a nineteen-year-old kid?"

"Unhh! I think you're missing the point here, DiCarlo."

Bobby pulled up in front of my house and cut the engine. He turned around in his seat, facing me. "I'm not missing the point. I'm changing the subject. Jesus, Brandy, I am so damn relieved to know these people weren't after you. Cut me a break here and let me enjoy it for a minute and a half."

"Bobby," I said, touched by his words, "I know you're just looking out for me, but there's some poor woman walking around out there who has "hit" men after her and she may not even know it. How are we going to find her before they do?"

"We?"

"Yeah. *What?*"

"Didn't you hear a word I just said? Look at you! You came this close to sleepin' with the fishes tonight. You haven't slept in weeks, your nerves are shot and now you're talking about plunging into another life threatening situation. What is wrong with you?"

I pushed open the car door. "Do me a favor. When you figure it out, let me know."

Chapter Four

Lynne Schaffer stopped me in the hall. It was Monday morning. I'd spent all of Sunday in bed, watching kick-ass movies like "Die Hard" and Walking Tall," getting vicarious thrills out of watching the good guys beat the tar out of the bad guys.

"You're filling in for Tamra today," Lynne said. "Be ready in half an hour."

Normally, this would have been great news. I've been dying for an opportunity to break out of the puff piece mold. But this just felt creepy. "Why?" I asked. "Where's Tamra?"

"How should I know?" Lynne groused. "Look, Alexander, you wouldn't be my choice, but you're here and there's no one else to fill in on such short notice. Oh," she added, "and see if you can lose the Goth look before you go on air. You look like something out of a Dracula movie."

I felt like decking her, but she did have a point. Pretty soon the bags under my eyes were going to need their own porter.

Eric was waiting for me when the show ended. "Nice job," he said, absently. "Listen, could you come into my office?" His baby face showed signs of strain. I felt sorry for him.

"What's wrong with Tamra?" I asked, taking a seat on the couch. "Why didn't she come in today?"

"I don't know," Eric said, "and to tell you the truth, I'm worried. I've been trying to call her all morning and I just keep getting her voicemail. This isn't like her. She's always been rock solid. I'm thinking maybe something happened to her."

My heartbeat kicked up a notch. "Have you tried calling her husband? He works at the university."

Eric nodded. "He's not there. They said he took the week off and won't be back until next Monday. Look, I've heard some rumors. Their marriage isn't so hot, but Tamra wouldn't bail on work. She knows it could cost her her job."

"Car accident," I suggested. "Maybe she was taken to the hospital and wasn't able to call." I knew if there had been a serious wreck we would have heard about it, but I was grasping at straws.

"I'm gonna need you to cover again tomorrow if we don't hear from her," Eric said.

I felt a little wave of excitement, which of course quickly turned into a massive wave of guilt. Being the product of a Catholic mom and a Jewish dad, it was a familiar feeling.

I left work at 4:00p.m making a detour on the way home. According to her personnel records, Tamra lived in Pennsauken, New Jersey, which was right across the bridge. I didn't know what I'd hoped to accomplish, but I figured it wouldn't hurt to at least drive by and see if her car was there. I pulled onto her street just as the last vestiges of daylight were slipping away.

Townshend Drive was a tree-lined cul-de-sac located in a quiet, upper middle class neighborhood. Her place was at the end of the block, a two story slate gray Cape Cod style house with an attached garage.

Tamra's car was parked in the driveway. I walked up the pathway, stooping to pick up the Sunday Times, and then I rang the doorbell and waited. Nothing. I went around to the side of the house and tried to peer in a bottom window, but the shades were drawn, no light coming from inside.

"What are you doing?"

I jumped a mile and spun around, knocking over a big clay pot. It looked expensive.

A skinny kid about eleven years old was sitting astride his bike, watching me.

"Hi," I said, brightly. "Do you know Tamra and Jeff?"

He nodded, inching closer. "I live right next door. What are you doing?" he asked again, this time with a proprietary edge to his voice.

"I'm looking for Tamra. Is she home?"

The kid shrugged. "Dunno. Jeff took off on Saturday morning. I saw him hauling a bunch of suitcases with him. He seemed like he was in a hurry."

"Did Tamra go with him?"

"I didn't see her. But if they were going away together," he mused, "why didn't they ask me to feed Mittens? Whenever Tamra goes away, she pays me five dollars a day to feed her cat."

"You wouldn't by any chance have a spare key, would you?"

"What for?"

Well, you see, as far as I know it's a felony to break into someone's home, uninvited. But if you gave me the key, it would knock it down to a misdemeanor.

It was probably just my imagination working overtime, but I wouldn't be able to sleep until I spoke to Tamra. She'd had a fight with her husband, she'd tried to reach me on Thursday night and now she's a no-show at work. Tamra's a consummate professional. She'd never jeopardize her job over a personal problem. She would have at least called in. Even Eric thought it was weird. I thought about calling the police, but what if it turned out to be nothing and I broadcast her marital problems all over town? The press would have a field day over it.

"What's your name, kid?"

"Ricky."

"Okay, Ricky, so here's the thing ..."

It took me fifteen minutes and twenty bucks to convince Ricky to let me borrow the key. He relented after I showed him my WINN I.D. card. "Hey, now I know who you are," he smiled triumphantly. "You're the lady who does all those crazy things around the city. Remember the time you visited a compost farm? You ate worms just like on Fear Factor. That was so cool."

Ricky took off with my twenty bucks and returned a few minutes later with Tamra's key.

"Wait here," I said, as he followed me to the door. "If Tamra is home, she may not be up for entertaining. She hasn't been feeling well, and I just want to make sure she's okay."

The first thing I noticed when I walked into the house was the stench. Like someone had pooped their pants. I stood just inside the foyer and called Tamra's name. There was no response, so I ventured further inside. It was dark and I reached along the wall for a light switch. Something brushed past my leg and I screamed, losing my balance and crashing into the wall.

"Are you okay?" Ricky stuck his head inside the door and flipped on the hall light. "Eewww. Somebody forgot to clean out Mittens' litter box. C'mere, baby." Ricky reached out and scooped up an orange tabby. It meowed piteously in his arms.

The downstairs looked to be in order; no dead bodies sprawled on the living room rug, no tell tale bloody butcher knife lying about in the kitchen sink. I should have been relieved but I wasn't.

Ricky came up behind me, cradling the cat in his arms. "Think I'll feed Mittens," he said. "I guess Tamra *did* go away and she just forgot to tell me."

"I guess so."

Even as I voiced agreement I knew it wasn't true. The house was beyond quiet, the air fetid and suffocating. A feeling of dread washed over me, taking up space like a third person in the room. Something was horribly wrong.

My instincts said to grab the cat and the kid and get the hell out of the house, but my conscience wouldn't allow it. Damn conscience. I instructed Ricky to stay in the kitchen, as I took a few reluctant steps up the stairs. When I got to the top I called her name softly, not really expecting an answer. I flipped on the light and worked my way down the hall.

There was a bedroom on the left. The king sized bed was unmade, the sheets and comforter all twisted together forming a huge lump. I held my breath and poked tentatively at it. Just sheets. I let out my breath and kept moving.

The room next to the master bedroom was set up like an office. Computer, fax machine, shelves crammed with books and framed pictures of Jeff and Tamra in happier times. A radio tuned to a classical station played softly in the background.

Finding nothing out of the ordinary, I moved on to the bathroom, peeked my head in and promptly threw up.

The water in the tub had turned pink, matching the Laura Ashley towels hanging from the rack on the wall. Tamara's naked body lay beneath the surface. Her head had slipped under the water, her hair a tangled mass of brown seaweed, her face almost unrecognizable, a grotesque, bloated distortion of her former self. It seemed redundant to check to see if she were really dead.

Stepping over my own vomit I braced myself against the doorframe. I tried to keep my voice steady, not wanting to alarm the kid. "Um, Ricky?" I called down the stairs.

"Coming."

"No, no. Tamra's here, but she's not feeling well." *Master of the understatement.* "She needs you to take the cat over to your house."

"Okay. Hey, do you want me to make some chamomile tea? Grandma says it's a miracle cure."

Sirens blaring, the police pulled up in front of Tamra's house. I don't know why they deemed it necessary to turn them on. At this stage of the game, there was no big rush.

Paramedics zoomed past me, racing up the stairs. Guess my layman's diagnosis of "dead as a door nail" wasn't good enough.

"Someone threw up," one of the cops observed.

"That would be me," I called from downstairs. "Sorry."

The house filled to overflowing with police, paramedics and the coroner. Outside, a news van was parked on the lawn. Bad news travels fast. I spied Ricky on the edge of the pathway, talking animatedly to a silver-haired reporter from a rival station.

A young officer approached me, holding a blanket. "Thought you might need this," he said, wrapping it around me. I had no idea how hard I was shaking until I tried to sit down on the couch and it fell away beneath me. The cop caught me before I hit the floor.

I told him everything I knew about Tamra, which unfortunately wasn't much. Her husband was out of town. They'd had a fight; she'd tried to call me. She seemed upset.

Upset enough to slit her wrists. She had reached out to me in the newsroom. She was my only friend there. And somehow, without meaning to, I'd failed her.

I drove myself home, ignoring some very good advice to ask someone to come pick me up. I was crying so hard I couldn't see out the windshield. The good news was I hadn't thought about the whole "somebody's trying to kill me" scenario in hours. There's nothing like a

65

decomposing corpse to take your mind off your own troubles.

Eric called on the way home. He'd already heard about Tamra. I half expected him to be mad that I didn't get an "exclusive." He was uncharacteristically kind and told me to take the next day off. He didn't have to tell me twice. I didn't relish running into Lynne at the office. She probably thinks I handed Tamra the razor, just so I could fill in for her.

I called John from the car and asked him to go over to my house to feed Rocky and Adrian. My head was splitting and I had to get some food in me, seeing as I'd left my lunch at Tamra's. There's an Italian restaurant on the corner of 16th and Passyunk Avenue that's famous for their cannelloni and Caesar's salads. I had just enough credit on my Visa card to eek out a meal and a tip. I figured after the day I had, I deserved it.

I pulled into the tiny parking lot and squeezed into a spot marked "compact". As I inched my way out of the car, I caught a glimpse of myself in the side mirror of the Lexus parked next to me. Two sunken eyes peered back at me from under a frame of stringy hair, accentuating the ghostly pallor of my face. I popped a breath mint and was good to go.

Normally I don't like eating alone in restaurants. I'm afraid people will think I have no friends. But at this point I was too tired to care. I got a table for two in the back and looked around like I was waiting for my date to show up. Okay, so I guess I cared a little. The waiter brought me a basket of bread and asked if I'd like something from the bar. I ordered a beer, thought better of it and made it a scotch. This was, after all, an occasion.

I started drinking before the meal came. Not one of my brighter ideas. It made me dizzy, and I went in search of the bathroom to splash some cool water on my face. It didn't really help, so when I spied a familiar figure a moment later, on the other side of the room, I thought it was the Johnnie Walker talking.

The man lounging against the bar looked deceptively civilized, his lean, five-foot ten-inch frame draped in Armani, concealing rock-hard abs and a .38 caliber pistol tucked neatly against the small of his back. He was alone, but he wouldn't be for long. Woman couldn't help but flock to him. I shrank back against a potted plant, trying to catch my breath, which had been knocked out of me by the unexpected thrill of seeing him.

Nicholas Santiago was the double whammy— transcendentally beautiful and a certified Bad Boy. It doesn't get any sexier than that. Nick and I met two months ago, and he's been bailing me out of trouble ever since. Ironically, the only thing he couldn't save me from was him.

It's not like he hadn't warned me. *"I'm not monogamous and I'm not permanent."*

And yet I'd jumped in looking. That night, the earth moved and my heart stopped and by the time it got going again, he'd moved on.

Last we'd spoken was about a month ago. John was there the day Nick had phoned, and he'd captured the aftermath with his Canon. Nick called to say he was going out of town on business. I didn't ask what kind of business. I'm sure I didn't want to know. If I believed a quarter of the rumors about Nick, I'd be scared. I believed all of them.

It was good that he was leaving. It would give me time to sort out my feelings. But the truth was I already knew, even if I couldn't admit it. Only now there was no room for denial. It was written all over my face in the photo. I was in love with the guy. Oh crap.

"Can I help you, ma'am?" A busboy stood beside me, balancing a tray full of dishware in his hands.

"No. Shh. I'm fine." I angled myself further behind the tree as a woman approached Nick and greeted him, European style, with two kisses, placed on either side of his cheek. *Pretentious twit. I'll bet she's not even really French. I hate her.*

The busboy didn't move.

"What? You've never seen a patron hide behind foliage before? I'm *kidding.* I lost an earring." Quickly I bent down to retrieve the non-existent accessory. I couldn't let him see me. Not like this. *If I could just find a way out of here…my meal hasn't come yet, so it wouldn't exactly be a "dine and dash"…*

"Hello, angel."

Uh oh. Could I pretend I didn't hear him? I guess not. I stood slowly, the scotch on an empty stomach wreaking havoc with my equilibrium. "Oh, Nick, hi. Fancy meeting you here." *Fancy meeting you here? What am I, Amish?*

Nick leaned over to give me a friendly peck on the cheek, and I took a wobbly step back, knocking into the busboy. The busboy teetered backwards, flapping his hands in a futile attempt to catch the falling plates. They made a sickening crash when they hit the tile floor.

"Um, sorry."

God, this couldn't be any more humiliating. Oh wait. It could. Nick's date joined us behind the tree. *Please don't introduce us, oh please don't introduce us.*

"Brandy, this is Pilar. Pilar, Brandy."

Note to self: Change name to something exotic. Possibly Tanisha.

We did the whole nice to meet you routine and then mercifully, Pilar remembered a pressing engagement and left. While they were doing their double-cheeked goodbye kiss, I flagged down the waiter and handed him my credit card, asking him to pack my meal to go.

"Do you have to rush off?" Nick turned back to me, his voice soothing, his look penetrating and for a moment I forgot that I'd just seen a co-worker dead—not to mention naked and that I had vomit in my hair.

"Well, uh..."

He guided me toward the bar. "Two coffees, please."

Oh, I get it. He thinks I'm drunk...which I am. Unhhh! There he goes bailing me out again! Does he have to be so damn gracious about it? And while I was on the subject of rhetorical questions, why was I feeling so angry with him?

The waiter came over and handed me my food.

"Gee, Nick," I said, backing my way toward the door, "it's been great seeing you. Well, take care." I gave him a little salute with my free hand and then wondered why I made such an asinine gesture. I turned and fled before I could do one more embarrassing thing and ran headlong into the glass door. I bounced off the glass and the cannelloni went flying, along with my pocketbook. My cell phone, pepper spray and stun gun sailed through the air as I hit the ground, my head landing with a clunk on the carpet. Then my phone started to ring. "Would you mind getting that?" I crawled to my knees, waving away help from the Maitre D'.

"Brandy Alexander's phone," Nick announced.

"Who is this?" I could hear the voice on the other end and it was not a happy one.

Nick turned the phone around and checked the caller I.D. "Detective DiCarlo. What a pleasant surprise. This is Nick Santiago."

I scrambled over to the phone and grabbed it out of Nick's hand. He smiled benignly as I said hello into the receiver.

"What's he doing answering your phone?" Bobby hissed. Bobby wasn't exactly a fan.

"Long story—and none of your business," I added. I'd had about as much grief as I could take for one day.

"None of my business? After what you put me through the other night?"

"I'm sorry," I said, on the verge of a major meltdown. "There's been another—" I hesitated—"development."

"Yeah?" His voice softened. "Do you want to tell me about it?"

"Eventually," I sighed. "Just not now. Did you ever find out anything conclusive about my car brakes?"

"No reports of other cars being tampered with," Bobby said. "No suspicious people spotted in the neighborhood except for that report from Heather, and Snake swears he did a thorough job on the brakes." Somebody had gone to an awful lot of trouble to silence the wrong person.

Nick reached out a hand to help me up. It was warm and reassuring and I wanted to hold it forever. His expression was that of mild curiosity, but I knew him well enough not to take it at face value. "When did you start packing heat?" he asked, holding the stun gun in his other hand.

"What? Oh. Long story."

"And none of my business?" he asked, handing me back the gun.

"It's really not that interesting."

"Try me."

I was sorely tempted to unburden the whole sorry mess on Nick, from my sleepless nights to the living nightmare of Tamra's suicide and the misguided attempts on my life. But something stopped me. And the truth is I had no idea in the world what it was.

"Come on," he said, finally, "I'll take you home."

"I don't need a ride, thanks. I have my car."

"And I have your keys." He held them up for me to see, leaving no room for argument.

I called Fran the next day to fill her in on everything that had happened—not because I wanted her to worry—I just knew she'd be furious with me if she found out from someone else. Franny thinks that now that she's pregnant she misses out on all the fun.

She met at Shorty's Rib House, the carnivore's equivalent to Disneyland. She said the baby needed the meat and I felt silly arguing with a six-month-old fetus, so I went along for the ride. I didn't think my stomach could take another jolt to its system, so I ordered the House Salad—iceberg lettuce with a radish on the side. Yum.

"So then what happened?" Franny asked, through a mouthful of barbequed beef ribs, bits of which were stuck solidly between her teeth.

"Nothing. I fell asleep thirty seconds after I got in the car. I can only hope I didn't snore."

"Did he kiss you goodbye?"

"No! We barely said two words to each other. And that's another thing. He's been back in town for God knows how long and he never even called me. I'm telling you, Fran. That night I spent with Nick was a fluke. He is *so* not interested."

"Don't be so sure." Franny gnawed thoughtfully on a bone. I could see the gears in her keen, analytical mind working overtime.

"What do you mean?" I asked, trying not to sound too excited and failing miserably.

"Well, Nick doesn't strike me as the kind of guy who waits for a woman to make up her mind—and let's face it, Bran, you're still emotionally joined at the hip with Bobby. I think you and DiCarlo should just do it and get it over with," she decided. "See if the old spark is still there."

"Jesus, Franny," I yelled, and a piece of lettuce flew out of my mouth and landed on her side of the table. "If I wanted that kind of advice I'd be sitting here watching Janine chow down half a cow instead of you."

"I hit a nerve, huh?" she grinned.

"No." *Yes.* "And anyway," I went on, lowering my voice to barely a whisper, "there's something a little more pressing I wanted to talk to you about."

Fran looked at her watch. "Better make it quick. I'm due back at the office in twenty minutes."

I took a deep breath. "It's about Tamra," I announced. "I think she was murdered."

I had plenty of time to think about it too, seeing as I was up all night again, so it gave me something new to dwell on besides where Bobby and I were headed and who Nick was sleeping with when he wasn't busy selling arms to third world nations or whatever probably illegal thing he did for a living.

The police were handling it as a routine suicide. As if deciding to end one's own life could ever be considered routine. But when I really thought about it, things didn't add up. Tamra just didn't appear all that depressed. Certainly, she wasn't thrilled the day her husband showed up at the restaurant, but she seemed more pissed off than suicidal. And she'd been so excited about a story she had been working on. I couldn't imagine her checking out when her investigation was going so well.

I called Detectives Moody and Hahn, the cops in charge of the case, with my theory about how Tamra had really died. I thought maybe they'd invite me to come in so we could pool our information, but all they'd said was thank you and they thought they could handle it from here. "But what about her husband?" I'd persisted. "Have you checked out his alibi? And what about a suicide note? Isn't it standard practice to leave some kind of message behind, explaining why they didn't want to live anymore? I mean, *come on, people,* what was her motivation?"

Detective Moody didn't feel inclined to discuss the subtleties of the suicidal mind with me. In fact, he suggested that I was looking for trouble where there wasn't any, as a way of lessening my own feelings of guilt over not being able to save my friend from herself. I made a counter suggestion for Detective Moody to perform an anatomical impossibility involving his head and his butt and then the line went dead. Must've been a bad connection.

"So what do you think?" I asked Franny, when I'd caught her up to speed.

She gave me a long look, and I swear there was pity in her eyes.

"You're not going to like it," she said finally.

"Then never mind."

"Too late," she said. "You already asked. Brandy, did you ever think there might be a little bit of truth to what that cop said about you feeling guilty? Not that you have anything to feel guilty about," she rushed on. "But you said yourself you barely knew this woman. Isn't it possible she was more troubled than you thought, and it just got to be too much for her?" Franny nabbed me with a look. "Hon, I think you may be plunging headlong into this whole murder theory as a way to avoid your own issues."

"What issues, Fran? I have no issues. I am issue-free." I folded my arms in front of my chest, my body language screaming, *"Woman on the verge of a nervous breakdown."*

"Fine," said Fran. "You're the picture of mental health. I've got to get back to work." She squeezed her way out of the booth, pausing to take one last chomp on a rib.

"Franny," I sighed.

"Yeah?"

"I'll admit I may have a few *teensy* issues where I *might* benefit from professional help. But if I'm right about Tamra and her death wasn't a suicide, don't you think she deserves to have the truth come out?"

"Even if you are right, Brandy, why does it always have to be you?"

Boy. First Bobby and now Fran. How could they ask me to just ignore two people who can't defend themselves? Jeez. Don't they know me at all? "If not me, Fran, then who?"

I thought about our conversation all the way back to my house. I mean it's not like I went looking for trouble. I didn't ask to be kidnapped and I certainly could have lived without the image of

Tamra's decomposing body…Y'know the average person could go through his entire life without experiencing even one of these events…How weird is that, anyway? I get mistaken for some unknown woman and almost killed because of it, and then my co-worker ends up dead…Talk about co-incidence…Shit! I am so stupid! I flung myself through the front door, grabbed the phone and punched in Bobby's number.

Chapter Five

Bobby didn't pick up. Damnit! I tried his cell, the station and his house. I even called DiVinci's Pizza, thinking he may have stopped in for a quick lunch. He wasn't there, but since I had them on the line I ordered a large pepperoni and a root beer.

While I waited for my pizza to arrive, I called Eric. "Have you heard anything more on Tamra?" I asked when he picked up the phone."

"Just that her husband's back in town. Lisa Stanley interviewed him last night. He's staying at his brother's. Apparently he's too broken up to stay at the house. She said Rhineholt appeared pretty devastated. They were coming up on their fifth wedding anniversary."

"When's the funeral?"

"Tomorrow. A small private service, family only, after the cremation."

Cremation. Shit.

I leafed through the phone book and punched in the number for the Philadelphia District Attorney's office.

"Giancola."

"Vince, it's Brandy." Vincent Giancola was my boyfriend in the third grade. He used to cheat off of me during spelling tests. He's an assistant D.A. now.

"Hey, I've been meaning to call you. My mother told me your parents will be in town on Saturday and your mother's invited me over for dinner." He hesitated a beat, and when he spoke again his voice turned raspy, like he'd swallowed a lemon. "The thing is," he said, "I think I'm coming down with something," which was followed by the fakest cough I've ever heard.

"Take something for it and be there, Giancola. If I have to suffer through my mother's lasagna, so do you." Bobby once said my mom's cooking could be considered a lethal weapon. Of course I defended her, but we *did* have a cat once that died under suspicious circumstances...

"Anyway, Vince, I'm calling about something else. You probably heard about the Tamra Rhineholt suicide out in Jersey."

"Yeah," Vince said quietly. "I heard you found her too. Of all the freakin' luck. Is there anything I can do for you?"

"As a matter of fact, there is. Can you stop a cremation and order an autopsy?"

"What? Are you, kidding me?"

"I wish I were."

"How soon can you get over here?"

"Twenty minutes. I'll bring a pizza."

"Okay, so you're telling me someone tried to run you over, they cut your break line, kidnapped you, stuffed you in a trunk and then left you for dead in a gutter, and you didn't tell the police...*why?*"

77

"I thought it would put a damper on Paul's festivities."

"You're nuts, y'know that?"

I was seated in Vince's office chair, polishing off the last of the pizza. Vince was behind his desk, pawing through one of the drawers. After a minute he extracted a half-empty pack of Camels and some matches. He picked up a small fan he kept stashed behind a mini fridge and set it on his desk. Then he lit up the Camel and took a long drag.

"Hey, isn't it illegal to smoke in a government building?" I asked.

As he flipped me the bird, there was a knock on the door and Vince's boss stuck her head in. "Put it out, Giancola."

I stifled the urge to laugh. He was mad enough at me already. "Look," I said, when she was gone, "my point is I think Tamra was the real target, not me. People mistook us for each other all the time. It's just too co-incidental that all those near-death experiences happened to me and then she winds up dead."

"So how do you know you *weren't* the real target, and she ended up dead by mistake?"

"Because the guy took a look at me close up and said they got the wrong girl. They wouldn't have let me go if I was the one they were after. Vince, you've got to talk to the Jersey police. The husband plans to have her cremated tomorrow. And did I mention he thought she was having an affair and they had a big fight at a restaurant?"

Vince smiled. "You may have mentioned it once or a thousand times. Look, Brandy," he said, drumming sausage-like fingers on the top of his desk, "you know I'd do anything in the world for you, but I can't go telling the

Jersey police how to run their department. They looked at the facts and determined it was a suicide. End of story."

"Well, could you at least call them and tell them what I told you?"

Vince took another long drag off his cigarette before tossing the butt into a Styrofoam cup. "Sure." He sighed deeply. "Just don't get too excited. Like I said if the cops thought there was foul play involved they would have jumped all over it."

"Thanks, Vincent. I owe you one."

"Does that mean I don't have to come for dinner on Saturday night?"

"If you don't show up I will hunt you down." I stood to leave when suddenly I thought of something. "Vince, Tamra came around here pretty regularly, right?"

"Yeah. I liked her. She was a good reporter."

"Well, right before she died she told me something big was about to break. What if she was killed because she knew too much?"

"So now you think her death might be related to a story she was working on?"

"Maybe. And don't give me that look, Vince. Do you recall any conversations you might have had the last time she was in here?"

"No...Yeah, come to think of it. She was asking a lot of questions about David Dwayne Harmon, the guy on death row who's scheduled to be executed next month. He claims he's innocent." Vince shook his head. "They always do."

The sun was setting as I left Vince's, and the anxiety that lately accompanied the darkness began to creep up on me. I looked in the rear view mirror. No one looked back. That's a good sign," I thought. Then I looked again just to make sure.

I knew I should go straight home, and I had every intention of doing just that, so I was as surprised as anyone when I found myself instead crossing the Betsy Ross Bridge into Pennsauken. I called John along the way and asked him to stop by my house and feed Rocky and Adrian.

"No problem. Where are you going?"

"Nowhere."

"What kind of an answer is that?" *A really stupid one. I should have just made something up.*

"I have some errands to run. I'll talk to you later," I said, quickly hanging up. He called me back as I knew he would, but I let it go to voicemail. How could I explain to John what I didn't understand myself?

I pulled onto Tamra's block and parked across the street. The house was shrouded in darkness, her car sitting forlornly in the driveway, as if it knew she wasn't coming back.

The thought made me irrevocably sad and I felt my eyes fill with tears. I quickly wiped them away, telling myself that inanimate objects don't have feelings—except, of course, for stuffed animals.

I reached into my bag for a tissue and my fingers grazed a small, metal object hidden under the weight of my pepper spray. *Tamra's key.* I'd forgotten all about it. "I really should return this to the neighbor's," I thought. They didn't appear to be home, but I figured I'd get out and stretch my legs and maybe wait for them.

I popped open the glove compartment and extracted a flashlight. It was dark on the street, I reasoned, and I didn't want to trip and fall. It was also freezing out, so I pulled my hood up over my head and slipped on a pair of gloves I found in my coat pocket. Quickly I scanned the street and, finding no one out there, I climbed out of the car.

As I approached the sidewalk in front of Tamra's, I was sure I heard a soft meow, which *could* have just been the wind, but why take chances. *What if her cat Mittens was stuck all alone in the house again? It would be so easy for Jeff to forget about her in the throes of his grief.* That settled it. I would simply go inside to make sure Mittens was okay and I'd come right out again. After all, by the time Jeff came home, the cat could starve to death. I took a cursory glance around and opened the front door.

Someone had tried to air out the place. The living room windows had been left open a crack, but even the crisp winter-night breeze couldn't mask the lingering odor of tragedy. I flicked on the flashlight and made a half-hearted attempt to look for a cat I already knew wasn't there. "Maybe she's upstairs," I announced, keeping up the ridiculous charade, on the off chance someone popped out of the closet with a video recorder. *"See, I'm just in here lookin' for the cat."*

What was I looking for, anyway? Did I really believe Jeff had murdered his wife, or was this, like everyone else seemed to think, just an elaborate way for me to assuage my guilt over my friend's death? As I am much more functional when I'm irrationally confident about my convictions, I decided to stick with my murder theory. I may be emotionally stunted, but my gut feelings are always dead-on. (No pun intended.)

I went into the bedroom and began opening drawers. It felt really uncomfortable rifling through the Rhineholts' personal belongings. Not that I'm averse to checking out other people's stuff—I'm inherently nosy—I just didn't want to get caught. I found an open box of condoms on the nightstand next to the bed and wondered if they had been used recently, in which case, their relationship was probably in a lot better shape than I had imagined.

I moved on to the office. It looked marginally different from the last time I had been in there, but I couldn't put my finger on why. "The computer screen is lit up," I suddenly realized. Who had turned it on? Had Jeff come by the house to sift through his dead wife's e-mails in search of proof of her infidelity?

As I thought about this, I noticed Tamra's cell phone lying on the floor, under the bookshelf. I held it in my gloved hands and scanned the menu for recent calls. Resting the flashlight on the table, I scribbled down the numbers for the last calls she'd made. I knew one of them by heart—my own.

Next, I hit incoming messages. A guy's voice, demanding and gruff filled my ears. "Goddamit, Tamra. You can't keep avoiding me forever." *Hmm…an angry bill collector, perhaps, or the mysterious— and evidently cranky Richard?* I checked for a callback number, but it was restricted. Message number two was from Jeff. *"Honey, I'm sorry about earlier. Can we please just talk about this? Call me. I love you."* His voice was soft and pleading and I began to feel very ashamed of myself for invading their privacy. I placed the phone on the computer table and looked around some more.

My flashlight battery was beginning to dim and I hadn't found anything incriminating yet. No bloody razor discreetly tucked away in his underwear drawer, no confessionary note proclaiming, "I did it, signed Jeff."

*Okay, assuming for a minute it wasn't Jeff, who else would have a vested interest in killing off Tamra...*hey, m*aybe her death was work related. What was that big story Tamra was about to break?*

I opened her desk drawer and there among a pile of unrelated news items, I found a reprint of an article about a man who had been convicted of raping and killing a college student, out in Manayunk. It was dated four years ago. Vince said Tamra been asking questions recently about a Dwayne Somebody on Death Row.

I stared down at a blurry mug shot of a large, muscular African-American man. David Dwayne Harmon. He appeared to be in his late twenties, shaved head, a small tattoo located above his left ear; good looking by anyone's standards, even *with* his homicidal tendencies. *Okay, that clinches it. I'm definitely going to hell.*

Tamra had highlighted parts of the article. I held the paper up to my face and tried to make out the words in the fading light, but was suddenly distracted by a faint rustling noise. My body stiffened. "Mittens?" I whispered hopefully. The noise was coming from just outside the door. I was surprised I could hear it over the pounding of my heart.

I grabbed my bag and reached inside for the pepper spray, knocking the flashlight onto the rug in the process. The light went out, leaving me in pitch darkness. I quickly crouched behind the desk, taking a fraction of a moment to ponder how I always seemed to end up in these predicaments. I guess my fourth grade teacher Mr. Brownstein was right on the money when he wrote on my report card, "lacks impulse control."

Oh God, the door was opening. I heard a soft intake of breath and suddenly the room was flooded with light. I stood and pressed hard on the pepper spray, aiming straight for the face that loomed in front of me. Too late, I recognized the uniform and gun that accompanied the command, "Don't move! Police." It was followed by a "Jesus Christ" and a few other choice expletives as the spray connected with his eyes.

His partner rushed into the room and tackled me to the ground, knocking the wind out of me. Squashed beneath his weight, I was hauled to my feet, hands bound behind my back and gasping for air.

Tears streamed down the first cop's face. I must've gotten him good because the rims of his eyes turned all red, like a white rabbit. So in my mind I started referring to him as Officer Bunny. "What the hell did you spray me with?" he barked, wiping his face on his sleeve. "It smells like Binaca."

"It is Binaca," I huffed, trying to catch my breath. "I couldn't find my pepper spray. I'm very sorry," I added. "I didn't know you were a cop."

"Tell it to the judge, sweetheart. You're under arrest."

"For what? Assault with a breath freshener?" *Oh my God. I'm in real trouble here. Why can't I just grovel like a normal person?*

"What's your name, ma'am?" Officer Bunny's partner interjected, and I could see he was making a concerted effort not to laugh.

"Brandy Alexander."

"You're kidding, right?"

I resisted the urge to say "bite me" and nodded toward my pocketbook.

"My identification is in there. Officer, what exactly am I being charged with?"

Cop number one did a quick check of my drivers' license. "Breaking and entering for starters. A neighbor saw you skulking around the property and called the owner. You have the right to remain silent." Boy that guy could really hold a grudge.

"Look, officer, this is all just a big misunderstanding. If you'll let me explain—"

He cut me off and read me my rights while his partner gave me the once-over. I thought I saw a glint of recognition in his eye. *He must have seen me on the morning news. Maybe he was a fan. This would be cleared up in a minute.* "Now I know who you are," he said finally. But before I could offer him an 8 X 10 color glossy photo, he turned back to his partner. "She's the nut who keeps calling the station saying the woman who lived at this house was murdered. It seems little Nancy Drew here wants to do our job for us." Seeing as he had a gun and the authority to haul my ass off to jail, I let the sarcasm slide.

I sighed. "The woman who lived here was a friend of mine. I was the one who discovered her. Look, I realized I still had her house key and I wanted to return it to her neighbor. But when I got here I became concerned that their cat was left for days all alone in the house, so I went inside to see if it needed to be fed."

"Why would you think that?" demanded a new voice. We all whipped around to see who had entered the room. It was Ricky, the buttinski kid from next door. "You were the one who told me to take the cat over to my house," he said. "Don't you remember?" Note to self: When the cops aren't looking, push Ricky down.

In the end, they let me go, but not before they called Bobby to have him vouch for me. They spoke for several minutes. At one point, Officer Bunny glanced over in my direction and nodded his head vigorously. He even chuckled a few times. For once I figured two guys having a laugh at my expense was a good thing.

He hung up the phone and uncuffed me. "DiCarlo says to go home and stay put. He'll meet you there."

"Thank you, officer," I said, rubbing the circulation back into my wrists.

"Ms. Alexander, if we catch you within thirty feet of this place again, you're going to jail. Is that clear?"

"Crystal clear." I didn't wait for an escort out.

I guess because DiCarlo ordered me to go straight home, I decided to stop at Paul's club on the way back from Jersey. I'd been promising to help him with the seating arrangements for his bar mitzvah party, but I'd been a little tied up what with trying to stay alive and all. Paul is co-owner of a nightclub in Center City. The party was going to be held there.

I found him perched at the bar, his head bent over the guest list. He looked up when I came in, relief flooding his face. "B-Brandy, I've been t-t-trying to c-call you. Where have you b-been?"

"I must've put my phone on vibrate and didn't hear it ring. Paul, calm down and tell me what's wrong."

My brother took a deep breath and let it out slowly. "Carla said one of her customers down at the beauty shop told her you'd k-killed yourself. She heard it on the eleven o'clock news."

"Carla's customer exaggerated. I wasn't dead. Only sleeping."

"That's not f-funny. I was w-worried sick about you. I mean I knew it couldn't be true, but where would Carla's customer get a story like that?"

"Paul, it was a co-worker of mine. I found the body. That's all. See? I'm fine." I peered over his shoulder, scanning the list. "Oh, you don't want to put Janine next to Phil Genardi."

"Why not? Hey, and don't change the subject."

I grabbed some honey-roasted peanuts off the top of the bar and popped a few into my mouth. "Janine and Phil dated two years ago. Let's just say it didn't work out, which is why he walks with a bit of a limp now."

Paul eyed me up and down, settling on my face. "You don't look so good."

"If that's supposed to be a compliment, it needs work."

He cut me a look and climbed down from the bar stool, leading me over to a booth. When my brother bought the place two years ago, he had it restored to its original condition, complete with red leather booths and mahogany tabletops. The club is his pride and joy. "Sit down," Paul said, letting go of my hand. I angled into the seat and he slid in next to me, gearing up for a lecture.

"Listen, Bran, I think you should to talk to a professional about not being able to sleep. Did you call Taco's cousin, like I said?" Taco is a friend from the neighborhood who plays in Paul's band. His cousin Sarah is a psychology major at Temple. She's a Junior, which would make her—oh—nineteen?

"I've got her dorm extension pinned up on my bulletin board." His look told me he was not amused. "Ah, c'mon, Paulie, cut me a break. Once Mom is here, I'll be swimming in parental concern. Say, Paul," I added, deftly changing the subject, "has DiCarlo mentioned anything about bringing a date to the bar mitzvah?" I picked up the guest list and did a quick check.

"No, why? And *quit* changing the subject!"

"No reason," I said. "Y'know, Paul, I don't think it's a good idea for your guests to bring dates. I mean this is your special day. Why would you want to share it with a bunch of strangers? And what if they steal something? Your whole day is *ruined*."

Paul snorted. "Yeah, that's a real concern. I hear Aunt Betty's bringing a seventy year-old klepto from Fishtown. He could run off with the chopped liver sculpture while we're dancing the hora."

I made a face. "Suit yourself, bro. I'm only thinking of you."

"And I appreciate it," he said, slinging an arm around my shoulder. "Now, do you want to tell me what's really going on in that head of yours, or should we continue to pretend you're fine?"

"Pretending's good," I said, avoiding eye contact.

"Bran," Paul gave my hair a gentle tug. "You're going to have to talk to someone eventually."

"Not necessarily," I argued. "Did you know there are some monks in Tibet who haven't spoken a word in over thirty years? They live perfectly contented lives without talking about every little feeling. We could learn a few things from those monks, Paul."

Paul heaved a big sigh. People tend to do that a lot around me.

It was after seven when I left Paul's, having decided that, for the sake of Phil and his one good leg, people should just choose their own seating. There was no parking on my street, because Mrs. Gentile's 1980 Coup D'Ville took up half the block. I don't even know why she keeps it around. She hasn't driven it since 1987, when her license was revoked (My mother has tried for years to find out why, but it's the best-kept secret since who shot J.R.). She has her grandson come over every Thursday, to move it from one side of the road to the other and back again for street cleaning.

I finally settled for the spot in front of the fire hydrant and was just about to climb out, when a car pulled up next to me and double-parked, effectively cutting off my exit. Bobby DiCarlo reached across the seat of his vintage Mustang and swung open the passenger door.

"Get in," he said.

I squeezed out of the driver's side of the Le Sabre, careful not to scrape the Mustang. He was mad enough already without me screwing up the original paint job on his car. I slid into the front seat, taking in the warmth and the smell of his aftershave, mixed with something else— wait—apple juice! I turned around and saw Bobby's daughter, Sophia, asleep in her car seat, a juice cup clutched firmly in her hand. Apple juice was trickling out of the pour spout and slowly making its way onto the leather upholstery. If Bobby noticed, he didn't seem to care. Boy, fatherhood sure changes a guy.

"So," I said. "What brings you here?"

"Didn't I tell you to go straight home?"

"Listen," I said, figuring his question was rhetorical, "thanks for talking those cops out of busting me. I was just there to return the key to the neighbor, when—"

He cut me off with a grunt.

"Honest!"

"Alexander, it's me you're talkin' to. I know you better than anyone does."

"You used to," I countered. "That was a long time ago. I've changed."

"Yeah, I can see that. You're much better at following orders now."

"Orders?" I yelled, forgetting all about the sleeping child.

"Shh!"

"Don't shh me, DiCarlo."

"Fine. Next time I'll just let them haul your butt off to jail."

He had a point there. The thing is, the more wrong I am, the more defiant I become. It's a real problem with me. I took a deep, cleansing breath. "Okay, Bobby, look. I appreciate you bailing me out. I really do. And I know you're just looking out for my best interest. But I can't let this drop. Tamra was my friend. Maybe we weren't all that close, but nobody else is fighting for her, so that just leaves me. I'm right about this. I know I am."

I started to climb out of his car, but he yanked me back in, hoisting me over the stick shift until I was practically sitting in his lap.

"You make me crazy," he hissed. Grabbing my face in his hands, he leaned into me and planted his lips squarely on mine. It was totally unexpected and completely thrilling. I let myself enjoy it for a brief moment, and then as I opened my mouth to protest, he slipped his tongue in, so I had no choice but to kiss him back. It was everything I remembered and more.

Suddenly the car became unbearably hot, so I unbuttoned my jacket and shrugged out of it, my mouth never leaving Bobby's. He pulled me closer and slid his hands under my shirt, inching their way north. *"I should stop him,"* the sensible part of my brain said, while the other part, the one in charge of my libido screamed, *"If you stop him I'll kill you."* His hands were almost at my breasts and I felt my stomach muscles contract in anticipation. Just a little bit farther and—

"Hi," a small voice piped up from the back seat.

I yanked my shirt down and peered over the top of the seat, where Sophia greeted me with eyes wide open. She stuck out a small hand and offered me a sip from her juice cup.

"Um, no, thank you."

I turned back to Bobby. "Do you know what we just did?" I whispered frantically. "We just made out in front of your two-year old. *That's sick.* We are *sick* people!"

DiCarlo grinned. "If my kid could put together a complete sentence, I'm sure she would say it's nice to see her old man enjoying himself for a change. I've waited a long time to do that," he added quietly.

"Was it worth the wait?"

"You tell me."

"I've gotta go," I said, my entire being still vibrating from his touch. I leaned over and yanked open the car door, but he pulled me back and kissed me again. Ten minutes later I opened the door for the third and final time.

"I guess you'll be burning up the phone lines tonight, telling your girlfriends all about this," he said, a look of smug satisfaction on his gorgeous face.

"Oh, grow up, DiCarlo!" I practically tripped over myself, running into the house to call Franny.

" ...and then out of nowhere he just grabs me, and then next thing I know, we're making out like a couple of horny teenagers in the front seat of his car. Oh, now don't give me that look. Like it's never happened to you?"

Adrian sat at attention by the foot of my kitchen chair, drooling over my every word—well, more likely, waiting for something to fall from my dinner plate onto the floor. Truthfully, he wouldn't have been my first choice to confide in, but Franny wasn't home and I *had* to tell *someone*.

I left the dishes in the sink and took my laptop over to the coffee table. I'd think about this new development between Bobby and me later on in bed, when I had more time to devote to it.

I typed in David Dwayne Harmon on Google and twenty-eight matches came up, among them, the oldest living alligator wrestler and a Rapper from New Hope. I added Death Row to the search and hit pay dirt.

It was all there, from his arrest four years ago for the rape and murder of a wealthy co-ed named Laura Stewart, to his conviction and the inevitable appeals that followed. Thanks to the miracle of computer technology, I was able to piece together a fairly complete picture.

On the night of the murder, Laura, an honors student of impeccable character went slumming with some friends at a bar in West Philly. According to eyewitnesses, Harmon, the bouncer at Marisco's Cantina, struck up a conversation with Laura and pursued her throughout the evening. Laura was polite to Harmon, but she was clearly uncomfortable. She and her friends left shortly after ten p.m. Her landlord found her early the next morning, when he entered her apartment to fix the heater. Cause of death was determined to be trauma to the head, caused by a blunt instrument. Laura Stewart was survived by her parents, Rita and Bill and an older brother, Ethan.

It was the sexual nature of Harmon's comments to Laura that red-flagged him and led to his eventual arrest.

His semen and blood were found on the victim and there were signs of a struggle. Harmon had a history of arrests, including aggravated assault and breaking and entering. He was on parole when Marisco's hired him—an apparent oversight on the part of the manager. Bet he's kicking himself now.

David Dwayne Harmon was on death row; scheduled to be executed next month. But what did that have to do with Tamra? She clearly had an interest in the case, otherwise, why all the questions to Vince? Maybe Harmon wanted to make a deathbed confession and picked Tamra to record his last words. Then again, according to the latest articles, he still maintains that he's innocent. Could Tamra somehow have become involved in trying to free the guy? I wondered if Harmon had any relatives in the area that might know the answer to this. I made a note to look them up when I got to work.

The phone rang and I ran to the kitchen to get it. It was my mom. She was calling from a Best Western, just outside of Charleston. Ever since she switched to the unlimited calling plan on her wireless network, she calls hourly, just to feel like she's getting her money's worth.

"Brandy, I got the most disturbing phone call from Doris Gentile."

"Mrs. Gentile has your cell phone number? When did you two become such great pals?"

"I gave it to her in case of an emergency. It's a good thing I did too. It seems she was taking out the trash this evening and she couldn't help but notice Robert DiCarlo's car double parked in front of the house."

Uh oh. "Really?" *Stay calm.* "How did she know it was Bobby? There must be dozens of 1968 red

93

convertible mustangs cruising the neighborhood. It could have been anyone's."

"Don't be ridiculous, Brandy. She said she saw you get out of your car and climb into Bobby's and when you finally dragged yourself out of there your shirt was all undone. Honestly, Brandy Renee, I don't know what you were thinking!"

Oh crap. How am I going to get out of this one? And why should I have to? I'm twenty-eight years old, for God's sake. I shouldn't have to explain my every action to my mother. I'm just going to have to tell her to back off. "Mom," I said.

"Yes?" It was amazing how much disapproval the woman could pack into one small syllable.

"Have you spoken to Paul lately? He's having second thoughts about the bar mitzvah. In fact, he mentioned something about canceling the affair and becoming a priest." Sorry, Paulie, but it's every man for himself.

I hung up with my mom and sat back down in the living room, turning my attention back to Tamra. Could her husband have killed her? He certainly had access to Tamra and a motive, seeing as he thought she was cheating on him. But he did leave that sweet message for her on her cell phone…unless he'd left it after he'd already killed her, to throw off the cops and make it look like he didn't know she was dead. *Yes, Brandy, biology professors are notoriously wily.* Just to be on the safe side I Googled him too.

Eric called as I perused a deadly dull paper on the life cycle of the amoeba, by Jeff Rhineholt, which led me to believe that if he did in fact murder his wife, he had probably bored her to death by reading her this paper. "Turn on the television," Eric said. "Channel 3."

It took me a minute to find the remote, because Rocky was using it as a teething ring. By the time I pried it out of her paws, it was time for weather and sports. "What's going on?" I asked.

"New developments in the Tamra Rhineholt suicide story. Looks like it may not have been suicide after all."

"What kind of new developments? Eric, are you telling me the police think she was murdered?" It was about friggin' time.

"Why are you acting so surprised? Rumor has it you've been going around town screaming "murder" to anyone who'll listen to you. So what have you got?" he asked.

"Not much," I admitted. "At least nothing concrete. Eric, was Tamra working on a story about that guy on death row who's scheduled to be executed next month?"

"You mean Harmon? If she was, it wasn't for me."

Hmm... "What do you know about her husband?"

"I met him once at the Christmas party last year. Seemed like a nice guy. I'd heard rumors that they weren't getting along. What did you find out when you broke into their house?"

Jesus, does everybody know about that? "I was just returning her house key!"

"Yeah, sure. Listen, come in early and we'll talk about this. You've been itching to get a real story. This may be the one."

"Really? Eric, you're not just jerkin' me around, are you? I mean, why me?"

"Alexander, it's no secret you're overqualified for the job you were hired for. And I know your heart's not in it. But you take even the most crappy-assed assignment and turn it into a piece that's worth watching. I want to see what you can do with something you actually care about."

"Thank you," I said, all misty-eyed.

"By the way," he added, not missing a beat, "will you go out with me?"

"Fuck off, Eric."

"Fair enough."

Chapter Six

At six a.m. I was startled out of a fitful sleep by a pounding on the front door. I had dozed off on the couch at around 2:00a.m. in the middle of reading another one of Jeff's mind-numbing biology reports. I shoved Rocky off my lap and scrambled over to the door. Adrian growled and pawed at the rug. "Shh." Cautiously, I stood on tip-toe and peered out the spy hole. A man with sandy colored hair and glasses peered back at me. *Holy cow, it's Jeff!* He looked mad.

My heart leaped into my throat as I slowly began backing away from the door. Rhineholt stopped banging and leaned on the bell. The piercing ringtone was extra loud, to accommodate my nearly deaf grandmother, who owned the place years ago, before my parents moved in. I'd have to get that fixed—if I lived that long. Jeff looked *really* mad.

It didn't appear that he was going to go away any time soon and the ringing doorbell was bound to start pissing off my neighbors, so I braced myself and called out, "May I help you?" Jeff stopped ringing and slumped against the door frame. I would have felt sorry for him had I not thought he was here to kill me.

"I need to talk to you," he said, his voice choked with emotion. I couldn't tell if it was overwhelming anger or sadness until he started to cry. *Crap.* I opened the door.

"I'm not sure that you should be here," I said, through the storm door.

"That's funny," he replied. "I'm absolutely certain you shouldn't have broken into my house last night, and yet there you were." *How many times did I have to explain this? I had a key!* "Look, my life has been hell the last few days, and last night it got worse. Do you know the police were at my door until all hours? They got a court order to stop the cremation. Because of you they won't even let me bury my wife. I just want to talk to you for a few minutes. I won't stay long," he added, starting to cry again.

"Hang on a second," I said. I ran back into the living room to grab my cell phone and pepper spray out of my bag, and then I opened the storm door and stepped aside.

"Thank you," Jeff said softly.

"I really don't know what you want from me," I said, following him into the living room. He sat down on the couch.

"I want to know why you think I murdered my wife. Haven't I been through enough already without you spreading your insane ideas about me all around town?"

I was one hundred percent shocked. The Jersey police had totally blown me off. Even my nearest and dearest friends thought I had a screw loose. I didn't know why the police suddenly decided to look more closely into Tamra's death, but it could not have been my doing.

"Jeff," I said. "I am so sorry about Tamra. I can't imagine how you must feel. But I don't for a minute think Tamra committed suicide. There are things you don't know that led me to this conclusion. I told the police my theory and what I saw on the day Tamra and I had lunch. I never pointed a finger at you. It didn't enter my mind to consider you a suspect. They drew their own conclusions about you."

"Oh, so you're just Googling me for the fun of it?"

"What?" I looked down at my computer screen. "Oh, that. I was just, um…" *Oh hell.*

We went into the kitchen and I made us some coffee. Since I didn't have a lot in the way of breakfast to offer my drop-in guest, I took some frozen Milky Ways out of the freezer and set them on the table. I waited a beat to see if he'd take one and when he didn't I dove right in. *Ah, sugar. The breakfast of champions.*

Jeff stared down at his coffee, his face contorted in unmistakable grief. "I didn't kill my wife," he stated flatly. "I loved her. I'm not saying our marriage was perfect. Far from it in fact. I guess you figured out I thought Tamra was having an affair."

"Was she?" I asked gently.

"I don't know. If she was, I pushed her into it. We'd been fighting a lot lately."

"What about?"

Jeff shrugged. "Nothing and everything. You know how it is. I guess we let our careers become more important than our marriage. The night before she—she died, I asked her if she wanted a divorce. She said no and I believed her."

"Then why did you leave? The kid next door said he saw you leaving your home with suitcases."

"I was going to a seminar. I never would have left if I'd known she was so unhappy."

"So you still think Tamra killed herself."

"She's had some problems with depression in the past. She'd been on anti-depressants. I don't know. What else could it be? Who would want to kill my Tamra?"

You mean besides you? For once, my filters were working and the words stayed in my head where they belonged. "Jeff, I said, instead, "did Tamra ever mention anyone by the name of Richard?"

He shook his head. "Not that I recall. Why?"

Ignoring his question I asked, "Did she ever talk to you about stories she was working on?"

"Sometimes. What are you getting at?"

I picked up the last Milky Way and popped it in my mouth. "Tamra was known for her hard-hitting stories. She may have made some enemies along the way. What if somebody wanted revenge, or wanted to stop her from exposing critical information about them?" Jeff's face crumbled and my heart went out to him. "I'm upsetting you. I'm sorry."

"You really think she may have been murdered," he said, as if seriously considering the possibility for the first time.

"I do."

"If the autopsy report proves you right, the police are going to go after me, aren't they?"

"They usually look at the spouse, first."

"Do you think I'm guilty?"

"I don't know," I said.

"Thank you for your honesty," he said, standing up. I stood too.

"Jeff, maybe the police will determine it was a suicide after all. But if not, there may be information on Tamra's computer at home—clues that could point us in the right direction and take you out of the loop as a suspect. Would you mind if I had a look?"

"I don't know. Maybe we should let the police handle this."

"Think about it," I said walking him to the door. "And Jeff—"

He looked up, his eyes welling up with tears. "I'm really sorry."

On my way into work, I called Vince. "Have you heard about Tamra Rhineholt?" I asked. "They've blocked the cremation, pending an investigation into her death."

"You asked me to look into it. I looked into it," Vince said.

"Thanks, Vince."

"Don't thank me. Thank DiCarlo."

"DiCarlo? What's Bobby got to do with it?"

"Bobby called me and we talked. I guess he thought there was something to what you were saying, so we both put in some calls. I think he figured if the police start investigating, you'll back off. I told him, 'fat chance.' Am I right?"

I wouldn't dignify that with an answer. Besides, he already knew what it was.

I walked into work and saw that a crowd had gathered at my desk. *That's so nice. Everyone's heard about my ordeal and they're rallying around me. This could be a real bonding opportunity.* Art looked over in my direction, his face positively beaming. Suddenly he burst into an off-key rendition of "For She's A Jolly Good Fellow" and the whole gang joined in. *Wow. They're really going all out.*

I smiled and waved back and was about to walk over when Megan stopped me.

"Brandy, what are you doing here?"

"What do you mean? I work here."

"But—I thought you were fired."

"Fired? Why would you think that?"

"Well," Megan blushed, "Lynne said Wendy was coming back to take over her old job as puff piece reporter, so naturally I thought…" Her voice trailed off as a large woman came up behind me, carrying a dessert tray. She was greeted with thunderous applause. "Everyone's pretty excited," Megan explained. "Wendy brought cheesecake."

Eric stuck his head out of his office and crooked his finger at me, beckoning me forth. "I put you down the hall," he said, "so you can have more privacy."

I looked around at the crowd, which was now descending upon Wendy. "I don't think that's a huge problem, Eric. Nobody talks to me anyway."

Seeing as I didn't have a nice slab of cheesecake to slow me down like everyone else did, I was able to get right to work. I picked up the phone and called Graterford State Prison, where David Dwayne Harmon was living out his last days. They confirmed what I'd already suspected. Tamra visited Harmon on three occasions, all within the past six weeks.

Encouraged, I called Heather at the Department of Records. "Heather," I said, when she got on the line, "I need a favor. Can you get me a copy of a transcript of a trial that took place four years ago?" The nice thing about Heather is she doesn't ask a lot of questions. I gave her the case name and she promised to look into it and get back to me. While I was waiting, I walked back to the newsroom.

Wendy had left the empty cake plate sitting on Tamra's desk. Tamra's assistant, Craig, stared down at the plate, looking absolutely miserable. *Maybe he didn't get offered any cheesecake either.*

I wandered over to him and sat down. "Are you okay?" I asked. Tamra had once mentioned to me that Craig was a unique hire, having come to WINN through a program that provides placements for what we used to call "special" students. She liked him a lot and was really protective of him. From the look on his face I'd say the feeling was mutual.

"I can't believe this happened," he said, close to tears. "I'm supposed to clean out her desk, but I don't know what to do with her stuff."

"I'll do it," I volunteered. I needed an excuse to go through her desk anyway. "I'm sure her husband will want her personal effects."

"Is it true that you were the one who found her?" he blurted out.

My stomach lurched at the memory. "Yeah," I admitted. "I can't get the image out of my mind."

"Oh, I'm sorry," he said, sitting down on the edge of the desk. "Sometimes I say things that are—you know—inappropriate."

"Well, I can relate to that," I told him.

Craig dropped his voice to a whisper. "I just can't believe she'd do something like this." He leaned forward until his head was practically in my lap. Somebody needed to explain to this guy about personal space.

"Can I ask you something, Randi?"

I let it slide. He had enough on his mind. "Shoot." I picked up the cake plate and ran my finger over it, scraping off the little bit of icing that was stuck to the rim.

"I heard on the news last night that maybe Tamra didn't kill herself after all."

"Yeah, I heard that too."

"I don't mean to bring up bad memories," he began, "but I've gotta know. I mean, you were there. You *saw* her. Do you think she could have been murdered?" His eyes widened.

"I don't know," I sighed.

"But why would anyone want to kill her?" he persisted.

"Craig, you worked closely with Tamra, so you probably knew more about her than I did." I thought for a minute. "Do you recall her getting any threatening phone calls lately, or possibly hate mail?" Reporters are always targets for disgruntled nut-jobs. It comes with the territory. Craig slowly shook is head. I'd check with Eric. If she lodged a complaint there would be a record of it.

Well, did you notice anything different about her, like a change in her personality?"

"Now that you mention it, she did seem sort of jumpy lately, but I just thought it's because she wasn't getting along with her husband. He used to call here all the time wanting to talk to her, and he'd get really upset when she wouldn't come to the phone. They had a terrible fight one night when he came to pick her up after work. Hey, maybe *he* killed her." The relief in his voice was puzzling.

"Do you remember what the fight was about?"

"He thought she was cheating on him. He called her awful names."

So, Jeff has a temper. I filed this away for later.

Craig stopped for a minute, thinking. "Randi, what will happen to Mittens if Jeff gets sent to prison? She's such a sweet cat. I'm worried that she might get sent to an animal shelter and they'll—you know." He put his index finger up to his throat and started sawing away, just in case I *didn't* know. "I really love Mittens. Do you think they'd let me take her?"

Boy, Craig sure was in love with that cat. When did he get to know her so well? I decided to ask him.

"Tamra used to send me to her house sometimes to pick up papers and stuff she forgot to bring to work," he explained.

"Oh. Would Jeff let you into the house?"

"No. He was never there. Tamra gave me the key."

So, Craig had a key, which pretty much gave him carte blanche to enter Rhineholt's house whenever he felt like it. Oh wow... maybe Craig killed Tamra... and then he set up Jeff to take the rap so that he could... gain custody of Mittens? Hmm...this may need some re-thinking.

"Craig," I said, moving on, "Tamra was working on a big story before she died, but Eric didn't know anything about it. Did she ever mention anything to you?"

"Why do you want to know?" Craig's voice took on a hint of agitation. His eyes shifted to the floor.

"I'm just—curious."

"Tamra didn't confide in me. I just ran errands for her, that's all. I—I've got to get back to work." He slid off the desk and stood up, carefully avoiding eye contact with me. "Thanks for taking care of Tamra's things for me. She was a nice person. She didn't deserve to die."

I spent my lunch break packing up Tamra's desk and going over her computer files. I worked uninterrupted, seeing as the gang took Wendy out for tamales. (They all snuck out while I was in the bathroom.) There was nothing in the files on Harmon. I wasn't surprised. Tamra was too professional to spend company time on a freelance story. What *was* surprising was Craig's abrupt reaction when I brought up the Harmon case. My question definitely hit a nerve.

Heather called, so I left early and drove over to the Department of Records to pick up the court transcripts. I could have asked Bobby or Vince to get them for me, but that would have meant admitting that I was going to pursue the story, and I wasn't ready for the lecture that would inevitably follow. Eric had enough faith in me to put me on this assignment—alright, Eric thinks with his dick and was trying to get into my pants—but the fact remains, he gave me a chance and I was not about to turn it down.

It was after 3:00 p.m. and I hadn't eaten lunch yet, so I stopped by Dunkin' Donuts for some coffee and an Old Fashioned. I took a seat by the window, pulled out the heavy manila envelop that Heather had given me and began to read. "The State VS David Dwayne Harmon."

A minute later I had the uneasy feeling that someone was watching over me. Fighting panic, I slowly raised my head, silently chanting my new mantra. "There's no one there. It's just my imagination. There's no-one—Aahhh!"

A light tap on my shoulder sent me flying backwards against the window. I hit my head on the glass and knocked over the coffee, splashing waves of wet heat onto my lap.

I looked up to see Alphonso Jackson grinning down at me, his dark eyes obscured by his ever-present sunglasses. Eyeing the wet spot between my legs he said, "I figured you'd be excited to see me, but I had no idea you'd be *that* excited." I blushed. Actually, I *was* that excited. Alphonso works for Nick. I don't know what his official job title is. Alphonso is a man of many talents—some of them even legal, I think.

"How're ya doin,' sweetcakes?" He pulled out a chair and slung his leg over it, making himself comfortable.

"Great," I lied.

Alphonso cut me a long look. "You tell a lie long enough, you start to believe it."

"Well, what's *that* supposed to mean?" I huffed.

"No offense, but you look like you've spent the last month in a crypt."

Before I could think of a snappy comeback, he stretched out a muscular arm and plucked the transcripts from my hand.

"Hey, give those back to me." I tugged at the papers, but it was like a Chihuahua wrestling a pit-bull.

David Dwayne Harmon," he read. "That dude is seriously bad news."

"You sound like you know him."

"Knew him. He was one of those guys made his presence known, y'know what I mean?"

I nodded. Having read the articles on him, I knew only too well.

"What's your interest in him, if you don't mind my asking?"

It's funny. I'd been warned about Nicholas Santiago since the day I met him, and not without good cause. But except for the fact that he's bound to break my heart, I

107

have absolute trust in him. By extension, I trust the people he trusts. And Nick trusts Alphonso.

I gave him the Readers' Digest version of Tamra's questionable suicide and my suspicion that her death might be tied into a case she was working on. "I haven't ruled out her husband, either," I added. "Then there's this mystery guy named Richard." I took a large gulp of coffee. "I'm just getting started and I can use all the help I can get, so if you know anything, now would be a good time to jump in."

Alphonso stared at me for a minute. At least I think he was staring at me. It was hard to tell with the sunglasses. "When was the last time you slept?" he asked, finally.

Six weeks ago, wrapped in Nick's arms. "Alphonso, I'm *fine*. But I do need to get to work on this, so if you don't have any useful information—" I finished the rest of the coffee and stood up. He grabbed my arm and pulled me back down.

"What do you want to know?"

"I don't know," I confessed. "I haven't read the transcripts yet."

My cell phone rang and I checked the caller I.D. Janine. I figured I'd ignore it, but when she called back fifteen seconds later I answered, mouthing "one sec" to Alphonso. While he waited, he entertained himself by finishing off my doughnut.

"Yo Neenie, I'm kinda in the middle of something—"

She cut me off with the promise of some major gossip. "You're going to want to hear this, Bran. I ran into Tina Delvechione at the Reading Terminal today and she said she's making dinner for Bobby and his little girl."

"Get out!"

"Wait, there's more. She also said that now that Bobby's available she's gonna make a play for him like she should've done in high school."

"That slut!"

"And that's not all. She also said she's going to the bar mitzvah with Bobby."

"DiCarlo asked her out?"

"No, Bran, listen—"

"I've gotta go." I snapped the cell phone shut. It rang again immediately, but I didn't pick up.

"So, Alphonso," I said, as my cell went to voice mail, "What are you doing next Saturday night?"

Oh my God. What was I thinking? I just asked Gangsta Rap's original poster boy to be my date for my brother's bar mitzvah. Oh man, I can just see it now. The usher walks him to his seat, hands him a yarmulke and says, "Sir, would you like me to check your Uzi at the door?"

Okay, so I panicked. I just couldn't go dateless. Not with Bobby bringing Tina! On the upside, Bobby would be so busy checking Alphonso's rap sheet he wouldn't have time to get it on with Tina. And who knows— maybe Alphonso and Tina will hit it off. I guess I was getting a little ahead of myself. The truth is Alphonso never even gave me an answer. He was too busy laughing.

I decided to make a quick run to the Acme before I headed home. My parents would be here any day now, and all I had in the house to eat was a bag of coconut flakes for those Christmas cookies I never got around to baking because I ate all the raw cookie dough.

As I cruised down Broad Street, I thought about Alphonso's parting words. *"Call Santiago. He knows everything that happens on the street. I'm sure he can get you the information you need."*

I was sure he could too. So why was I so reluctant to call him?

"Because he hasn't called you," said a little voice inside my head.

"Pride goeth before a fall," chirped a new little voice.

"Oh shut up," replied the first one. *"If she calls him she'll look desperate."*

"If she calls him, she'll get the help she needs with her investigation. And maybe find true love!"

"Yeah, right," I said, jumping into the fray, *"like that's gonna happen. Look, you guys, I know Nick cares for me, but he's made it clear that he's not looking for emotional attachments. I don't know if he's capable of loving anyone."*

Okay, it's one thing to talk this through with my dog and cat. They only want the best for me. But having a three-way conversation with imaginary people is just plain silly—not to mention a little frightening.

When I got home I made a quick dinner of tomato soup and Ritz crackers and then I settled in on the couch with the box of stuff I'd taken off Tamra's desk. Earlier in the day I'd pocketed a small notebook I'd found stuck between the pages of an old *U.S.A. Today* that was stuffed in the back of her drawer. I took it out and thumbed through it.

Most of the pages had been torn out. The remaining few were filled with scribbled notes. Two in particular stood out—*"background check on A.B. Mitchell. Where is he now?"* and *"Call K. Morgan to confirm appt."* Tamra had doodled Laura Stewart's name right next to it, with circles and arrows pointing to the phone number. The appointment was set for two days ago, an appointment she never got to keep.

A.B. Mitchell sounded familiar. *"Anthony,"* I *remembered. Anthony "Boner" Mitchell.* He was mentioned in one of the old newspaper articles I'd read about the trial. Mitchell was a friend of Harmon's who'd testified that Harmon bragged to him about murdering Laura. It was Mitchell's testimony that sealed the deal for the prosecution. Apparently, Tamra had been looking for him. I wondered if she found him.

K. Morgan didn't ring any bells, so I picked up the phone and dialed the number in the notebook. A machine picked up. The voice was female, young, around my age. "This is Kylie. Please leave a message." I left my name and number and said I was a colleague of Tamra's and I asked her to call me.

I still had the phone in my hand when it rang again.

"Yo." It was Bobby. I was dying to ask him about Tina, but I wouldn't give him the satisfaction of thinking I was jealous, which I most certainly was not!

"Hey." I said. "I was going to call you. Vince told me what you did. Thanks for putting pressure on the Jersey police. I heard on the news they're doing an autopsy."

"Yeah, it only made sense. And now that they're involved, you can finally back off."

"Yeah," I lied.

"Listen, I thought I'd come over."

Panic washed over me like a tidal wave over the Titanic. "Here? Now? Why?"

I still hadn't processed last night's game of tonsil hockey and to tell the truth, I was scared to be alone with

111

him. Franny was right. I had some unresolved issues with Bobby, but this was no time to resolve them. It was much too soon. Only I didn't think common sense was any match for the hormonal surge I felt at the moment.

"I just want to see you," he said, smelling my fear and pouncing on it. "Do I need a reason?"

"Um, now isn't a good time. I'm, uh, I'm having a party. The gang from work's here—Hey, buddy," I yelled across an empty living room, "use a coaster. That's what they're there for. Listen Bobby, I've gotta go. Juan's making Margaritas." I hung up the phone and the doorbell rang.

I stood on tiptoe and peeked through the spy hole. Bobby grinned back at me.

I sighed. "Go away."

His grin got wider.

"Ah, come on, let me in. Please?" Now the dimples were showing and I knew I was toast. I opened the door.

Rocky ran up to Bobby and began sniffing his shoe. He scooped her up in his arms and petted her with strong, sure hands. She purred with deep contentment. *Shit. I'm jealous of my cat.*

"Shouldn't you be home with Sophia?" I asked.

"I had the day off and we spent the whole day together. She's over at Fran and Eddie's for the night. They wanted to see what they're in for when their kid shows up."

He put Rocky down and unzipped his leather jacket and extracted a small bouquet of wild flowers. He handed them to me.

"What's with the flowers?" I asked.

"I'm wooing you."

"You're *'wooing'* me?" I went into the kitchen to find an empty spaghetti sauce jar to put them in.

"Yeah," he said, following me. "How am I doin'?"

"What makes you think I want to be wooed?"

I filled the jar with water and stuck the flowers in it. Then I picked it up and carried it back into the living room. I was about to set it down on the coffee table when Bobby came up behind me and worked his hands around my waist. "Oh, you want to be wooed all right," he said, nuzzling my neck.

"Get away," I breathed. "I have work to do."

He continued to nuzzle, brushing soft lips against my skin. "You like this."

"I do not."

"Then why are your nipples getting hard?"

"Shut up. They are not!" *Oh God, they are!* "Bobby—"

"Shh." He gently turned me around and pulled the jar out of my hands, setting it on the table. Then he lowered his head and lifted my chin until our mouths were a hair's breath apart. "Listen," I croaked, struggling to be the voice of reason, "I don't think—"

"Good idea," he whispered. "Don't think." And his mouth came crashing down on mine. *Oh boy!*

Chapter Seven

We were just getting warmed up when the phone rang again. *Damnit.*

"Don't answer it," Bobby grunted. We'd moved to the couch, displacing Rocky and Adrian, who had been curled up together on top of the afghan. Bobby flopped down on the cushions, pulling me along with him until we were lying side by side. At the moment he had his hand under my shirt and was making a one-handed attempt to unfasten my bra. I wasn't about to stop him, but I wasn't going to help him either. That way, when I recounted it later for Fran and Janine I could claim at least partial innocence.

The phone kept on ringing, and I was about to throw it against the wall when I remembered about Kylie. "I've got to get this," I groaned. "It might be work." I pushed against Bobby's chest and rolled him off the couch. He sprawled on the floor, eyes closed, breathing deeply, his lips moving in a silent count to ten. It took every ounce of strength I had to keep from joining him on the floor.

"Hello?" I said into the phone.

"Brandy, this is Kylie Morgan. You left me a message?"

"Oh, hi," I said, tucking in my shirt. "Thanks for calling back. Um, could you hang on for just a second?" I held my hand over the receiver. "Bobby, I've got to get some papers from upstairs. I'll be right back." I dashed up the steps two at a time.

Now was not the time to tell him I was assigned to this investigation. I thought about when *would* be a good time. *Possibly never.*

I took the call in my bedroom. Kylie confirmed that she did have an appointment with Tamra to talk about her friendship with Laura Stewart and her recollections of her. She agreed to meet with me the following day.

I hung up the phone, walked into the hallway and ran smack into Bobby. "Hi," he grinned, backing me into the bedroom. "Now, where were we?"

"Whoa! We weren't *there*," I said, yanking his hand out of the waistband of my pants.

"But that's where I want to be." His voice had gone all husky and serious and it went straight to the pit of my stomach. He put his arms around me and I could feel how serious he was through the crotch of his jeans. "I've got to be honest with you, sweetheart, except for Sophia, my life has been shit these past few years." Before I could say anything he added, "I did it to myself, I know. And I screwed you over in the process. But the way I look at it, we've got a chance to start over. And this," he said, pulling me toward him, "would be an excellent place to start."

He began a slow assault on my neck; open-mouthed kisses that left me breathless and wanting a whole lot more. I strained against him and we fell back onto the bed. Soon, my shirt found its way to the floor and Bobby's wasn't far behind. *"You go girl,"* said the little voice in my head, and I was about to do just that, when another voice, louder and oh so familiar began calling my name.

"Brandy, we're heeerre!"

"Holy shit, it's my mother!"

I bolted upright, grabbed my shirt and began a frantic search for my bra.

"How the hell did they get into the house?" Bobby barked, scrambling around for his pants.

"Shhh! They'll hear you. I left a key under the mat, in case I wasn't home. They're not supposed to be here until tomorrow!"

"Brandy, are you up there?"

I stuck my head out into the hall. "Hey, you're here! Great! Give me a second and I'll be right down." I turned to Bobby. "You've got to get out of here!"

"Whadya think I'm *tryin'* to do?" He grabbed his shirt off the floor, yanked it over his head and started for the door.

I hauled him back inside the bedroom. "You can't go out that way. They'll see you."

Bobby sank back down on the bed. "Well, what do you expect me to do? Climb down the trellis?"

I walked over to the window and opened it.

"You can't be serious."

"Hey, it was good enough for you twelve years ago..."

"Jesus, Brandy, we were just kids then. We're adults now. We're entitled to do...what adults do."

"Brandy Renee!" The voice was coming closer.

Bobby leaped up and bolted toward the window. "Man, I forgot one thing," he whispered.

"Yeah, what's that?"

"Your mom's scary." He gave me a quick kiss and climbed out the window.

Bobby was wrong. He'd forgotten *two* things and my mother was holding them in her hand. "Whose boots are these?" she asked, entering my bedroom.

"Mom!" I said, throwing my arms around her. "I'm so glad to see you. Those are Paul's. You know how forgetful he is. Where's dad?" I took the shoes from her and set them on the floor. "You must be exhausted." I turned her around and directed her to the top of the stairs. "I'll be down in a minute and we'll have a nice long chat. 'K?"

I shut the door, ran to the window and looked out. Bobby was standing on the sidewalk, looking up at my bedroom window. He was barefoot. I opened the window and tossed out his boots, accidentally hitting him in the head. I winced.

"Brandy," my mother said through the closed door. "Next time tell Bobby to use the front door like a normal person. You aren't kids anymore."

It was like they'd never left. Within a half hour of their arrival, my dad was sitting on the couch, remote in hand, alternating between the History Channel and the Food Network (my dad has a little crush on Rachel Ray). My mother had commandeered the kitchen and was preparing her "famous Spaghetti Marinara" for Saturday night's dinner. I tried to warn her that Rocky has a "thing" about red sauce and if she didn't keep an eye on her, the secret ingredient in the meal would likely end up being cat fur. She told me to "get the damn cat" off *her*

117

counter and then she sent me to my room. (Swear to God.)

Kylie Morgan sat at a table in the back room of the Country Club Restaurant, located in the Northeast section of the city. I recognized her immediately by her description. Long blond hair pulled back in a pony tail, wearing a navy blue hooded sweatshirt with the name of her school emblazoned on the front. She was a grad student at Drexel University, working part time at a senior center on Cottman Avenue.

"Thanks for agreeing to meet with me," I said, after the introductions had been made.

"Oh, no problem. Actually, I was curious," Kylie admitted. "When Ms. Rhineholt contacted me, I'd told her I didn't know Laura all that well. I don't think anyone did. She said she wanted to meet with me anyway; that I might recall something that, at the time, I was maybe too traumatized to think about. I was there the night Laura met that guy at the bar," she clarified. She lowered her eyes, remembering. "We had to talk her into coming out with us. She seemed so tightly wound all the time. We thought she could use a little fun in her life, you know? Afterwards, we all felt so responsible...I just don't know what I could tell Ms. Rhineholt—or you—that I didn't already tell the police."

I studied her a minute. "You said you were curious. About what?"

"Well, two things really." Kylie let out a nervous laugh. "It seemed so obvious that David Dwayne Harmon is guilty. I mean all that evidence. And he had a history of violence..." I was very familiar with Harmon's background. I'd been up until four in the morning going over the transcripts of the trial. He was not a nice guy by anyone's standards. "So if a jury of his peers convicted him," Kylie continued, "why would Ms. Rhineholt think he might be innocent?"

So that was it. Tamra must have somehow become convinced that the state had prosecuted the wrong person. Holy cow. The guy is set to fry in less than a month. Oh man, what could Tamra possibly have discovered that would help prove Harmon's innocence?

"You said there were two things you were curious about," I reminded Kylie. "What was the other one?"

"Well, I know this is none of my business" she blushed, "but I was wondering. What would make a successful person like Tamra Rhineholt want to kill herself?"

And that's the million dollar question.

Country Club Restaurant is famous for their cheesecakes. They're way better than Wendy's, I'm sure of it, so I got a whole one to go. It helped to soften the blow of Kylie not being a whole lot of help.

"Kylie," I said, taking one last stab at it as we stood in the parking lot, "I know you'd said Laura was difficult to get to know. That she kept to herself, didn't share her personal life with you. But there must be something. No matter how insignificant it seemed at the time."

Kylie squinted her eyes at the harsh winter sunlight, thinking. "I don't know if this is what you're looking for, but I remember giving Laura a ride home from school one day. We were riding around near down town, and you know the big Lutheran church at the corner of 17th and Maple?" I nodded. "Well, there's this small, red brick apartment building right next door to it, and as we're driving by, Laura goes, "That's my shrink's building. Dr. Applebaum."

"Her shrink? Are you sure?" There was no record in the transcripts of Laura going to a therapist, and I was pretty sure that in a murder trial the defense would be interested in that bit of information.

"I'm sure," said Kylie, shaking her blond ponytail.

"Did you mention it to the police?"

"No. It was a fleeting remark. Right after she'd said it, she'd changed the subject really quickly, like she was sorry she'd let it slip out. I—I didn't think it was anything worth mentioning."

"I'm sure you're right," I said, feeling sorry for her. She felt guilty enough already.

So, unbeknownst to the general public, Laura Stewart was seeing a therapist. I wondered why he hadn't come forward after she was killed. Well, I was going to find out.

I sat in the car and punched in 411 on the cell phone. There was no listing for a Dr. Applebaum on Maple, however, the directory showed one for a Peter Applebaum. I jotted down the number and was about to call him when I thought better of it and decided to check it out in person. One of the advantages of being on television is people tend to feel like they know you and are more likely to open up.

On the way over I rehearsed what I was going to say. What with doctor-patient confidentiality and all, I didn't know how much Dr. Applebaum would be willing to share. This was just a shot in the dark anyway. For all I knew, Laura was a bed-wetter or addicted to on-line shopping. Not exactly the deep dark secret I was looking for, but it was the only lead I had.

Peter Applebaum lived on a quiet street in a quaint four-plex, half-hidden by ancient, giant Maple trees. I walked up to the mailboxes and checked for Peter's apartment number. 1A.

I rang the bell and waited. A few minutes later the door opened and I was greeted by a middle-aged man in a wheelchair.

"Oh, hello. I thought you were U.P.S. I was expecting a package."

I tried not to stare at the wheelchair. The man was good-looking, with an athletic build and a nice, friendly smile. I concentrated on that and smiled back at him. "I'm sorry if I disturbed you. I was looking for a Dr. Applebaum."

His smile faded slightly. "May I ask why?"

"Are you Dr. Applebaum?"

"Actually, Dr. Applebaum was my wife. She died several years ago."

My heart took a dive into my stomach. "Oh, I'm so sorry." I didn't know what to say after that. It seemed insensitive to do anything but leave. Luckily, Mr. Applebaum was a fan of early morning news shows.

"You look familiar," he said. "Aren't you uh…wait, I've got it," he scrunched his face up in concentration. "Whisky?"

I laughed. "Brandy. Alexander, WINN news." I extended my arm and he gave me a warm handshake.

A few minutes later I found myself sitting in Peter's living room, a spacious area that opened up into the kitchen. There were stairs leading to a second floor, "Traci's old office," he explained to me. "We bought the place upstairs so that she could work from home. Patients used to come in through the staircase outside. I keep thinking one day I'll get one of those stairway lifts for inside the house, but since Traci's been gone, I just haven't been able to bring myself to go up there." Once again, I was caught not knowing what to say. It took everything I had not to burst into tears.

"So, how can I help you?" Peter started.

I explained to him about Tamra's death and the story she had been working on before she died. "Tamra was convinced that David Dwayne Harmon, the guy who was convicted of the murder, is innocent."

"I'm sorry, I don't understand," Peter said. "What does all this have to do with my wife?"

"I met with an old friend of Laura's, the girl who died. She said that four years ago, Laura was seeing a therapist. A Dr. Applebaum. Apparently, Laura was a patient of your wife's. "I don't know if you still have those patient files around, but if so, would there be any way I could get a look at them? I'm hoping that somewhere in Laura's files there's a clue that would substantiate Tamra's theory about Harmon. I'm not looking to make a name for myself," I felt compelled to add. "I'm just trying to find out what really happened. Tamra was my friend. I think maybe she was getting too close to the truth about who really killed Laura so she was murdered. And if I can't prove it, Harmon's going to be executed for a crime he didn't commit."

Peter sat back in his chair, thinking. "I wish I could help you," he said, finally, but I don't have Traci's files anymore."

"What happened to them?"

"Traci had a living will," he explained. "In it, she specified that if she died unexpectedly, her patient files would go to her colleague, Dr. Ann Levi. This is common practice," he added. "I'd be happy to give you Dr. Levi's number."

"Thanks. That would be really helpful."

As I got ready to leave, the part of my brain that's supposed to keep me from shooting off my mouth malfunctioned and I heard myself asking Peter about how he lost the use of his legs.

"Car accident," he said. "That's how Traci died." He began to well up and I instantly regretted my question.

"I'm sorry. It was rude of me to ask."

Peter shook his head. "No, it's been four years—I should be over it by now, but sometimes the guilt just eats away at me. It was my fault," he ended, choking on the words.

"It was an *accident*," I said, having no idea how to comfort this man.

"It could have been prevented if I hadn't been so stubborn. We were in Traci's car and I'd insisted on driving. I thought she was too upset to drive." He gave a rueful snort. "We'd been burglarized the night before—actually, Traci's office was. Goddamn drug addicts. They broke open her cabinets and stole all the drug samples. My mind was on the break-in. A car came out of nowhere and—" He looked up giving me a grim smile. "I guess I could use a trip to Dr. Levi's myself."

Dr. Levi was in her office when I called. I introduced myself and told her that Peter Applebaum suggested I get in touch with her. After filling her in, I asked if she was still in possession of Laura's files.

"I'm sorry," she said, "but I never received those files."

"Oh, but I thought that Dr. Applebaum turned all of her patients over to you."

"She did. As far as I know, Traci was only seeing five patients at the time of her death. I took all of them. There was no mention of a patient named Laura Stewart in any of the paper work I received."

Maybe Dr. Applebaum destroyed the file when she heard that Laura had been killed. But if Laura had been seeing a psychiatrist over some major issue, she probably wouldn't have just tossed the file. Presumably, if she thought something Laura had told her was in any way linked to her death, she would have gone to the police when she found out Laura had been murdered. Unless... she didn't have time to go to the police. What was it Peter had said about his wife's accident?

I thanked Dr. Levi and hung up. Then I punched in Eric's number. "Do me a favor," I said when he picked up.

"Where are you calling from?" he asked.

"I turned on the engine and blasted the heat. "My car. Listen, I need you to look something up for me. Four years ago, a local psychiatrist named Traci Applebaum and her husband were in a car accident. He survived but she didn't. Can you get me the particulars of the police report? I think this may be tied in to Tamra. I'd do it myself," I lied, "but I'm checking out another lead and I need this info ASAP." *Boy, if lying was fattening, I'd look like the Goodyear Blimp.*

The thing is I didn't want to go through my usual sources, meaning Bobby and Vince. They're kind of under the impression that I'm out of the loop now, and that's fine by me. My job is hard enough without those guys giving me grief about it.

Plus after my little escapade with Bobby, I wasn't quite ready to see him. As soon as my parents had gone to bed last night, I'd called Franny.

"Are you awake?" I asked.

"It depends on what you want to tell me."

I made her swear on her first-born child that she wouldn't breathe a word of what I was about to confess and then I launched into the specifics of my evening.

"You actually hit him on the head with his own shoes?" she howled with laughter. "What is that, some kind of kinky, new mating ritual?"

"I'm serious," I huffed. "I don't know what got into me."

"From what you just told me, *nothing* got into you, which, I might add is a little disappointing, seeing as the only thrills I'm getting these days are vicarious ones."

"Fran, this isn't helping."

"Alright. So you fooled around a little. No big deal. Bobby's a free agent, you're a free agent. You're entitled to have some fun."

"Yeah, you're right," I reasoned. "It's about time I started having some fun. I deserve it."

"So," she asked, "was it?"

"Was it what?"

"Was it *fun*?"

"God, yes!"

"Then what's your problem?"

"I guess I don't have one."

Only why did I still feel like I did?

Just as frostbite began to set in, Eric called back.

"I've got the police report," he told me. "What are you looking for specifically?"

"The date the accident took place and could you check to see if there was any mechanical malfunction that could have caused it?"

"Hang on a minute… preliminary findings… blah, blah, blah… Okay, it says here 'broken brake line.'"

"Are you sure?"

"No, I'm making it up. What was the other thing you wanted to know? Oh yeah, the date. May 4th."

And we have a winner! Dr. Applebaum never turned Laura's files in to the police because she was in a fatal car accident two days after Laura was killed. And not just any accident. Her brake line had snapped, just like mine.

I needed some time to think about this. "Eric, I've got to go." I hung up the cell just as a new thought occurred to me. *The burglars weren't after drugs when they broke into Traci's office. That had to have been a cover-up for the real prize— Laura's file.* If I was right, and it looked like I was, someone murdered Laura, stole her files and arranged her doctor's death. Fast forward four years, they go after me, thinking I'm Tamra, then they kill her in order to keep the truth from surfacing.

My head was reeling from these new revelations, which was probably why I didn't notice the guy with the ski mask sidle up to my car and smash in the window. Shit!

Bits of flying glass pelted the side of my face as a gloved hand clamped down on my neck. In an instant he thrust his other arm through the gaping hole in the window and grabbed for the door lock. I tried to pull him off me but he was too strong. I twisted sideways, loosening his grip on me. Blindly I fumbled around in search of the car keys. They were still in the ignition. As I reached for them, he let go of my neck and stuck his head inside the car, grabbing for the keys. His masked face was mere inches from mine. I raised my elbow and aimed straight for his windpipe.

The force of the blow stunned him long enough for me to turn on the engine and drop it into gear. I gunned it and took off, with half of him still stuck inside my car. He ran alongside, spewing expletives until I stopped short, trying to shake him loose. He stumbled and fell to the ground and I tore out of there, never looking back.

Ten minutes later, the surge of adrenalin that had propelled me into action abandoned me. I pulled over and parked, oblivious to the graffiti filled buildings and urban filth that lined the street. The wind had picked up and whipped through the car as I sat huddled behind the steering wheel. My throat hurt and I had a pounding headache but I was still alive, which was more than I could guarantee for the guy I'd left lying in the road.

I found my cell phone and was about to punch in 911, when I noticed a torn piece of dark leather material sitting in my lap. I picked it up and turned on the interior light so that I could examine it more closely. It was the tip of a glove. It felt wet and sticky, with chunks of glass clinging to it. Gingerly, I opened it and peeked inside. *Eewww!* Bile rose up in my throat and I flung it onto the floor and bolted from the car.

As I stood shivering on the sidewalk, wondering what the resale value is for a twenty-year old La Sabre equipped with a shattered window and a severed human finger, I began to take note of my surroundings. Suddenly I realized that I'd been on this street before, on this very block, and I was filled with an overwhelming sense of relief.

Halfway down the street I spied what I'd been looking for. I ran toward a pristine storefront, stopping short as the door opened and ten or so young guys in martial arts attire poured out the door. They were speaking Spanish, sweating, laughing. I shrank back to let them pass. When the last one filed out, I lost my nerve and turned to leave, but I didn't get very far. One man had remained in the doorway. Now he reached out and gently pulled me to him. "Hello, angel. Rough day?"

Chapter Eight

"...and then to top it all off, there was a *bloody finger lying* in my lap! It's still in the car by the way, if you wouldn't mind helping me get it out."

Nicholas Santiago flashed me a lopsided grin and my stomach flipped. "One thing at a time, darlin'. Let's first take a look at those cuts on your face." He knelt down in front of me and gingerly brushed the hair away from my cheek.

I was curled up in the red velvet armchair in the back office of his martial arts studio. The studio I was convinced was a front for all sorts of nefarious operations, but I was willing to overlook them for the moment.

Nick gently lifted my chin. I pulled back, embarrassed. I'd caught a glimpse of myself in the floor-to-ceiling mirror as we first walked in and, well let's just say that between the red blotches on my face and the snot pouring out of my nose, I wasn't looking my best.

"Nick, really, I'm—"

"Are you going to tell me you're fine?" he asked mildly. "Because I'll believe you if you do."

I looked away, not wanting him to see how scared I really was.

129

He turned my head, forcing me to meet his gaze. "But I won't think any less of you for needing help," he continued softly. "You know you can tell me anything, angel."

I did know and I was through fighting it. "Nick, I need your help."

Wordlessly, he got up and poured me a shot glass full of amber liquid. I didn't bother asking what it was. I really didn't care. I downed it in one gulp and it helped to stop the shaking.

While I busied myself getting good and blotto, Nick sauntered over to his desk and extracted a small bottle from the bottom drawer. He doused a cotton ball with its contents and positioned himself in front of me again. "This is going to hurt," he warned, swabbing my cheek with antiseptic. It stung like crazy but the pain was offset by the feel of his hand on my leg. He was so close I could smell the heat wafting off his caramel-colored skin. *Jesus, I'm sitting here with glass embedded in my face and I'm so turned on I could explode. What is wrong with me?*

"That should do it," Nick said, getting to his feet.

"Thanks. I just couldn't face another trip to the E.R."

Nick raised an eyebrow. "Another?"

"This hasn't been my week. Listen," I said, extricating myself from the chair, "I've taken up enough of your time. I should go."

He gently pushed me back down. "Not yet, darlin'. We have some business to take care of."

"We do?" I gulped.

Nick picked up the phone and punched in some numbers. While he was waiting for whoever it was to pick up, he said, "Have you called the police yet?"

"No, I—"

"Good." He began speaking into the phone in rapid-fire Spanish, pausing to ask me exactly where I'd left the guy who had attacked me.

"Nick, no." I've seen first-hand Nick's brand of justice and although I was sorely tempted, I'd just as soon not be the cause of another dead body added to his resume. "Let the police handle it."

"Sit tight, I'll call you back," he said in English, hanging up the phone.

Suddenly, it was all too much. I sank back into the chair again, drawing my legs up and curling into a ball. I was so close to tears I could taste them. "Nick, I didn't come here to be rescued." *Well, I did, but I hated myself for it.* "Hey, you're not one of those guys who gets off on helpless women, are you?"

He threw back his head and laughed. "Let's review the facts here. A guy tries to attack you and he ends up lying in the road, with nine and a half fingers. I wouldn't exactly categorize you as helpless." He scooped me up off the chair and sat down, bringing me along with him. "You have great instincts, angel. But you've been through a lot in the last few months and it has to be taking its toll on you."

I sat up, spoiling for a fight. "Are you telling me to butt out too? Because I've had my fill of people telling me that lately."

"No," Nick said calmly. "I'm telling you to be careful. And to accept help when you need it. It doesn't make you weak to need someone every once in a while."

"Who do you need, Nick?" The question just popped out of me. I really didn't expect an answer.

He grew quiet for a moment. Then he kissed the top of my head and eased me off his lap. "Let's take care of that car window."

We decided to grab something to eat, but first we took a detour in Nick's 1964 XKE Jaguar to check out the scene of the crime. We didn't find anyone sprawled in the street or squashed like road kill in the oncoming traffic. We got out and looked around. Not even a tire mark where I'd peeled rubber. "Do you still want to report it?" Nick asked. "It's your call."

I weighed my options. If I report it to the police I could end up looking like a nut job, or give my parents matching heart attacks and effectively ruin Paul's bar mitzvah. If I don't report it, I can go home and pretend it never happened. In my current state of mind it was a no-brainer.

Nick and I settled into a booth at Mai's Vietnamese Restaurant, a little hole-in-the-wall located about two blocks from his studio on Spring Garden. We'd dropped my car off at Nick's body shop and the guy promised to have it back to him in no time. We took the finger with us.

The server at the restaurant knew him, *of course.* She was young, beautiful and looked like a Bond Girl. *Stupid exotic looks. I hate her.*

Nick ordered soup and spring rolls which sounded good to me so I ordered some too.

The soup came and we both dug in. "I just don't get it, Nick. Tamra's dead. Whoever did it must know they finally got it right. Why are they still after me?"

"They may have gotten wind somehow that you're taking up where your friend left off. For better or worse you've earned a reputation in the past few months. You've been involved in some pretty high profile cases." He paused and shook some red pepper flakes into his soup. "Whoever's behind this knows their secrets aren't safe with you in the picture. Eventually, you're going to 'out' them."

I lifted my eyes to him. "Yeah? Well, I think so far they've got the edge on me."

"My money's on you."

The server returned to our table, bringing our meal. Nick smiled and thanked her, which, in my mind translated as, *"I'll be back as soon as I dump the albatross."* I guess my self esteem could use an upgrade.

I looked down at my plate, expecting to find a greasy, pork-filled fried wonton and found instead what appeared to be fresh salad wrapped in steamed wonton dough.

"What's this?" I asked.

"Spring rolls," Nick said, biting into his. "I thought you wanted them."

"I did. Only, I thought they'd be, I don't know— more—exciting." I picked one up and bit into it. Yep. Salad. It was really disappointing.

"If you want more excitement, try the sauce. But I've got to warn you, it's spicy."

He dipped his spring roll into a gooey reddish mixture and took a bite. Then he dipped it in once more and offered it up to me. It felt more like a challenge than an invitation, so naturally I had to accept it.

"I like spicy. I live for spicy. Bring it on." I took a bite and instantly my mouth was on fire, blazing a trail right up my nose. I spit the spring roll into my napkin and grabbed my water glass, taking humongous gulps.

Nick's mouth curved into a wicked grin. "Let that be a lesson to you, darlin'. Be careful what you wish for, because you just might get it."

Somehow I didn't think he was talking about the sauce.

In the hopes of regaining some sense of professionalism, I decided to change the subject. "Are you familiar with a guy named Anthony Mitchell?" I asked.

Nick shook his head. "Doesn't ring any bells. "Why?"

"He was a friend of David Dwayne Harmon's. His nickname is 'Boner'."

"Ahh. 'T-Bone Mitchell.' 'Tony the Bone.' The guy had a lot of street names."

"Had? What happened to him?"

"He disappeared a few years back. Legend has it some of Harmon's homies took him out after he testified against him in court."

I eyed him. "What do you think?"

Nick leaned back in his seat, resting his arm on the top of the booth. "There's another theory floating around, but it was never substantiated. He may have been paid to testify in that trial."

"You mean lie."

"Like I said, it's just a rumor."

"Any chance I could meet the folks who started that rumor?"

"Maybe. I'm acquainted with a few guys who ran in the same 'social club' as Harmon and Mitchell. They may be willing to talk to you. But I recommend you don't go alone—or unarmed."

A shudder ran through me. It was easy to forget the company he kept. It was also dangerous.

I sat back in the booth, pretending to study the paintings on the wall behind Nick's head, but the truth was I couldn't take my eyes off of him. His hair was pulled back in a loose ponytail, revealing the tiny silver cross he wore in his left ear. On his wrist was a silver band. I don't recall ever seeing him without it. One day I would ask about its significance but not tonight. He hadn't shaved in a day or so and a slight shadow edged his jaw line. He was undeniably beautiful and yet it wasn't his most compelling quality. Damned if I knew what was. I only knew that it kept me coming back for more.

We'd just finished up our meal when in walked a familiar face. Two, actually. Mindy Rebowitz and her totally whipped husband, Terrence. Mindy and I had gone to high school together. She was a cloying, obnoxious brat back then and time had done nothing to improve her. What was she doing slumming in this part of town, anyway? *Oh crap, she was headed our way.* I grabbed a menu out of the hands of the guy seated at the next table and buried my face in it, but I wasn't fast enough.

"Brandeee. I thought it was you. Don't you just love this place? I read about it in *Philadelphia Magazine*." She nodded her blond bobble-head at her husband. "Terrence, get a table near the window," she ordered, making a beeline for our booth.

"Oh, hi Mindy," I said, with as little enthusiasm as humanly possible.

Mindy's sharp blue eyes did a quick appraisal of Nick. "Who's your attractive friend?" she cooed. *Gack. Who talks that way?*

Nick stood, taking her hand and she practically slipped into a coma. "Nick Santiago," he smiled. "And you are--"

"I—um…"

"Mindy," I supplied, rescuing her. I stood up too. "Listen, we were just leaving."

"Oh. Do you have to rush off?" She looked like she was about to cry. I really couldn't blame her. Nick has that effect on women.

"Oh, great! Now the entire world is going to know I was here with you tonight," I grumbled as we walked back to Nick's car.

"Is that a problem?" He was smiling, clearly amused.

"You don't understand," I said.

"Explain it to me."

"I live in a fish bowl," I began. "My parents are in town…Bobby's going to hear about it…I…oh, never mind."

Nick leaned against the hood of his car, pulling me to him in a playful embrace. "So, are you and Detective DiCarlo an item now?"

"No, of course not," I stammered. "Well—*maybe*."

"Then I guess I shouldn't be holding you," he whispered in my ear.

"No, you *should*. I mean *you can if you want to*." *God, I sound like an idiot.* I took a deep breath. "What I meant was Bobby and I are friends—and you and I are friends. And friends *hold* each other sometimes. Right?"

"Right." Nick gazed down at me, his look intense, the light of the moon casting an unlikely halo around his head. "And sometimes they do more." I felt the heat pooling in my belly as he cupped my face in his hands and kissed the living daylights out of me.

"Two guys in two days? Way to go, Alexander!"

"Yeah, well, it certainly beats my old record of two guys in two *decades*."

I sat, feet tucked beneath me, on the closed lid of Janine's toilet seat, watching as she slathered her face in green clay. She was giving herself a facial. I'd stopped in to see her on the way home from retrieving my car from the body shop. She knew something was up the minute I'd walked in the door. "Okay, spill it," she said. "Have you and Bobby done 'it'?"

"No! Why would you think that?"

"You have a hickey on your neck the size of Lake Erie."

"I do? Oh crap." I ran to her mirror. *I do!* I began massaging my neck, hoping it would somehow miraculously disappear, but that just made it worse.

"So if it's not Bobby, then… "

I sighed. "We need to talk. But you can't tell anyone. Swear to me, Janine."

"My middle name is 'Discretion'," she said, making the sign of the cross.

"Your middle name is Christina. And you're not that good with secrets, Neenie, but I really need to tell someone."

"And Franny wasn't home?" she laughed.

"No. I mean I don't know. But this one's for you."

Franny and Janine are my closest girlfriends in the world. Separate but equal. When I need good, strong,

137

heads-up advice I tell Fran. When I want a non-judgmental ear to vent to I go to Janine.

I started at the beginning and told her everything. About Tamra and how I'd been investigating her death and how Franny and Vince and Bobby had warned me off it but I wouldn't listen. And how I'd gone and almost gotten myself killed, but for some unfathomable reason I had no intention of stopping. And then I told her about Bobby and Nick.

"So who gave you the hickey?"

"Nick."

"Cool."

"That's it?"

"You might want to apply a cold compress," she said, pointing to my neck. "Twenty minutes on, twenty off. And if that doesn't do the trick, Maybelline makes a terrific concealer." Wow. No lectures, warnings or judgments. Just total, Zen-like acceptance with a helpful hint thrown in for good measure. *Which is why I chose Janine.*

It was after nine p.m. when I finally pulled onto my street. I took a few extra minutes to grab the stun gun and pepper spray from my pocket book and check the street for stalkers and then I made a mad dash for the house. I was exhausted and wanted nothing more than to crawl into bed without having to pretend that everything was okay. I sent up a silent prayer that my parents had turned in early, but I guess God was busy with more pressing matters.

I opened the door and Adrian shot toward me, barreling through a thick cloud of cigar smoke as a chorus of male, middle-aged voices shouted hello to me. My dad was hunched over the dining room table, flanked by three old lodge buddies. A pile of poker chips sat in the center of the table. Sam Giancola emerged from the kitchen carrying a tray of hoagies from his deli, followed by Jerry Morgenstern and six Heinekens.

"Hope you don't mind, doll," my dad said. "The boys wanted to get the old gang together. Hey, pull up a chair and join us."

"Um, thanks, Dad. Maybe later. Where's Mom?" I asked. *Maybe I could sneak up to my room before she knew I was home.*

My dad cast an apologetic glance around the table. "She's in the kitchen making her special homemade brownies."

"Cripes," Sam grumbled under his breath. "Do we have to eat them?" I knew how he felt. Even I wouldn't eat my mom's brownies. They taste like mud pies rolled in chocolate.

I gave my dad a kiss on the cheek and walked into what used to be my kitchen. On the counter sat a pair of Campbell Soup Kids salt and pepper shakers that belonged to my grandmother when she owned the house and a hideous plastic flower arrangement that I'd buried in the basement.

"Brandy, honey," my mother said, as she scoured the stove within an inch of its life. What my mom lacked in culinary skills she made up for in obsessive cleanliness. "I thought you'd be home for dinner."

"Sorry, Mom," I said, feeling fourteen again. "I was working."

"What kind of a boss doesn't let a person come home for dinner? By the way, did you see this box of knick knacks I'd left for you when we moved to Florida?"

"Oh. Gee, I'd wondered where they'd gone."

"Good thing I found them," my mother said. "You needed some color to brighten up the place. Now doesn't this look much better?"

"Much better," I agreed. "Listen, Mom, I really appreciate all the nice things you're doing for me. But—"

"Honey," she replied, cutting me off. "You're a responsible adult and I wouldn't dream of treating you otherwise. Now go upstairs and clean your room. It's a mess."

Kevin L. Starnes sounded exactly like Apu from the TV show The Simpson's. This was all the more disturbing seeing as he was a white guy born and raised in Pittsburgh. Starnes was the latest in a series of less than stellar court appointed legal representatives assigned to David Dwayne Harmon. I got his name from a recent newspaper article.

"Visiting an inmate on Death Row isn't as much fun as one might think," he said, in a clipped, "cartoon Indian" accent. "There are many bad people there and you may be cavity searched."

"Thanks for the heads-up. Can you get me in?" I didn't relish the idea of any of my cavities being searched, but I had to talk to Harmon.

Nick was right when he told me to be careful what I wished for. Starnes arranged for a visit. No cavity searches but the guy sitting across from me in the visitor's center was freakin' scary. It looked like Harmon had been on the losing end of a knife fight. There was a scar on his face that he didn't have in the pictures I'd seen of him. It cut a diagonal line from his forehead to his lower lip, causing, I suspected, nerve damage and setting his mouth in a permanent sneer.

The glass partition and leg shackles didn't do much to allay my fears about being there, but his warm greeting more than made up for it.

"Fuck *you* want?" he spit into the phone. *Okay, no need for full sentences. I'm cool.*

I smiled and picked up the receiver, dropping it once and causing ear-splitting damage on his end. "I'm Brandy Alexander," I told him, when he was through cursing me out. "I was a colleague of Tamra Rhineholt's. She thought you were innocent and so do I. I want to try and help you, if you'll let me."

Harmon dropped his voice to a whisper. It made my skin crawl. "Why do you want to help me? You got a thing for me? Is that it? You lookin' for some lovin'? Be happy to give it to you." He spread his legs, surreptitiously grabbing his crotch with his free hand. "I'll give it to you real good."

I blew out a sharp burst of air. Looking directly into his eyes, I spoke slowly and calmly into the phone. "Listen, David. May I call you David? Or would you prefer 'Shithead'? I'm here because a friend of mine died trying to save your sorry ass. So if I can figure out who really killed that girl, I'll know who murdered Tamra. Saving you is strictly incidental. If there was a way around that, I'd take it in a heartbeat."

Harmon leaned forward. His rage was swift and palpable. "You talk big with this glass wall between us. I get you alone some time—"

I stood. "It's been real."

Just as suddenly he relaxed in his seat, his face splitting into a wide grin. The mood swing was unnerving. "That's some mouth you got. But I like you. I do. What you want to know?"

I took out a notepad and we began.

According to Harmon, Tamra Rhineholt started out doing a piece on capital punishment, but after hearing his story about incompetent lawyers, a flawed judicial system and an admittedly unsympathetic defendant, she was convinced he'd gotten a bum rap. Harmon hadn't put much stock in Tamra championing his cause. Over the years he'd seen "do gooders" come and go. She was just another face in the crowd. He refused to get his hopes up, even when she told him she may be getting close to the truth. He told her not to bother him until the day she knew for sure. That day never came.

"All along my lawyer told me to plead guilty. Said the best he could do would be to bargain it down to a lesser charge. The man didn't want to work for his money."

"So why didn't you plead guilty? I mean wouldn't you have been better off?"

"Shit. I didn't kill that woman and I wasn't gonna say I did. Don't get me wrong. I messed up a few people in my time, but I never killed nobody. She came on to me that night. In front of her friends she act like she wasn't interested. But I seen her in there before. Only she act like it's the first time she ever set foot in the place. So I slip her my phone number before she leaves and she calls me later on and invites me over. She was one wild bitch. Kept wantin' me to do shit to her. Damn, I felt like I should've paid her for all that fun. Tell you the truth I never even knew her name."

"Wait. Back up," I said, trying hard to keep the revulsion out of my voice. "If she called you, there would have been a record of it. Why wasn't that introduced as evidence?"

"Because my cocksuckin' lawyer never bothered to check the phone records. I told him to but he didn't. Then he says it wouldn't have made a difference anyway."

"Are you serious?"

"Damn right I'm serious. Happens all the time. Hey, you think I'm the only one in here got screwed by the system? This joint's filled with guys who'da been better off representing themselves than to trust some court appointed asshole who hates you for breathin'." He gave me a long look. "So what do ya think *you* can do for me, little girl?"

I was torn between utter loathing for the man and feeling like a terrible injustice had been done to him. "I'll get back to you," I said.

The guard gave me the high sign to wrap it up, which I was only too happy to do. Harmon was leering at me like I was Playmate of the Month, and although deeply flattered I just couldn't see us having a future together...*although I did still need a date for Paul's bar mitzvah...*

"Oh. One more thing," I remembered. "Anthony Mitchell. Any idea what happened to him?"

Harmon shrugged. "Heard he came into some money and spent it all on blow. Maybe he dead. If I ever get out of here, he gonna be."

Chapter Nine

It was lunch time so I stopped off at Barnes and Noble on Rittenhouse Square and headed up to their café. It was really convenient, seeing as it was *only* fifteen miles in the opposite direction of where I was going and, coincidentally, across the street from Nick's apartment. Okay, so maybe I was hoping he'd be there picking up the latest issue of "Mercenary Weekly" and we could make out again.

I think it's important to eat a balanced diet, so I ordered a mocha cappuccino (there's milk in it, right? Milk is a protein) and a hunk of chocolate chip banana bread (fruit equals fiber). Then I ate the four Hershey's Kisses I found in my coat pocket, because what's lunch without dessert? And anyway, I needed the energy boost.

The thing is I still wasn't sleeping. I'd thought that having my parents in the house would help, but it just made things worse. I'd woken them up the first night they arrived, screaming "Someone's trying to kill me." My dad took it literally and ran into my room, minus pajamas and wielding a Star Wars plastic light saber he'd found in the back of Paul's old bedroom closet. I didn't want to risk a repeat performance, so last night I set my alarm to go off every hour so I'd wake up before I hit the dream stage of my sleep cycle. It wasn't a very practical solution, as it took me half an hour each time to fall asleep again. But at least I didn't have the added horror of seeing my dad in the buff.

I took a seat near the window and gazed across the ice covered branches of frozen trees to the apartment building across the street from the Square. Suddenly, the wrought iron security gate swung open and two figures emerged. One was female, about five foot eight. She was encased in tight, form fitting jeans and a three quarter length, dark leather coat, a stark contrast to her silken blond hair. Her companion was male, wearing faded jeans and a gray hooded sweatshirt. Even from a distance I knew it was Nick.

My pulse zoomed into overdrive as I stood with my face pressed against the glass trying to get a better look. Suddenly, their arms were wrapped around each other's necks and they were kissing. Apparently, they both had lungs of iron and saw no need to come up for air. My heart dropped into my stomach.

I have to stop them before they keel over from lack of oxygen! I grabbed my cell phone and punched in Nick's number. A split second later I came to my senses and slammed the phone shut. Too late. Nick heard the ringing and reached into his pocket for his phone. He flipped it open and checked "missed calls" on his caller I.D. *Oh Jeez. Now he knows it's me.*

I fully expected him to stick the phone back into his pocket and resume the lip lock. Instead, he began punching in numbers. A second later my phone rang.

"Hello?"

"Hey, angel."

I felt really stupid and sad and I was struck with a sudden urge to start bawling my head off. I fought to keep it all under control. "Oh um, hi, Nick. Sorry... I didn't mean to call you. I—I must've hit the wrong number."

"Are you okay?" There was genuine concern in his voice.

"Yeah, I'm fine. Sorry," I said again and hung up. He called back immediately, but I didn't trust myself not to blurt out something dumb, so I didn't pick up.

A cab pulled up to the curb. Nick opened the door and the woman got in. He didn't kiss her goodbye.

I called Janine on my way to the office. "Can you believe it? He was kissing her less than twenty-four hours after he kissed me."

"Yeah, but you were kissing Nick less than twenty-four hours after you kissed Bobby. What's the difference?"

I didn't know, but I was sure there was one.

There are about two hundred websites that boast access to old phone records. I know because I spent the afternoon researching every blessed one of them. Most were defunct, some offered highly illegal services and the few legitimate sites I found were cost prohibitive on a cable news budget. I briefly entertained the thought of asking Nick to get the information I needed, but I couldn't get past the thought of him and that woman. It's one thing to know something intellectually. But seeing it with your own eyes is a whole other deal.

I finally went with "Insta-search," a popular site for stalkers and other would-be felons. They faxed me the information in less than an hour.

I took out the notes I'd jotted down at the prison and checked for Harmon's old phone number against the list of Laura's outgoing calls. A third of the way down the page I spotted it. At 11:14 p.m. on the night of May 2nd a two-minute phone call was made to Harmon's number. It was reasonable to assume that Laura had made that call. *So at least Harmon was telling the truth about Laura calling him that night.* It didn't prove much else, but it was a start.

I scanned down the list of numbers. There were relatively few calls on the page. It made me feel bad to think that Laura didn't have anyone to talk to. Out of curiosity, I punched in the first phone number on the list. It was no longer in service. The second one connected me to the registrar's office at Drexel University. I hung up and dialed the next number on the list.

After three rings a man's voice answered. "Dante's Garden where *every* night is Ladies' Night. How can I help you?"

Dante's Garden? As in the male strip joint? I thought I'd dialed wrong so I hung up and tried again. I hadn't dialed wrong. *What was Laura doing calling a place like this?* I quickly scanned the list. There were several more calls, all to the same number.

"Oh. Um, hi," I said into the phone. "What's your address?"

Okay, the way I saw it, I didn't have any choice. I'm an investigative reporter now. So if getting information on Laura meant spending time with hot, gorgeous naked guys gyrating around to cheesy music while women stuffed dollar bills into their jock straps, well that's a sacrifice I'd just have to make. I hung up and called Franny, Janine and Carla because I knew they'd want to be there to support me every step of the way.

Craig came by my office at around three p.m. I'd just finished calling the local E.R.'s to inquire if anyone with a missing finger had come in for medical assistance. At the moment, said digit was residing in the mini fridge in Nick's office. If I could find its rightful owner, maybe I could bargain body parts for answers.

Craig had come around to the other side of my desk. Now he was peering over my shoulder while I typed up my notes from my visit with David Dwayne.

"Um, did you need something?" I asked.

"Someone came by to see you," he announced, never taking his eyes off my computer screen. "He's a detective so the guards had to let him in."

I shut down the screen. "Did he leave a name?"

"Uh huh. Detective DiCarlo. Are you in trouble?" he asked.

"Depends. When he asked where I was, what did you tell him?"

Craig shrugged. "I told him the truth. I didn't know where you were."

"Then no, I'm not in trouble."

"He called you Brandy."

"Who?"

"Detective DiCarlo. He said, 'Tell Brandy to give me a call,' like he knew you or something. But he called you the wrong name."

"Oh. That. Listen, Craig, there's something I've been meaning to tell you..."

I had one thing left to do before I left for the day. Something I'd been putting off all afternoon. In order to get the full picture of who Laura Stewart was, I had to talk to her family. This is the thing I hate most about being a reporter. The part where you track down innocent, grieving people, shove a microphone in their face and demand that they tell you how devastated they feel about whatever tragedy has befallen them.

I don't mind sticking it to people who deserve it. In fact that's why I wanted to be a reporter in the first place. To right the wrongs and be a voice for those who can't speak for themselves. I know it sounds corny, but it's true. But in this case, it meant dredging up horrible memories of the loss of a loved one. The only solace this family probably had was the knowledge that their daughter's killer had been caught and would soon be put to death. And I was about to take that away from them. Somehow I didn't think they'd welcome me with open arms.

I didn't have the heart to confront Laura's parents head-on. Instead, I looked through the Philadelphia phone directory for her half-brother, Ethan. According to the old newspaper clippings, his last name was Girard. At the time of Laura's murder he was an intern at Childrens' Hospital. I found a listing for an obstetrician named Dr. Ethan Girard out in Bryn Mawr and put through a call.

Dr. Girard's receptionist answered and informed me that he was with a patient.

"Would you like to make an appointment?" she asked.

"Yes," I said. I thought it best to meet with him in person. I figured he'd be less likely to turn me down if I were already sitting in his office, than if I just explained to him what I wanted over the phone.

"Is this for an existing patient?" she chirped. If Tinker Bell could speak I imagined she would sound just like this woman.

"No, actually I'd just like to interview Dr. Girard."

She didn't seem surprised by my request. I guess with Harmon's execution set for next month, I wasn't the only reporter looking to speak to the victim's brother.

"Interviews are scheduled on Monday and Thursday mornings," she explained, confirming my suspicions. "Doctor Girard has a cancellation for this coming Monday at 10:30 a.m. if that's convenient for you."

I booked the appointment, relieved that I had the weekend to gear up for the interview.

"See you then and congratulations!" she added sweetly.

"For what?" I asked, but she had already hung up.

"Wow." Carla leaned forward on the table, her arm outstretched so far I thought it would pop right out of its socket. Frantically, she waved a five dollar bill in the air as if she were hailing a cab. Only it wasn't a cab she was hailing. It was a guy. A bare-chested, bare-assed hunk of human male perfection. And he was headed our way.

We were seated at one of the side tables located right off the stage at Dante's Garden. I'd opted for a seat toward the back, preferably in a dark corner near the exit. But Janine had insisted on up close and personal. Franny, Janine and Carla were whooping it up alongside dozens of other uninhibited females and one lone guy who kept pantomiming a phone to his ear and mouthing "Call me" to all the male strippers.

Carla was tanked on rum and coke, her beehive listing like the Leaning Tower of Pisa. Zeroing in on her, the dancer reached the edge of the stage and air humped to the beat of the music, his considerable attributes dangling above her. Carla's eyes began to widen in either terror or anticipation, I really couldn't tell which. Then without warning she jumped to her feet and rushed the stage.

"Don't tell your uncle," she yelled, ripping open her shirt and stuffing the fiver into her bra. He leaned down to meet her and plucked it out with his teeth. The crowd went wild. I slid under the table, (my natural response to anything embarrassing) and stayed there until he headed back upstage.

What I really wanted to do was slug down a straight shot of bourbon, but I was working and needed to sound at least a little bit coherent when I talked to the club manager. I couldn't stop thinking about Nick and it didn't help that he'd called again. I ignored the call. I knew I was being childish, but I was never going to win any prizes for maturity anyway.

At 11:00 p.m. I took a bathroom break and then wandered over to the bar. Joe Allen, the manager was there. He was a short, burly man in his late fifties. At the moment he was wrestling a drink out of a very drunk patron's hand. "You've had enough for one night, honey." He nodded to the bartender. "Take some money out of petty cash and call her a cab."

I waited while Joe turned the woman over to the bouncer and then went up and introduced myself. He smiled at me. "Hey, I know you," he said. "You're Brandy Alexander from that morning show. Are you doing a piece on the club?" He looked around. "Where are the cameras? Come on, I'll buy you a drink. What do you want, doll?"

I liked Joe. He reminded me of my Uncle Marty on my father's side of the family. I smiled back at him. "I'm fine with this," I said, holding up my Coke. "But I would like to talk to you if you've got a minute."

We went into Joe's office where I took out Laura's picture and showed it to him.

"Do you recognize her?" I asked.

Joe stared at it, scratching his head. "Yeah. She looks familiar. I can't put my finger on why though."

"Her name was Laura Stewart. She was murdered about four years ago. Maybe you saw her picture in the paper?"

"Maybe." After a minute he shook his head. "Nah, that's not it. Wait. *Now* I remember. She used to be a regular here. You say she was murdered?"

I nodded.

"I'm not surprised. This chic was a real weirdo. She'd come in about two, three times a week. She was always alone. She'd sit over there in the corner of the bar, not talking to anyone. It was kind of spooky. Reason I remember her is she used to call here before she came in to make sure this one particular dancer would be here that night. She'd even asked for his phone number so she could call him directly, but we don't give out personal information on our boys. I figured if he wanted her to have it, he'd have given it to her. Danny used to say she had some strange tastes, if you catch my drift."

"Who's Danny?"

"Danny Lang. The guy she used to come see perform."

"Is that all she'd do is watch him dance? Do you remember if they had any contact outside of the club?"

Joe cut me a look. "This is a legit business here. We don't promote anything except some good, clean fun for the patrons. Whatever arrangements Danny made with this chic were off the clock, y'know what I mean?"

"Does Danny still work here?"

"He quit about eight months ago. Listen, Danny's a good kid. I don't want to make trouble for him by implying there was anything improper going on between him and this Laura girl."

It was a tad late for that, but I kept my mouth shut. "Do you know how I can get in touch with Danny?" I asked instead.

"I've got his home phone number." He hesitated. "Look, I don't feel right just giving it out to you. How about I take yours and ask him to call you?"

I routed around in my bag for my business card and handed it to him. "I don't mean to put you on the spot, Joe, but this is important. Tell him either he talks to me or he talks to the police."

I thought about Laura all the way home. Her friends, the few she had anyway, had described her as quiet, shy and reserved, while David Dwayne Harmon insisted she was an insatiable sex addict with an appetite for kink. This was confirmed tonight by what Joe had told me. For all I knew, this guy Danny was the one who killed Laura.

Damn! I just couldn't believe that no one had thought to follow up on Harmon's claim that Laura had pursued him. It was an automatic assumption that he'd been lying. Granted, the guy was pond scum, but it's the constitutional right of every American citizen to have adequate council, even the grossly unlikable.

I would have pondered this some more, but at that moment my cell phone rang. I pulled up to my street and parked one handed while I answered the phone with the other. It was Bobby. Oops. I'd forgotten to call him. "Hey, what's up?" I said.

"I'm about to make your day, sweetheart. I got a call this afternoon from a buddy at the Pennsauken precinct. The autopsy results are in."

"And?"

"And it looks like you were right. They've turned it over to homicide."

"I knew it!" I yelled.

"Okay, calm down," Bobby said. "There's more."

Having turned off the car engine, I was rapidly turning into a Popsicle. "Listen, don't go anywhere. I'll call you right back."

I flew into the house, almost tripping over Adrian who was sprawled on the living room rug like a tiny beached whale. He looked up at me with baleful eyes, his tummy distended beyond normal capacity. Lying next to him was half a meatball. The poor little guy was seriously in need of an Alka Seltzer. "Didn't I warn you to stay away from my mom's cooking?" I whispered.

I dashed upstairs to call Bobby back when I heard my mother's voice calling to me from the kitchen. "How was your book club meeting?"

I stopped mid-dash. "Fine. Great. We all cried when Mr. Darcy finally declared his love for Elizabeth. Mom, I'm really tired, so—"

My mother walked into the living room, ladle in hand. She'd been hard at work lovingly creating tomorrow night's meal which sadly, was bound to be inedible.

"Honey, a friend of yours called tonight. A Nicholas Santiago."

"He did?" *Omigod! Omigod! Stay calm. Don't give anything away.* "Did he happen to leave a message?"

"Well, naturally he was calling to speak to you, but somehow we got to talking and—"

"You talked to him? What exactly did you say?"

"Oh Brandy, don't be ridiculous. How am I supposed to remember every word of our conversation?" *My mother has a mind like a steel trap. She can recall conversations she had in the 4th grade.* "The point is he seems like a very nice boy, so I invited him to join us for dinner tomorrow night."

"You what? He's not coming, is he?"

"He most certainly is. In fact, he insisted on bringing the wine."

Nick can't be serious about coming over tomorrow night...or can he?

I sat closeted in my room fruitlessly dialing Nick's number. The phone kept going to voice mail, finally forcing me to give up and leave a message. "Nick, it's Brandy. I'm sorry I haven't called you back, but I've had, um...pink eye...It can be very debilitating." *Oh God is there any way to erase this?* "Anyway, I just wanted to say that it was very nice of you to humor my mother by telling her you'd come for dinner, but it's totally unnecessary. I'm sure you have better things to do, so—" BEEP. *Shit.* "Hi, it's me again. Anyway, we're not even *having* dinner tomorrow night. My mother drinks a lot and she gets mixed up. So, uh, I'll talk to you later. Bye." *Unhhh!*

I dialed Bobby next. He picked up on the first ring, his voice a soft blend of Philly and his Chicago roots.

"Did I wake you?" I climbed into bed and snuggled under the covers. Rocky and Adrian had beat me to it and were fast asleep at the foot of the bed.

"Nah," he yawned. "I was just lying down with Sophia. Sometimes she gets scared at night, so I stay with her until she falls asleep. What took you so long to call me back?"

"My mother. Don't ask. So what did the autopsy report show?"

"I wasn't able to get the specifics," he said. "Something about chloroform in the blood stream, cardiac arrest. Whatever it was, it was enough to convince the D.A. that foul play was involved." Bobby breathed out a slow puff of air. It was the sound he made when he was trying to keep his cool. But I knew him too well and braced myself for the worst. "The autopsy showed something else, Bran. At the time of her death Tamra was pregnant."

A shock ran straight through me. "How far along was she?"

"I don't know. A couple of months I think. Like I said, I don't have all the details. I just thought you'd want to know."

I was quiet for a minute as I digested this new information.

"Hey, you still there?"

"Yeah." Something had been nagging at me and now it worked its way to the front of my brain. "Bobby, do they know who the father is—I mean was?"

"I assume it was her husband's. Why?"

"When I was at their house I noticed an open box of condoms on the nightstand. Why would they have condoms around if they were trying to have a baby?"

"Maybe they *weren't* trying. Maybe they were using protection but she got pregnant by accident. Rubbers aren't foolproof." I knew he was speaking from personal experience. Even though Bobby loved his little girl more than life itself, the pregnancy wasn't planned and, given the choice, it's not the path he would have chosen.

"Okay, here's a thought," I said. "What if it turns out Jeff wasn't the father? Jeff thought Tamra was having an affair. What if he knew she was pregnant and suspected the baby wasn't his—"

"That would be one hell of an incentive for him to kill her," Bobby cut in.

"Are the cops going to run a DNA test on the baby? I should call and tell them to."

"Great idea. Cops love being told how to do their jobs. Look, Brandy, you were right all along about Tamra and I'm sorry I gave you such a hard time about it. But I want you to promise me that from here on in you'll let the professionals handle it."

Yeah? Well, David Dwayne Harmon left his fate up to the "so-called" professionals and look where he ended up. I wasn't about to drop this. Not by a long shot.

"So," Bobby said, not waiting for an answer, "I haven't seen you on-air the last couple of days. Are you taking some time off while your parents are in town?"

"Um, no, actually, I've been re-assigned. My boss thought I'd be more useful in another department. I'm doing a little investigative work."

"Yeah?" he said, his voice guarded. "What kind of investigative work?"

"Oh, I'm just following up on a story for a colleague. Nothing too eventful." *Not exactly a lie. Nothing's happened*

157

to me in at least twenty-four hours. That's uneventful given my track record lately.

"Oh. Well, I'm glad to hear you're taking it easy. I've been worried about you."

"No need to be. Really." I didn't know whether to be touched by his concern or pissed at the vote of "no confidence." At any rate, he wouldn't be happy with the news that I was taking on Tamra's case. I figured I'd better hang up before guilt took over and I ended up confessing everything to him. Hell, he probably knew I was lying anyway.

I lay in bed, unable to sleep. I couldn't stop thinking about Jeff and Tamra. Could the mild mannered biology professor really have killed his pregnant wife? I wondered if the police had been able to track down the illusive Richard. Was he Tamra's secret lover? Was he the father of her unborn child? And what was it Bobby had said about chloroform? *It was found in her system.* Chloroform is what the kidnappers used to drug me with when they thought I was Tamra. That had to have taken a lot of pre-planning. Assuming Jeff killed her in a moment of unbridled jealousy, he wouldn't have gone to all the trouble to have her kidnapped, taken to some unknown destination and then drag her dead body back to their house.

The more I thought about it, the less possible it seemed that Jeff had murdered his wife. It was just too coincidental that Tamra was investigating Laura Stewart's death and the next thing you know she winds up dead.

Oh crap. I'd forgotten to mention to Bobby that Craig had access to Tamra's house before she died, although I doubted that he had anything to do with her demise either. The poor guy had the mental acuity of a cantaloupe. He didn't seem capable of pulling off something like this. Plus, Craig's affection for Tamra was genuine. I couldn't imagine him doing anything to hurt her.

I tossed and turned for about an hour, making a "To Do" list in my head. *Track down Danny Lang. Talk to Laura Stewart's brother. Find the guy who tried to kill me. Find the other guy who tried to kill me. Round up a suitable date for Paul's bar mitzvah. Solve Tamra's murder. Solve Laura's murder. Learn to tap dance.*

At four a.m. Adrian hopped off the bed and began whimpering and scratching at the bedroom door. I opened it and he made a beeline for the hallway, bounding down the steps so fast he looked airborne. Chalking it up to the meatball he ate earlier, I followed him down and let him out the front door to do his business.

Adrian paused on the porch, head cocked, ears straining forward. Cautiously he took a step down and sniffed the ground around Mrs. Gentile's Azaleas. He was after something, the neighbor's cat probably, but I was freezing my butt off and just wanted to get back in bed. Suddenly he slipped around the side of the house and disappeared.

"Damnit, Adrian," I whispered, stepping off the front porch. Suddenly, my frozen body turned into a sweaty wreck as I realized I wasn't alone. But before I could invite the scream that was stuck in the back of my throat to come forward, I felt the imprint of large hands on my back and with one swift movement I was knocked head-first into the azalea bush. As I struggled to right myself I slipped backwards on the icy pavement, my feet sliding out from under me. "This is going to hurt," I remember

159

thinking, just before my head crash-landed on the sidewalk.

Chapter Ten

Something not quite heavy was weighing me down. I tried to open my eyes but the effort it took was more than I could afford to expend. My head felt like it had been split wide open. I checked for a crater and found instead a goose bump the size of a fist located behind my right ear. I groaned just to hear the sound of my own voice.

The weight on my chest shifted and soon I felt moist, heated breath followed by a soft, wet tongue on my mouth. "Oh please don't let it be human," I thought, completely grossed out and in a good deal of pain. Forcing my eyes open, I came face to face with Adrian. He was planted on top of me, his paws kneading my chest, his furry little muzzle clamped down on mine as if he were trying to perform CPR.

I nudged him off me and sat up. Someone had dragged me off the sidewalk and onto the porch. My head was throbbing and I was cold to the bone but, hell, I wasn't dead, trapped in the trunk of a car or in the process of being strangled so, all things considered, I was in pretty good shape.

As I rolled over onto my knees, my hand brushed against an envelope that had been stuffed under my hip. I had trouble making out what was written on the front of it.

You'd think with double vision I'd be able to see twice as well, but such was not the case.

I had a whopper of a concussion and had to get to the E.R. fast.

I considered my options. Wake my parents. Oy. Neither one of them is very good in a crisis. Once when I was a little girl I got my finger stuck in the sliding glass door of our beach house down in Jersey. My mother began screaming at the top of her lungs and my father fainted. I had to pull it out by myself and then I sealed the cut with Elmer's Glue... I could take a cab, but I already felt like I was going to vomit and cabs smell funny. I finally settled on the one person I knew would be awake at this ungodly hour and be cool enough to handle it. I grabbed Adrian and went back inside the house to call my Uncle Frankie.

Uncle Frankie understands me. He'd spent enough time being the black sheep of the family when he was a kid to recognize a kindred spirit. He was already at the gym but he came and got me. I stood outside, decked out in my Hello Kitty footsie pajamas and my dad's old pea coat. I'd stuffed the envelope into my coat pocket. I figured whatever was inside wouldn't be good news, so I'd wait on opening it until I got back from the emergency room. I was kinda hoping Dr. Sanchez wouldn't be there. It was just too embarrassing.

Uncle Frankie didn't ask a lot of questions on the ride up, but on the way back, when he knew I wasn't in imminent danger of dying, he demanded full disclosure.

"...so you can see why Bobby can't know about this. He thinks I'm too 'fragile' right now, which is so ridiculous. Oh, and let's not mention anything to Paul either. At least not until his car comes back from the body shop."

Uncle Frankie cut me a look. "What happened to Paul's car—never mind. I'm pretty sure I don't want to know." He let a minute pass and then he said, "What's up with you and DiCarlo anyway?" His voice had taken on a slightly macho Italian edge that belied the casualness of his question. But it was an honest question and it deserved an honest answer.

"Beats the hell out of me."

Thankfully, when I got home my parents were still asleep. I went upstairs and took the envelope out of my coat pocket. My initials were scrawled on the front. With shaking hands I extracted the neatly folded paper that had been tucked inside. The note, typewritten in a commonly used font, was short and to the point. "David Dwayne Harmon is a killer. He deserves to die. Stay out of it or suffer the consiquences." *Well, what the hell is that supposed to mean? Plus they misspelled consequences.*

I stuffed the note back in the envelope and shoved it under my mattress. Then I sat down on the bed to make sure it didn't escape. "Okay," I decided, when rational thought returned. "I should call the police." Only what would I tell them? *Somebody pushed me?* If they had intended to do actual harm it would have been a lot more then a shove.

My guess is whoever delivered the note did not expect me to come waltzing out of the house at that moment. And they could have left me to freeze to death on the sidewalk. But instead they took the trouble to stick me back up on the porch where I'd be relatively out of harm's way.

I stood and slid my hand under the mattress and retrieved the note. *Who even knows I'm working on this story?* I picked up the phone and called Eric.

He answered on the third ring. "Hello?" He sounded like I'd woken him from a deep sleep. I envied him.

"Eric, it's Brandy. I know it's early, but I've got to talk to you."

"Hang on," he said. There was a whispered apology, obviously not meant for me and then a rustling of sheets. Finally he got back on the line.

"What's up?"

"I've got some news on Tamra," I said, ignoring the fact that I'd just dragged him out of a warm bed where someone named "Sweet Buns" anxiously awaited his return. "The Jersey police have ruled Tamra's death a homicide. They should be going public any time now." Eric gave a low whistle.

"And that's not all," I added. "She was pregnant."

I filled him in on the details ending with my early morning visitor. "Who else knows that I'm following up on Tamra's story?" I asked.

Eric hesitated. "You mean besides everyone at the station?"

Great. That narrows the suspects down to about two hundred and fifty full and part time WINN employees—not to mention all the people I interviewed and managed to piss off in the course of a day. One thing I was pretty sure of. Whoever wrote me that note was not out to hurt me—at least not yet. The note was a warning—and an amateurish one at that. Still, I figured I'd better tell the police, so if it turned out I was wrong and the note wasn't just an empty threat, I'd have something on record.

I decided to call Mike Mahoe. He was a friend of sorts, but not close enough that he'd feel obliged to lecture me. I caught him at the station just as he was leaving.

"Yo," he said. "What's up?" So I told him.

It's hard to imagine a six foot five inch cop whining like a three year old, but Mike had it down pat. "Aw, c'mon Brandy. Don't put me in the middle of you and DiCarlo. If I keep something like this from him and he finds out—you know what a hothead he is when it comes to you."

"Okay. Look, I'm sorry I got you involved. The note was probably nothing anyway. Just somebody who wants to see justice done and they got a little carried away. Forget I told you. Just please don't mention it to Bobby."

"Oh man," he muttered. "Bring it in. I'll keep it on file. But if DiCarlo finds out—"

"He won't. And thanks Mike."

I felt better in the afternoon, so I decided to run some errands. I went downstairs and found my mother holed up in the kitchen, cleaning out the refrigerator. "Do you have any oregano?" she asked.

"Um, not unless you left it here when you moved."

My mother shook her head in utter disbelief. "Brandy, a good cook always has fresh oregano on hand. Your friends are coming over tonight and they're expecting a wonderful home-cooked meal."

"No they're not. *I mean* they just really want to see you guys. The meal is a bonus!"

I walked into the living room. My dad was seated on the couch watching Rachel Ray. "Good save," he whispered. Glancing toward the kitchen, he handed me thirty bucks. "If you're going out, pick up a dozen cannoli from Termini Bros., would you? We're all gonna starve to death otherwise." He rolled his eyes heavenward. "God bless your mother, Brandy. She's a wonderful woman but a lousy cook."

I swung by Snake's garage to check on Paul's car. It was still sitting up on the pedestal, but at least he was working on it. "How's it going, Snake?"

"Be cheaper to scrap it and buy your brother a new car. The body work alone is gonna cost you a fortune." *Gee, I was hoping the answer would be more along the lines of "everything's going swell and it'll be ready by dinner time. And by the way, since you're as cute as a button, I'm throwing in the brake job for free."* I settled for a promise that the car would be drivable by sometime next month and headed off to the bakery.

My head was starting to ache again so I cruised down South Street, looking for the Chocolatier's shop. I read somewhere, probably in the Journal of the American Medical Association—or maybe it was in a pamphlet put out by the Hershey Company—that chocolate relieves headache pain. It also produces some kick-butt endorphins and after another sleepless night I needed a little pick-me-up.

The shop is down the block from Lucinda's gallery. I drove slowly so as not to miss a parking space. *Okay, there's the gallery...I wonder if John's in there? Ooh. Look at the crowd in front of the window. She must've put up a new display. Wow, it looks like one of John's pictures. How cool is that? Hey...wait a minute...that looks like...Oh John, you are so dead!*

I double parked and bolted from the car, pushing my way through the door of the gallery. A beanpole of a woman wearing black eyeliner that would make a raccoon turn green with envy slinked up to me, tapping her wristwatch. "I'm afraid the gallery is closed, dear."

"Yeah, well, the thing is, you've got my face hanging in your window and I want you to take it down."

She studied me for a moment, no doubt debating whether to call the cops or Mental Health Services. "Excuse me?" she said finally.

"Look," I said, walking over to window. The photo was perched on an easel. I spun it around and stuck my head up next to it. "See? Same face. I didn't give you permission to hang it there." I picked up the photo and began to walk toward the door.

"Hey." Lucinda grabbed me by the arm. She was stronger than she looked and it really hurt. "Where do you think you're going with that? I'm calling the police."

I looked out the window. "No need," I sighed. "They're already here." To be precise they were in the middle of the street towing my car away.

Lucinda let me go after I explained I was suffering possible brain damage. Then she escorted me to the door and locked it behind me. When I looked again the photo was already back in the window.

Uncle Frankie bailed me out—again. Luckily, his buddy owns the towing place and it only took an hour to get the car out of hock. Then I raced over to Termini Bros. to pick up dessert.

It was after four by the time I got back with the cannoli. "Look, Lorraine," my dad said, feigning surprise. "Brandy brought dessert home. Now you don't have to go to the trouble of making that pie."

"It's no trouble. I love to bake. You know that. Brandy," she said, wiping flour off her hands. "Get the cat off the counter and set the dining room table. People will be here in less than two hours and I still have to strain the carrots."

"We're having strained carrots?" I asked. I knew my mom had trouble thinking of my friends and me as adults, but this was going too far.

She gave me an exaggerated sigh. "Don't be ridiculous, honey. They're for the baby."

"What baby?" I all but shouted.

"Oh, didn't I tell you? I invited Bobby and his little girl. The more the merrier, I always say."

That's not what she *used* to say. She used to say, "Keep away from that goddamn hoodlum." But ever since Bobby became a single dad, he's risen in her estimation to somewhere bordering on sainthood.

I spent the next two hours trying to make myself look presentable, only to come to the conclusion that it was a lost cause. Every scary thing that had happened to me in the past few months seemed permanently etched on my face. I felt like shit and worse yet, I looked like it.

I knew I couldn't go on like this, feeling all sorry for myself. I needed a major attitude adjustment. After all, people get kidnapped, shot at and strangled every day and you don't hear them whining about it. (Granted, the majority of them are dead, but still...). I was just going to have to stop being such a wuss and learn to roll with the punches. Okay! I felt much better after putting it into a healthy perspective.

John was the first to arrive, which was good because I didn't want to have to kill him in public. "Brandy, I swear I didn't know Lucinda was going to do that. I am so sorry... you say there was a crowd around it? About how many people do you think—just a rough estimate would be fine."

168

I socked him hard in the arm. "I hate you. My life sucks."

"No you don't and no it doesn't." John replied and went off to help my mom in the kitchen.

Vince came in next with a six pack of Bud and sat down on the couch with my dad to watch the Flyers' game. I grabbed a beer and tried to get into watching it too, but the truth was I was so tired I couldn't even tell who they were playing against.

Paul called and said he was running a little late. One of the bartenders at the club called in sick at the last minute and he had to wait for the sub to arrive. "Okay, Paulie. But please get here as soon as you can, okay? Mom's trying to organize a game of Charades after dinner."

Eddie had a sinus headache so Fran drove over with Janine. They'd gotten into a big fight in the car because Fran and Eddie decided to ask Eddie's sister and her husband to be the baby's godparents. Janine had thought she was a shoe-in. "I'm your twin, for God's sake. If God forbid anything happened to you, I could step right in and the baby wouldn't even know the difference."

"She has a point there, Fran."

Franny shot me a look. "Shut up."

"You shut up."

My mother stuck her head into the living room. "Girls. Is that any way to talk? Be nice to each other or no dessert."

"Jesus," I said when she was gone. "Do you see how insidious that woman is? She hits town and suddenly we're nine years old again, fighting over who gets to wear the crown in "Pretty Pretty Princess."

"Fran would probably just hand it over to Eddie's sister," Janine muttered under her breath. It was going to be a fun evening.

Frankie and Carla arrived next, followed by Bobby. He was carrying Sophia in his arms. She looked like a porcelain doll all bundled up in a pink snow suit and *Dora the Explorer* bedroom slippers. "I'm afraid she's a little cranky, right now," he apologized. "She fell asleep in the car on the way over here."

"Oh she's just perfect," my mother cooed, stretching out her arms to take the little girl from him. "Bobby, help yourself to a beer. Brandy, get Bobby a beer."

"That's okay, Mrs. Alexander. I'm fine for now." He flashed her a smile that could melt the panties off a mannequin and my mother blushed. *She actually blushed.*

I went into the hallway to hang up coats. Bobby followed me in and closed the door.

"So, all through flirting with my mother?"

"We need to talk," he said, his voice dangerously calm. *Uh oh.*

"About what?" I asked, and made a big deal out of looking for hangars.

"About this." He drew an envelope from his back pocket. "Oh and by the way, Mike says to tell you 'Sorry'."

"Look, I can explain." I stalled, trying to think up a really good lie.

"Goddamn it Brandy, you said you'd butt out of this."

"No." Suddenly I was royally pissed off. "You *told* me to butt out. Bobby, this is my job. I've been assigned to find out what really happened to Tamra. You can't tell me not to do my job."

"Everything alright in there, honey?" It was my dad. I guess he was wondering why I'd locked myself in the closet and was arguing with the coats.

"Fine, Dad. Be out in a minute. Look," I whispered, "I'm glad this is all out in the open. I'm an adult and I get to make the decisions about my life." Just then the door bell rang. "That must be Paul. Can we talk about this later?"

Bobby took a deep breath, but it did nothing to temper his mood. "Listen to me. I can't keep chasing around after you, trying to keep you safe. You're worse than my two year old."

"Oh yeah? Well, *bite me*, DiCarlo!" I ripped open the door and ran smack into Nick. As promised, he'd brought the wine.

Startled, I jumped back and slammed into Bobby, sandwiching myself between the two of them like the proverbial rock and a hard place.

"Sorry I'm late," Nick said smiling. "Hello, angel." He bent down and kissed me on the cheek. "How's the pink eye?"

"What? Oh. All cleared up."

Nick nodded toward Bobby, who looked about ready to pop an aneurism. "Detective DiCarlo."

"Santiago," Bobby replied, barely containing his hostility. "Excuse us a minute, will ya?" He took my arm and pulled me back into the closet.

"Why didn't you tell me you invited him?"

"I didn't invite him," I spluttered. "And as a matter of fact, I didn't invite you either." I yanked open the door and stalked off into the living room. I found Nick in the kitchen, introducing himself to my mother. She held tight to his hand, her mouth hanging open ever so slightly as

171

her eyes roved over his exquisite features. *What is with my mom tonight? First Bobby and now Nick. She must be going through some sort of hormonal resurgence.* Eyeing me she dropped his hand, stammered something about it being hot in there and rushed off to turn down the furnace.

"So, Nick, what do you do for a living?"

There were eleven of us crammed around the dining room table, twelve if you counted Sophia, who had fallen asleep in her booster seat, her little cheek mashed against her plate of strained carrots. Once again I was jammed between Bobby and Nick. Carla sensed the tension and tried to diffuse it by telling "an amusing story about a dye job gone wrong at the beauty shop." She ended with, "I guess you had to be there."

My mother sat across from us, keeping up a steady monologue about the hideously embarrassing things I did as a baby. When she got to the part about how, when I was four I peeled off all my clothes and ran down our block belting out the theme song from *Sesame Street*, my dad took pity on me and tried to change the subject.

Vince looked up from the hunk of lasagna he was attempting to hide under his salad and waited for Nick's response. Nick's been flying just under the radar at the District Attorney's Office for years. They couldn't prove he was up to anything illegal, but they weren't entirely convinced that he wasn't. To tell the truth, I was sort've curious to see how he'd respond to my dad's question myself.

"I own a martial arts studio on Spring Garden," Nick said. He looked across the table at my mother, locking eyes with her. "Mrs. Alexander, do you mind if I have another helping of lasagna? It's been a long time since I've had a home cooked meal."

Wow. Nobody saw that one coming. Even Vince was impressed.

At around nine p.m. Bobby got a call from the station. Some kids had found a corpse in a dumpster and he had to go check it out. I walked him and Sophia to the door.

"Look, I'm sorry about before," I told him.

"Yeah, me too." He cast an eye back toward the dining room. "I'll see ya later."

Paul called at ten and said he just couldn't get away so he suggested we move the party over to the club. "Great idea," Janine said. "I'm gonna call Tony and see if he can meet us there."

Parking was at a premium so Frankie, John, Vince and Carla decided to car pool. I was bone tired but the idea of lying in bed, waiting for the nightmares to kick in didn't seem all that appealing to me. "I'm in," I told them.

"Good," Nick said. "I'll drive you."

"Oh—well—uh—okay. Coming Mom?" All evening I had successfully managed to avoid being alone with Nick and I wasn't about to blow it now.

My mother glanced over at my father who had fallen asleep on the couch and was snoring to beat the band. "I've got all the excitement I need right here," she said.

"Oh, then if *you're* not going—"

"No, you go," she insisted, "and take a doggie bag for your brother."

Nick opened the passenger door and I slid into the seat, leaning over to unlock his side of the car. My stomach was doing back flips. It was dangerous to be alone with him. And yet my own mother had (albeit unintentionally) handed me over to him on a silver platter.

173

All that separated us was a two pound bag of ground beef and noodles that I clutched firmly to my chest.

Nick eyed me and started the engine. "Your parents are nice," he said.

"Yeah. They are."

And then came the sucker punch. "So are you ready to tell me why you've been avoiding me?"

"I told you. I had eczema."

"Pink eye," Nick said. He cut the engine. "You told me you had pink eye."

"*What-e-ver!* Listen, I hope you don't mind, but I'm really not up for going out tonight. Do me a favor and drop this off for Paul, okay?" I tossed him the lasagna, ripped open the car door and jumped out never looking back.

"...and then I threw the bag of leftovers at him and ran out of the car."

Janine shouted to be heard over the din of the club. I could hear Carla in the background singing along to the lyrics of "Starry Eyes Surprise," and getting them mostly wrong. "Brandy, get over it. So he kissed another woman. Jeez. If I got mad every time my boyfriend kissed another woman—"

"First of all, Janine, Nick is not my boyfriend. Second, you don't have a boyfriend, and third, if you *did* have a boyfriend and he kissed another woman, you would rip out his tongue and served it on a deli tray with kosher pickles and rye bread!"

Janine considered this for a minute. "True. But don't you think you might be overreacting just a little?"

"Yes," I said, miserably. "I do. It's official. I'm a crazy person."

"Honey, I'm not arguing with you. You'd better get some sleep before you have a complete psychotic breakdown. Listen, Tony wants to dance. I'll check up on you tomorrow."

I laid in bed until after midnight, but every time I closed my eyes my chest would get so tight I couldn't breathe. I wouldn't take anything to help me fall asleep because I'm not so good with medication. I tend to lapse into a coma with anything stronger than aspirin. So I tried counting backwards from a hundred, counting sheep and counting Hershey's Kisses. Then I got up and *ate* some Hershey's Kisses.

"I can't go on like this," I said to Rocky. She rubbed her little body against mine in agreement.

"You know what you have to do," she seemed to say.

"You're right, per usual," I told her. I pulled on some jeans and a sweatshirt, grabbed my pocketbook and headed downstairs and out the door.

Maybe I should have called first, but I didn't want to lose my nerve and frankly I couldn't risk a rejection. I pulled the La Sabre into the loading zone in front of Nick's building and turned off the engine.

Now what? I couldn't get into his building without getting buzzed in, so I took out my phone and punched in his number. It rang three times before it went to voicemail. I disconnected and tried his cell. He didn't pick up. *Was he avoiding me?* The knot in my chest tightened as I contemplated the possibility that I had pushed him away for good. Hot tears that had threatened for so long finally erupted and spilled down my cheeks. I closed my eyes and leaned against the cold glass window.

Someone was chasing me. I tried to run but my legs were rooted to the spot. A hand reached out, grabbing me, choking me. I could feel my heart pounding, hear its erratic beating in my ears. The hand pressed harder on my throat and the beat of my heart grew louder. Just when I thought my heart would burst, I awoke with a violent shudder.

Nick stood just outside the car door, tapping lightly on the window. I was flooded with gratitude at the sight of him. He had changed into workout clothes, and despite the cold night air he was coatless, his t-shirt soaked with perspiration.

I rolled down the window. "Hey," I said, shyness creeping up on me like an uninvited guest.

"Hey." He gazed at me with dark, piercing eyes and any shred of pride I had dissolved in an instant. Driven by desperation, the words, naked and honest tumbled out of me.

"I haven't slept in a month and you're the only person I feel safe with. Can I stay with you tonight?"

"That may be a mistake, darlin'," he said, pulling me out of the car.

Chapter Eleven

We were silent in the elevator on the way up to his apartment. Nick leaned against the back wall, his arm draped loosely around my shoulder, his look inscrutable. Suddenly I began to get nervous. *Maybe I should've thought this thing through a little more. I mean who in their right mind takes advice from their cat, anyway?*

The elevator stopped on the fourth floor and he took my hand and led me down the hall. Something went all gooey inside of me as we held hands. When we got to the end of the corridor he stopped, pausing to unlock the door to his apartment. He opened it and stepped aside to let me in. It smelled like espresso and chocolate.

"Make yourself at home, angel. I'll be right back." He stripped off his shirt and disappeared down the hall. A minute later I heard the shower running. The clock on the kitchen wall said one-thirty.

I didn't know what to do with myself, so I wandered around and ended up in the spare room. The sleeper couch was open and the bed was unmade. I went back into the living room and sat down at the baby grand piano that stood in the corner of the room. I knew that Nick could play. I'd heard him once when he thought he was alone. It was dark and soulful and a little bit heartbreaking. I wondered who had taught him and it struck me how little I knew of his life—how little he shared.

In about ten minutes Nick reappeared, dressed only in pajama bottoms slung low on his hips. His hair was damp and hung in waves around his face. He walked over to the piano and sat down beside me and I felt the heat rise to my cheeks as he turned me toward him. Taking my face in his hands he ran his thumb softly along my bottom lip. "Now. What makes you think you're safe with me?" he said. And then he kissed me.

I sank into his chest and kissed him back with no other thought in my brain than the simple need to be close to him. We kissed for a long time; passionate, heart-stopping kisses and then he scooped me up in his arms, (just like you'd see on the cover of a Harlequin Romance, only I was wearing jeans instead of a long flowing white dress and my boobs weren't popping out of my top) and he carried me into his bedroom.

Nick laid me gently on the bed and stretched out beside me. "This is it," I thought. "I want him. I need him. *To hell with everything else.*"

I yawned deeply and closed my eyes, waiting for him to take me. Then I waited a little bit more. When nothing happened, I opened my eyes. Nick was leaning on one elbow, watching me. I yawned again. "Um," I said. "Did I read this wrong?"

"No, angel. You didn't. It's just that when I make love to a woman I like her to be conscious. I'm funny that way."

"Oh, but I—"

"Shh, querido," he whispered, placing gentle kisses on my cheeks and eyelids. "Shh."

I woke up seven hours later wrapped in Nick's arms, my head resting on his bare chest. Some time in the night he had replaced my sweatshirt and jeans with one of his long sleeved cotton tees. I didn't remember the exchange but felt nonetheless embarrassed. I did a surreptitious check. No bra, but I still had my panties on. *Thank God.*

As I lay curled up in the crook of Nick's arm, I suddenly realized two things. One—I'd slept through the entire night without a single scary dream and two—Nick had a hard-on. The latter was pressing against my leg in a pleasant sort of way.

I raised my head off his chest and he opened his eyes. "Good morning," he smiled, and before I could work up a self-conscious protest on the state of my breath, he leaned over and kissed me on the mouth. I guess I had nothing to worry about because he pulled back to look at me and then he kissed me again—tongue this time. He tasted wonderful.

After a few minutes Nick sat up and adjusted his pillows so that they were propped against the headboard. His stomach was exposed and I could see the faint line of fuzz that led down from his belly button and disappeared into his pajama bottoms. To the right of it were the faded remains of a jagged, silvery blue scar, about three inches long. I traced it lightly with my finger. "Appendix operation?" I asked.

"Something like that." There was a barely perceptible shift in his mood and I let the subject drop.

"So how are you doing this morning, angel?"

I sat up too, pulling the blankets around me. "A lot better. Thank you for not throwing me out," I added quietly.

He laughed, taking my hand and lacing his fingers through mine. "The thought never crossed my mind."

"I guess I've been a little stressed."

"You could hardly tell. So," he said, after a moment, "now that the police have labeled your friend's death a homicide, are you still working on your own investigation?"

"How did you hear about Tamra—never mind. Silly question." Nick knew everything.

"Well?"

"I don't know." I told him. "I still think there's a tie-in between the girl who was killed four years ago and Tamra and I want a chance to prove it." I shrugged. "I know I should back off. At least that's what everyone around me wants." I cast my eyes downward, the words stuck in my throat.

Nick fixed me with a look. "And what do you want, Brandy Alexander?"

"What do I want? I want to believe that the system works for everyone—not just for the people who have the right skin color or can afford the best legal representation. Mistakes were made in Laura Stewart's murder trial, Nick. Mistakes born of sheer laziness. And nobody questioned it because it's easier to accept that a lowlife like Harmon was guilty than to offer him a decent defense. Where is the moral outrage?"

"I'm looking at it." He cut me a wry smile.

I went beet red. "Sorry. I'll climb down off my soapbox now."

"Never apologize for caring, angel. I admire you beyond words for it."

I went all "gooey" inside again and quickly changed the subject. "Nick, remember when you said you were acquainted with some people who knew Anthony Mitchell?"

"What about it?"

"I want to talk to them. Can you arrange it?"

He nodded. "As long as I go with you. These people don't always play nice."

From a distance I heard the faint ringing of my cell phone. "Oh Jeez, it's probably my mother. I forgot I told her I'd go to mass with her this morning." I jumped out of bed and ran into the living room just as the phone stopped ringing and went to voicemail.

"Mom, I'm here," I said, interrupting the message.

"Where's here? Why aren't you home getting ready for church?"

"Oh, church. Right. The thing is I had to come in to work."

"Since when?" She sounded dubious.

"Mom, really. I'm a very important person here at the news—place. I'm needed at all hours of the day and night."

My mother dropped her voice to a whisper so that God wouldn't overhear. "Brandy, tell me you didn't sneak out of the house in the middle of the night to be with Bobby DiCarlo."

"What? No! Of course not. Listen, mom, my boss is on the warpath and—uh-oh here he comes now. Give my love to Father Vincenzio." *Give my love to Father Vincenzio?* I hung up before she threatened to "ground" me.

181

Nick had business to attend to. I wasn't bothered by the fact that he didn't offer any details as to what kind of business. However, the fact that he added a Kevlar vest underneath his jacket in order to attend to this business bothered me plenty.

He walked me to the door, stopping to retrieve something off the table in the foyer. "You might want to consider hanging on to this for a while," he said.

I looked down at the .22 caliber pistol he held in his outstretched hand and I shook my head, knowing I'd never use it. "I appreciate the offer, Nick, but I'd probably just end up shooting myself."

"I could ask Alphonso to keep you company," he suggested, sticking the gun into the waistband of his pants.

Alphonso babysat me once before. I think he'd rather have brain surgery.

Nick stood against the door post and tugged on the front of my jacket pulling me toward him. Then he leaned into me, slipping a thigh between my legs and covered my mouth with a long, lingering kiss. "I'll call you as soon as I can arrange a meeting with Mitchell's ex-pals," he said. "In the meantime, watch your back."

I nodded, barely able to breathe.

"And darlin'?"

"Yes?" I whispered, feeling the liquid heat in his eyes.

He shot me a wicked grin. "The next time you come by for a sleepover, take a nap first."

It was raining as I climbed back into my car. Good thing. I needed to cool off. I hadn't gone to Nick's looking for sex. At least I don't think I did. But walking away without it seemed anti-climatic…no pun intended.

I looked at my watch. Eleven-thirty. I'd have just enough time to sneak back into the house and take a shower before my mother got home from church. With any luck, I'd be gone again before Father V. got there. It's not that I really have anything against the guy. It's just that the last time I saw him I was rolling around face down on the pavement outside of Saint Dom's Church with Bobby DiCarlo's soon-to-be-ex-wife. It was not my most dignified moment. Plus, I think he was rooting for her.

I found my dad in the kitchen, sharing a plate of Scrapple with the dog. He looked up when I came in and offered me some. Scrapple is supposed to be a true Philadelphia delicacy. Personally I'd rather eat worms.

"Thanks, Dad. You enjoy it." I sat down at the table and began picking at the eggs on his plate. They were sunny side up and perfectly shaped with no slimy gunk on top. My dad is an excellent cook, but he acts helpless in the kitchen when my mom's around. That man really loves her.

I tugged his plate a little closer to me. "I could make you some eggs of your own, if you want," he said, eying his breakfast.

"No, no. This is fine," I told him, digging in.

After the eggs were gone I went upstairs and showered and changed. As I started back downstairs I heard my brother's voice in the hallway. He was asking my dad about the Mercedes. Oy. I turned around and tried to sneak back up the steps but I wasn't fast enough.

Paul stood at the bottom of the staircase looking up at me. He had shaved off the goatee he'd been growing, leaving only the mustache. It was a 1970's look best suited for actors with stage names like "Dick Longo."

"Hey, Sis. Where's my car? I didn't see it on the street."

183

I turned around and headed back down the stairs. "That's because it's not out there," I said, stalling my head off. "I told you I was getting it tuned up."

"No you didn't and it was tuned up two months ago."

"Did I say tuned up? I meant reupholstered."

"Y-you what?" Paul sputtered, turning a vicious shade of red. "That car has all its original parts!"

"Sheesh! Paulie, I'm joking. I went out after work on Friday with some friends from the station and I left the car there. It's perfectly safe."

Paul thought about this for a beat. "Didn't you say everybody at works hates you?"

"Well, that's just mean, Paul. Dad, Paul's picking on me."

At that moment Adrian came to my rescue by barfing up a chunk of Scrapple. "I've got to take him out. I'll be back in a little bit." I yanked on my jacket and grabbed Adrian's leash.

"I'll come with you," Paul told me. Obviously he wasn't buying the whole "Left the car at work" scenario. Note to self: Stop lying.

I opened the front door and a miracle appeared in the form of Heather Koslowski and Mr. Wiggles. Heather's had a crush on my brother since she was six. Unfortunately for her the feeling isn't mutual. "Hi Paul," Heather said, ignoring my dad and me. "I thought I saw your car pull up."

Mr. Wiggles sat down on the porch, decked out in a tiny trench coat and a water proof beret. He looked mildly embarrassed.

"Hey, Heather," I said, eying my brother, "Paul and I were just going to take Adrian for a walk. Would you like to join us?"

184

"Um, actually," said Paul, "I'm just gonna hang out here and talk to Dad. You go and enjoy yourselves."

I clipped Adrian to his leash and stepped outside.

It was still raining so I yanked up the hood on my jacket just as a white Toyota Corolla turned the corner onto our block. Instinctively I shrank behind the lamp post, my guts twisting into a leaden mass of paranoia. Maybe it was just my imagination, but I swore the Toyota slowed down fractionally as it passed my house. I tried to see who was behind the wheel but the windows were completely fogged up. *Was someone looking for me?* More likely, they were gawking at Mr. Wiggles who had just taken a major dump on the sidewalk. Still, I wasn't quite able to dismiss the feeling.

"Are you okay, Bran?" Heather asked.

"Yeah, I'm fine. Listen, about that mechanic you saw working on my car. You haven't seen him around here lately, have you?"

Heather stopped walking and put on her thinking face. She is one of those people who finds it difficult to do two things at once. "Nope. Haven't seen him."

I was only marginally relieved and it occurred to me that I should be actively looking for the guy instead of trying to avoid him. "Heather," I said, suddenly recalling something. "Weren't you an Art Major in high school?"

"Yeah. Why?"

"Do you think you might be able to draw a picture of that guy you saw?"

We headed back to Heather's house. Forty minutes later I walked back out with a sketch of the man she had seen crawling out from underneath the Mercedes. The way I figured it, whoever the guy was, he had to know something about cars to be able to do the kind of damage he had done. Maybe he was a professional mechanic. I knew it was a long shot, but it wouldn't hurt to show his picture around to local auto shops. Maybe someone would recognize him.

My cell phone was ringing when I walked back into my house. I ran to grab it, leaving Adrian to drip dry in the hallway.

"Yo." It was Bobby.

"Yo." I wasn't sure where we stood after last night. On the one hand he'd been pretty pissed off that I'd been keeping things from him. On the other hand, he should be used to it by now. "What's up?" I asked.

"I booked a slot for you at the shooting range for this afternoon. Are you free?"

I didn't know how I felt about spending the afternoon with Bobby. Especially on the heels of spending the night with Nick. My feelings were all mixed up and I needed time to sort them out. "I don't think I can make it, Bobby. I'm supposed to have lunch with my parents and Father Vincenzio."

The front door opened and in walked my mother, followed by our parish priest. He greeted me with a curt nod. "Brandy. We missed you at church this morning."

"Yeah, sorry about that, Father. It couldn't be helped."

His eyes settled on me and I looked down at my shoes. "Your mother tells me that you were working. Will I be seeing you at confession any time soon?" he added and I swear he was smirking. *Well, of all the nerve! Implying that I would lie to my own mother. I was just going to have to do a better job of it in the future.*

I turned back to the phone. "What's that? There's another crisis down at the office and you need me immediately? I'll be right there!"

Bobby nearly busted a gut laughing. "If there is a hell, you're going straight to it, Alexander."

"Shut-uh-up."

My mother's jaw dropped open. "That is no way to speak to your boss, young lady."

"I guess I should have asked you this before you picked up a loaded pistol, but are you still mad at me?"

Bobby hadn't said much on the way over to the shooting range. He'd been up half the night dumpster diving for evidence and his nerves were pretty well shot. The corpse those kids had found last night turned out to be a fifteen year old hooker who'd been beaten and strangled before getting tossed head first into a six foot pile of garbage. I could read Bobby well enough to know he was sick to his stomach over this case. And since he couldn't do anything to change what had happened to that girl, he was going to make damn sure nothing happened to me.

Bobby picked up some ear protectors and a pair of goggles and handed them to me.

"Do I seem mad?" he asked.

"Yeah. *A little bit.*"

"Maybe you're just feeling guilty," he said.

I opened my mouth all set to deny having anything to feel guilty about, but we both knew that wasn't true. I'd withheld important information from him. It was stupid and maybe I even regretted it. But I wasn't in the mood to listen to another lecture on all of my flaws. I stuck the goggles over my eyes and picked up a gun. "I'm never going to use this, but show me what to do anyway."

I started out with a .22 and worked my way up to a .45. I put one hand over the other and squeezed off a couple rounds. The recoil on the larger gun was so strong it felt like my arms would pop right out of their sockets.

"Good," Bobby said. "Now try it with your eyes *open.*"

"I glared at him. "Very funny."

"Imagine that. And I wasn't even trying to be. Keep your eyes open," he reiterated. "You've got a lethal weapon in your hands."

The place was empty except for two nineteen year old rookies at the other end of the room who kept shouting "freeze muthafucka" just before they'd pull the trigger. By the time they were finished, I understood why some animal mothers eat their young.

Bobby was a lot more relaxed on the ride home. Spending an hour shooting the crotches out of paper bad guys seemed to be just what he needed. He pulled up in front of my house and turned off the engine. "You did good today," he said.

"Thanks." I was never going to be Annie Oakley, but at least now I wouldn't run screaming from the room at the mere sight of a gun.

I wanted to ask Bobby a question, but now that we were back on an even keel, I didn't want to stir things up again. However that little voice inside me had different ideas. "So," I ventured, "are you going to do anything about that note I got the other night?"

"It's already at the lab. If there are any decent prints maybe a match will show up in the database."

"I really don't think we're dealing with a hardened criminal here, Bobby. It felt more like the guy was just out to deliver the message and I got in the way."

"Yeah? What makes you think that?" *Hmm. He's not mad. He's listening. I'm starting to see where working out with a semi-automatic might be considered therapeutic.*

I leaned back against the door, making myself comfortable. "It's the only thing that makes sense. I surprised him and he reacted. If the guy had wanted me dead, I would be. Besides, what would be the purpose of leaving me a note if he was trying to kill me? And anyway, the message seemed too benign. Too vague. Like the person wasn't used to playing the tough guy role and hadn't fully thought out the plan. I honestly think whoever wrote it is in a whole different league than the guys who kidnapped me or the one who got his finger torn off when he broke into my car and tried to strangle me—"

Bobby cut me off, his voice deadly calm. "What did you say?"

Oh shit. I forgot he didn't know about the finger. I was going to have to get file folders to keep all my lies and secrets straight.

"Where's the finger now?" he asked when I finished filling him in. To his credit, he didn't blow up, although the little vein in his temple was throbbing in triple time.

"It's in Nick's mini-fridge at his office."

The mention of Santiago's name didn't do much to improve Bobby's mood. "Get it for me," he said through gritted teeth. "If the tip of the finger is intact we might be able to come up with a name to go with it. Is there anything else I should know about, while you're at it?" he added.

"Only that Heather sketched a picture of the guy who screwed with my brakes. I figured I'd take it around to local mechanics to see if anyone recognizes him."

"Good idea," he said begrudgingly. "Get me a copy. In fact—" He stopped mid-thought.

"What?"

"Nothin'. I was gonna say let the cops handle it from here, but I'd just be wasting my breath, wouldn't I?"

"Pretty much," I admitted. "But I swear I'm just going to ask around. I'm not going to get involved with anything dangerous."

"Speaking of dangerous," Bobby said, "what's going on between you and Santiago?"

His voice was neutral, but there was no mistaking the implication behind his words. My antennae shot up. "Uh, where did that come from?"

Bobby shrugged. "You've been spending a lot of time with him and I want to know what his intentions are."

"You want to know what his *intentions* are? What are you, my father? No, make that my *grandfather*."

"I'm serious here, Brandy. I have a right to know what's going on."

Hey, where did he get off deciding on the company I keep? Did I go marching over to his house, demanding full disclosure on his "intentions" regarding Tina Delvechione? Okay, so maybe my righteous indignation was fueled by the fact that I was as much in the dark about Nick's intentions as Bobby was. I know Nick said that he couldn't offer me anything beyond friendship and an occasional roll in the sack, but he made me feel special in ways I couldn't even begin to explain. So I'd be hard pressed to explain it to anybody else.

190

"Look, Bobby. Nick and I are friends. But if there *was* anything going on beyond that, well, I'd say that's between Nick and me. You got a problem with that?"

Bobby sat up in the seat, his jaw muscles clenched so tight he looked in danger of breaking a couple of teeth. "Yeah. As a matter of fact I do. The guy is bad news. And if you're falling for that creep, somebody needs to straighten you out before you get hurt or worse."

"Oh. And you think it's *your* job? Well, I've got a news flash for you, DiCarlo. It's not. Who I choose to spend time with and *how* we choose to spend that time is none of your business."

"You made it my business when you kissed me the other night," he growled.

"You kissed me! And anyway, we never should have gone there. We talked about this and we agreed it wasn't a good idea."

"Yeah, well, I've changed my mind. I know you still have feelings for me and it's no secret I want you back. So all bets are off, sweetheart."

Bobby leaned forward, our knees touching, his eyes locked on mine. My insides responded with a familiar rush and I tried to turn away but he wouldn't let me. He reached out and cupped his hand behind my head, his lips perilously close to mine. "I'm going to keep on reminding you of how good we are together every chance I get," he murmured. It was a really big reminder.

Chapter Twelve

"I swear to God, Fran, if Vincenzio hadn't come along and tapped on the car window, we would have done it right then and there in broad daylight. Mrs. Gentile was taking out the trash and saw the whole thing. My mother is so mortified she's refusing to leave the house. It's a stinking mess…and stop laughing. It's not funny."

"Yes, it is."

Yeah, actually I guess it was.

After I swore to my mom that I'd go to church next Sunday to confess my sins, (which seemed redundant, seeing as Father V. was there for a goodly portion of it) I took the rest of the afternoon to deliver copies of Heather's sketch around to local auto shops. At 4:30 p.m. I started thinking this was a really dumb idea, and then at 4:45 p.m. I hit pay dirt.

I'd been cruising down Germantown Avenue when I spied Ditto's Car Repair at the corner of Germantown and Belmont. I pulled into the alley just as a guy with a military buzz cut, wearing a grey mechanics coverall was closing up shop. I parked behind a blue, 1968 corvette that Paul would have killed for and got out of the car, taking the copy of Heather's sketch with me.

He walked toward me, wiping grease laden hands on a towel he kept in the back pocket of his coveralls. The name on his shirt said Mel. "Sorry, we're closed. But if you want to park it here tonight, I can take a look at it in the morning."

"Oh, thanks, but actually, I'm looking for someone." I handed him a copy of the picture. "Do you by any chance know this guy?"

Mel took the sketch from me and held it up in the dimming light. "Yeah. I know him. His name's Zack Meyers and he's a real jerk."

My heartbeat quickened. "Does he work here?"

"Used to," Mel said. He was fired about three months ago. The inventory kept disappearing. He was stealing the owner blind. Nobody could prove anything for sure, but we all knew it was him."

"You wouldn't happen to have an address for him, would you?"

He looked me up and down. "Are you a cop?" he asked.

"Nah," I said, shaking my head. "Listen, it sure would help me out if I could locate this guy. He screwed me over pretty good too and I'd really like to find him."

I followed Mel back into the office. Thumbing through an old Rolodex, he extracted a card and handed it to me. "If you go looking for Meyers, take somebody with you. The guy's got a real temper. I wouldn't want to see him use it on you."

My impulse was to drive directly over to Meyers' house and beat a full confession out of him. However, the saner side of me, glimpses of which I was still able to conjure up upon occasion, prevailed, and I decided to think things through a little more.

I had to tell Bobby I now had a name and an address. But first, I had to confirm it was the right guy. If I could get a picture of him, I could bring it back to Heather to I.D. Once I knew for sure it was the same man she had seen under my car, the cops could bring him in for questioning. It was too dark outside to get anything useful accomplished tonight. But early tomorrow morning I'd go over and stake out his place.

My parents weren't home when I got back to the house. My mom had left a note saying they'd been invited to play Pinochle at the Giancola's and there was dinner in the fridge. I opened the refrigerator and took out a container and opened the lid. Uh-oh. Smorgasbord Stew. It was something my mom had concocted when Paul and I were young; the ingredients consisting of whatever leftovers existed in the refrigerator at the time and were in danger of exceeding their shelf life. I emptied the container into the garbage disposal and made a box of chocolate pudding.

It was nice to have the house to myself for a change. I went into the living room with the entire sauce pan of pudding and popped in a movie. *The Princess Bride.* Somewhere around the time when Vizinni started ranting to the Dread Pirate Roberts about never getting involved in a land war in Asia I fell asleep.

I woke up an hour later and turned off the movie. It was 10:30 p.m. and Adrian needed to go pee. I took out my stun gun and stayed close to the front door while he made his deposit on Mrs. Gentile's Azalea bush.

The night was clear and crisp. I breathed in deeply and scanned the block checking for signs of anything amiss. About four houses down on the other side of the street I spotted a white Toyota Corolla. I know every one of my neighbors' vehicles and this wasn't one of them. My guts twisted in fear as I flashed on the white Corolla that had cruised down my block earlier in the day. I whistled for Adrian and he came trotting back inside. I slammed the front door shut and locked it. *Is someone spying on me? Should I call the cops? Bobby? Nick? My mommy?*

While I was debating this the doorbell rang. I jumped a mile. Clutching the stun gun in my hand I balanced on tiptoe to peer out the spy hole. My parents peered back at me. I opened the door to let them in. "Why didn't you use your key?" I asked, forgetting all about the faux cell phone I was holding.

"Oh, honey," my mother said, wrestling it out of my hand. "I need an upgrade on my phone. Does this one take pictures?" She held it up and aimed it at my father.

"No, Mom. Don't!" I grabbed it back from her before she zapped my dad into tomorrow. "Um…I'm expecting a call." I said goodnight, ignoring the "Where did we go wrong?" look that passed between my parents and went upstairs.

Grabbing a pair of binoculars out of my bedroom closet, I crept over to the window and pulled the curtains back slightly. The white Corolla was still out there. I could barely make out a shadowy figure sitting behind the wheel. I dragged a chair over to the window and sat down. It was going to be a long night.

At around 3:00 a.m. someone emerged from the car. He looked to be about 5 feet nine or so, wearing a bulky, hooded jacket. His back was to me and by the way he was standing, I'd say he was taking a bathroom break. He finished up and got back in the car. I fell asleep after that and when I awoke at six, the car was gone.

I pulled on some jeans and a long sleeved tee shirt and threw on a hooded sweat shirt on top of that. Then I grabbed the binoculars and my digital camera off the dresser and headed downstairs.

Rocky was in the kitchen scooting a hockey puck around on the floor. *Where'd he get a hockey puck?* I bent down to pick it up and discovered it was actually one of my mom's homemade biscuits. Seeing as it looked like a piece of blackened rubber, I could understand how my kitten might mistake it for sports equipment. I thought about letting her play with it some more, but I doubted my mom would find the humor in that, so I tossed it into the garbage disposal where it joined the stew.

When I got outside, Heather and her dog were just getting back from their morning stroll. She waved hello and crossed the street to meet me. I was anxious to get underway but I didn't want to be rude, so I started walking backwards to the car to sort of let her know I was in a hurry. "Thanks for all your help yesterday," I called out to her, making a big deal out of opening the car door and tossing my stuff inside. I slid behind the wheel and stuck my key in the ignition.

"Did you find the guy you were looking for?" she asked.

"I'm not sure. I'm on my way over to his house now to try to get a picture of him. When I get back I'll show it to you." I started up the car.

"Take me with you, Brandy."

I turned off the ignition. "What?"

"That way you won't have to take a picture," Heather said. "I'll know him if I see him. It'll save you time."

She had a point. But not a strong enough one to endure what could turn out to be hours on end of her company, riding shotgun in the Le Sabre.

"Heather, why would you want to come along? I mean who knows how this guy will react if he catches us spying on him. This could turn out to be really dangerous."

Heather looked down at her feet. "Brandy, I'm thirty-one years old and I've never had a boyfriend. I still live with my parents, my job bores me to tears and Mr. Wiggles is my only friend. And he just barely tolerates me. Your life is so exciting. Just once I want to do something crazy."

I sighed. "Don't you have to go to work?"

She whipped out her cell phone. "This is Heather. *Cough. Cough.* I'm not coming in today." She hung up and looked at me. "Please?"

"Oh, what the hell," I relented. "Ditch the dog and climb on in."

Zack Meyers lived at Front and Duncannon Avenues, across the street from a high school. His neighborhood is an older, more dilapidated version of mine, with double wide porches, bars on the windows and aluminum awnings stretching across the tops of the entrances to the houses.

We parked a few doors down across the street and I cut the engine. Heather had changed from her work clothes into what she imagined the well dressed spy was wearing these days—black turtleneck, black jeans and a black ski mask. I told her to lose the ski mask, unless she was planning to rob a bank afterwards.

I'd felt really sorry for her after she told me that Mr. Wiggles was her only friend, so I'd stopped at Starbucks along the way and bought her a Mocha. Then I drove by Dunkin' Donuts and picked up half a dozen of the powdered jelly-filled. I'd never been on a stake out before, but it just seemed like the right thing to bring along and I wanted to look professional.

"This is fun," Heather said, slurping her mocha. "We should hang out more often."

"Yeah," I agreed, swept away by a sugar-induced euphoria. I'd already eaten all three of my doughnuts and Heather still had one left. I eyed the bag longingly.

"You can have it if you want," she said.

"If you're sure," I said and took it out of the bag before she had a chance to change her mind. I bit into the doughnut and raspberry jelly squirted out the side, landing on my chest. I looked like I'd been shot. Note to self: Take etiquette lessons.

Time went really slowly after all the doughnuts were gone. I knew Meyers was at home. I'd called his house line when we first got here. Judging by the way he answered his phone, the guy was definitely not a morning person.

"Well, we can't just go marching up to his door and ring the bell," I said, "so we've got to find a way to lure him out of the house. But how?"

"Yo Bran," Heather said slowly. "Remember that Halloween about fifteen years ago, when you and Bobby DiCarlo went around the neighborhood lighting bags of dog poop on fire and then ringing door bells and running away?"

"Hey. Why do I always get blamed for everything? That was *not* me."

"Sure," said Heather. "Anyway, remember?"

And suddenly I knew why the Universe conspired to make me bring Heather along. I smiled at her. "Has anyone ever told you you're a really smart cookie?"

"You're the first," she said, smiling back at me. "Thanks."

Okay, even though our goal was not to get some poor schlub to stick his foot in a pile of flaming dog poop, the same principle applied. I handed Heather the binoculars and told her to wait inside the car while I gathered some dried twigs to fill up the doughnut bag. Then I crept up to Meyers' porch and laid it down on the top step. People would be leaving for work soon so I had to hurry. I have to admit I was a little nervous. Bobby had always been the one to do the actual torching. I was just the "Lookout." I took a book of matches out of my pocket and struck two at once, touching the burning tip to the paper bag. The bag was slow to ignite. That was good. It would give Meyers a chance to stamp out the flame before it set the entire neighborhood on fire. Once I got it going I rang the doorbell a bunch of times and then ran like crazy back to the car.

I almost made it too, except for that icy patch on the sidewalk. For the second time in a week my feet flew out from under me and I landed on my butt on the muddy ground. Heather stuck her head out the car window. "Are you okay?" she asked. I could tell she was trying hard not to laugh.

I hauled myself up and scrambled back into the car. "Don't say a word," I warned her. She made a sign like she was zipping her lips and throwing away the key.

Suddenly, the door to Zack Meyers' house flung open. Although we could barely make out the bulky figure inside, we heard him loud and clear. "Goddamn kids!"

"Get ready," I said to Heather. She lifted the binoculars to her eyes. I set my camera to zoom lens and poked my head out the window.

Dressed in a ratty old robe, Meyers took a tentative step out his front door. I looked down at his feet. He was barefoot. How the heck did he think he was going to put out a fire with bare feet?

I began clicking away on the camera while Heather fiddled with the focus on the binoculars. Meyers looked up, debating his options and I got a clear shot of his face. I turned to Heather. "Did you get a good look at him?" I asked. She nodded, the binoculars trained on the man standing on the porch. Only she wasn't looking at his face. Her aim was significantly lower. I dropped my gaze down too, to see what had grabbed her attention. Oh crap.

Meyers had whipped open his robe and was now playing fireman, hosing down the flames with a steady stream of urine.

"Heather!" I yelled. "Unless he was waving hello to you with his dick you're not going to be able to identify this guy unless you look at his face!"

Heather went beet red. "Oh. Sorry, Brandy. I don't get to see this very often...or ever." Reluctantly she raised the binoculars upward. "That's him," she shouted. "That's the guy I saw under your car."

Bingo!

I picked up the camera and reviewed the pictures I'd taken of Meyers, figuring the police might want them. He didn't look familiar to me, however something on his face

200

caught my eye and suddenly this queasy feeling came over me and I thought I was going to lose the doughnuts. Right below Meyer's left eye, a chunk of skin had been gouged out of his cheek. I flashed back on the night I was kidnapped and the precise moment the "Clear Knuckles" made contact with human flesh. Holy cow.

Meyers finished his business and went back inside the house. I pulled out my phone and punched in Bobby's number. He was just getting ready to head off for work and he sounded harried. I could hear Sophia wailing away in the background. Boy, that little girl had a set of lungs on her. "What's wrong with Sophia?" I asked.

"She's mad because I told her she couldn't eat her breakfast out of the dog's bowl."

"Why not?" I asked. "I mean, if the dog is done with it…"

Bobby did a big sigh. "Do you need something? Because now's not a great time."

Actually, this could work to my advantage. I could tell him what I'd done and he wouldn't have time to yell at me about it. I filled him in on the morning's activities, ending with my suspicion that Meyers was the one who grabbed me in the parking lot. "So when are the cops gonna come and arrest him?" I said.

Bobby laughed. "In a perfect world, sweetheart. Swing by the precinct and we'll get yours and Heather's statements and then we'll send someone out to talk to this guy."

After a pit stop at the police station, we drove straight home. I was due at the doctor's office to interview Laura's brother and I still had to get changed.

"Thanks for taking me with you, Brandy," Heather said, as we got out of the car. "This was the best day of my life."

I got a lump in my throat, which I'm sure was because I'm getting a cold.

Dr. Ethan Girard was movie star handsome. He had the astonishing good looks of a young Gregory Peck and the charm to match. Personally, I couldn't imagine going to a doctor who looked that good. Our family physician, Dr. Powers, is about a hundred and four and deaf in one ear, but at least I'm not embarrassed to take off my clothes in front of him. Of course, he can't see me anyway what with the cataracts and all.

I sat across from Dr. Girard, discreetly crossing my legs as if I expected him to vault over the top of his highly polished cherry wood desk and commence to giving me a pap test. The nurse had escorted me into his office. Girard stood, shooting me a brief, quizzical look like he couldn't quite place me. Being a C list television personality, I get that a lot. "I'm Dr. Girard," he said, recovering. He flashed me a smile any orthodontist would be proud to take credit for. "It's nice to meet you."

He was familiar to me too. His voice anyway and I mentioned this to him.

"Are you a fan of NPR?" he asked. "I have a spot once a month on Saturday mornings. 'Ask the Doctor.'"

"Oh, that must be it," I said, wanting to appear like someone who listened to National Public Radio instead of the Oldies station.

"So, tell me," Dr. Girard said, settling back in his leather bound chair. "When are you due?"

"Due for what?" I asked.

"I'm sorry. Didn't you tell my receptionist you were here for an interview?"

"Yes I did. And to be honest, I was surprised to hear you were granting interviews. This must be a very emotional time for you and your family."

Dr. Girard's face clouded over. "I think there's been a misunderstanding. Emily told me she booked you for a prospective doctor's interview. If you're not pregnant, why are you here?"

Realization dawned and my heart sank to somewhere below my rib cage. The poor guy thought I was looking for an obstetrician. Oy. "Dr. Girard," I began, "I am so sorry for not making myself clear. I'm a reporter and I'm here to talk to you about David Dwayne Harmon. As you're no doubt aware, he's scheduled to be executed next month."

Ethan Girard's lips thinned. "I don't mean to be rude, Ms. Alexander, but I'm sure you'll understand if I ask you to leave. As you said, this is a very painful subject for my family and me. Our feelings on the matter of Mr. Harmon's execution are not open for public scrutiny." He began to rise out of his seat, even as I sat rooted to mine.

I had to convince him to talk to me. "Dr. Girard, I can't even pretend to understand the suffering your family has been put through, and I would never intentionally add to it. But there's something I think you should know. If you would just please give me a few minutes of your time—I'll be as brief as possible."

"No, let me be brief. About two months ago my stepfather had a massive stroke. He's been in Hillgarden Convalescent Home since then and communicates by blinking his eyes and shaking his head. The day of his stroke, someone came to visit my parents—a reporter by the name of Tamra Rhineholt. I assume you're familiar with her."

I nodded, speechless.

"She misrepresented herself. Told my parents she was doing a story on 'Old Philadelphia.' My stepfather comes from a rather prestigious background. Anyway, when she got there Rhineholt told them the real purpose for her visit. She said she believed that the man who had been convicted by the courts for the rape and murder of my sister was innocent. The idea was ludicrous. There was enough evidence to convict that man ten times over."

"But what if it was false evidence?" I asked. "Wouldn't you want to know?"

"Were you there at the trial, Ms. Alexander?"

"No," I admitted. "I wasn't."

"The man's own lawyers wouldn't let him testify because they knew the truth. There was no doubt in anyone's mind that he was guilty. And then, two months before he's scheduled to die, this—this woman comes skulking around my parents' home, stirring up horrific memories. And for what? A career boost? She couldn't possibly think he was really innocent. And if that weren't enough, she went on to defame my baby sister's character. She made absolutely vile accusations about her. Rhineholt alluded to the idea that Laura was some kind of sex-crazed co-ed and that any number of men could have killed her. According to my mother, Rhineholt stopped this short of blaming Laura for what happened to her that night. My stepfather was devastated. Laura was the light of his life. He used to call her his little kitten."

Girard turned away, deep in thought. "My mother lost her only daughter and now thanks to Rhineholt, she could lose her husband too." He looked back at me, his voice thick with emotion. "I'm a doctor, Ms. Alexander. I bring life into the world. But God help me, I want that man dead."

"Did you want her dead too?" I asked softly.

"What?"

"Dr. Girard, are you aware that Tamra Rhineholt was murdered last week?"

Girard stood, his handsome face distorted by quiet rage.

"Get out," he said.

So I did.

"What the hell were you thinking?"

Why does everyone keep asking me that? I was standing in Eric's office, watching as he paced a hole through his rug.

"Ethan Girard's family could buy and sell our station and you practically accused him of murdering Tamra. He's already called here threatening a harassment suit."

"I didn't accuse him. I *asked* him. Big difference." The truth is I had no idea why those words had popped out of my mouth and I felt really awful about it. Girard was obviously in a lot of emotional pain. It hadn't been my intention to add to it.

"Look, Brandy, I'm not saying don't do your job. But for Christ's sake, be a little more sensitive." Eric paused, eying me up and down. "And while you're at it, could you do something with your hair? It looks like birds nested in it."

Okay, so my timing was terrible. But the more I thought about it, the less far fetched my question to Girard really was. After all, he had practically come right out and blamed Tamra for causing his stepfather's stroke. Maybe he got carried away by his grief and went crazy. You hear about this kind of thing all the time. The Press hounds decent, law-abiding citizens until they can't take any more and they just snap...on the other hand, Tamra's murder seemed too well planned to be an act of spontaneous revenge.

My thoughts were interrupted by the sound of Lynne Schaffer's voice, shrill and demanding, just outside the door. I walked into the hallway and found her with Craig. He looked to be in the throes of a nervous breakdown. Papers were scattered everywhere, with Craig on all-fours haphazardly trying to retrieve them. Lynne loomed above him, shouting insults at the poor kid. All she needed was a whip and thigh high boots to complete the tableau. "I'm s-so sorry, Lynne," he stuttered. "It was an accident."

"What's the problem?" I asked, bending down to help him.

"This cretin crashed right into me. That's what we get for hiring the handicapped," Lynne muttered to no one in particular, as I'm sure I was included in her assessment of the hired help.

Technically I did not push her down. I just sort've accidentally bumped into her when I stood up and in a blink she was on her ass. "Ooh, sorry, Lynne. You okay?"

"You did that on purpose," she screamed, struggling to right herself.

"Prove it." I scooped up the rest of the papers and helped Craig to his feet.

Craig looked up gratefully. There were deep circles under his eyes. It was like looking in a mirror. "I have to get this script over to the set," he said. "I'm late. They're waiting for me."

I put a protective arm around his shoulder. "Come on. I'll walk you."

Something was bothering Craig and it wasn't just the run-in with Lynne. I knew it by the way he kept sneaking looks in my direction, like he was expecting me to implode at any minute. An uneasy feeling settled over me. If he had something to say I wished he'd just come out and say it.

As if he could read my mind, Craig turned to me, the words tumbling out in a rush. "I know you're trying to find out who killed Tamra, but you have to stop. I—I don't want you to get hurt."

My nerves went on red alert. "Craig, do you know something? Because if you do—"

Craig gave his head an emphatic shake. "I don't know anything," he said, grabbing the script pages out of my hand. "I have to go."

"No, wait," I said. But he'd already disappeared through the set door.

I stood there, dumbfounded. Obviously, Craig was worried about me. But was it out of general concern for my safety, the way you'd warn someone not to play in traffic? *Or did he have specific information that my health was about to be severely compromised?*

I thought back on the events of the past few days; the misspelled note warning me not to interfere in Harmon's execution, the white Corolla parked across the street from my house. Craig looked about ready to keel over from exhaustion. Could it possibly be from one too many late nights parked outside my door? I was about to find out.

207

It was lunchtime, and in an effort to soothe Lynne's wounded pride, Eric was springing for hoagies. Seems Lynne was still pissed about me pushing her down. Well tough. She'd been beggin' for it.

Eric sent Craig to pick up lunch. I waited as he entered the elevator and punched the button for Lower Level parking and then I took off running down the stairs. When I got to the bottom I hung back until Craig emerged from the elevator. He dragged his feet slowly, as if carrying the weight of the world on his shoulders. I trailed him while he worked his way through the parking structure. After a few minutes he finally reached his car. A white Toyota Corolla. *Big surprise.*

What the hell was Craig doing stalking me? Oh my God. Could he be in cahoots with Zach Meyers? What if it's Craig's finger that's sitting in the ice tray in Nick's mini fridge? I shut my eyes and tried to envision Craig bending down, picking up the script pages. Nope, all digits were present and accounted for. That was a relief. Anyway, in my heart I couldn't imagine Craig purposely setting out to hurt anyone.

I knew I should call Bobby and let him in on this latest development, but I just couldn't bring myself to rat Craig out. He was scared, and in his own weird way I believed he was trying to protect me. But from who?

I stayed hidden until Craig pulled out of the lot and then I went back upstairs. I nabbed Eric in the hallway. "Hey, Eric, what's the name of the work placement program Craig came to us through?" I asked.

"Helping Hands. Why?"

"I thought I'd give them a call and let them know what a great job he's doing."

The truth is I didn't trust my own instincts anymore. Was Craig the innocent soul I believed he was or some diabolical monster who was faking mild retardation in order to gain the trust of the people around him?

I typed in Helping Hands on my computer. According to their website, the organization had been in existence since 1994 and had been honored last year by the mayor at his annual Humanitarian Awards dinner. There was a lengthy article accompanied by a picture of their Board of Directors. The board was comprised of about twenty people who were virtual strangers to me along with one very recent acquaintance. Dr. Ethan Girard. *Well, what do you know.*

A very nice lady named Mrs. Wyland answered the phone. Yes, she knew Craig quite well. He'd been a part of the program since he was sixteen. She was pleased to hear he was doing so well at the station.

"I was looking over your website and I noticed my friend's obstetrician is on your board of directors. Dr. Girard?"

"Oh, yes. He is such a nice man. He's been very active in our fund raising efforts."

"Boy, that sounds just like him," I chuckled. "How active is he in the daily operations of Helping Hands?"

"What do you mean?"

"Oh, well, for instance...is he involved in matching up your clients with local businesses?" *I found it entirely too coincidental that Dr. Girard, who considered Tamra to be public enemy number one, was a board member for the same organization that placed Craig at WINN. What if Girard planted Craig there in order to spy on Tamra?*

"Generally speaking there's not a lot of contact between our clients and the board," Mrs. Wyland

209

informed me. "Primarily, the board raises money so that we can keep our doors open. Oh, but we did have a wonderful event about three months ago—an old fashioned pancake breakfast, and our clients got a chance to meet their benefactors. You should check out our photo gallery. It's on the website."

I took Mrs. Wyland up on her suggestion and clicked on the photo gallery. There were dozens of shots of the event but only one that held my interest. It was a picture of Dr. Girard seated at a banquet table, his plate piled high with pancakes. He was smiling into the camera. And smiling right alongside him was Craig.

I called personnel to see how long Craig had been working at the station. Turns out he'd been there a little over a year. Granted, it would be a stretch to think that Girard planted Craig at the station a year ago, on the off chance that he would some day need an informant. But the connection was too strong to be coincidental.

The pancake breakfast was three months ago, which was around the same time that Tamra began her investigation. Maybe Girard and Craig met at the breakfast and during the course of polite conversation he found out that Craig worked at WINN. A month later Tamra visits Laura's dad and upsets him so much he has a major stroke. At which point Girard contacts Craig and somehow convinces him to help exact revenge on Tamra.

I wandered down the hall to run my theory by Eric.

"Let me get this straight," he said. "Your prime suspect in Tamra's death is a philanthropic obstetrician, and your only proof is a picture of him yucking it up with Craig over some flapjacks?"

It didn't sound stupid when I was hashing it out in my mind. Maybe the jelly doughnuts were clouding my thinking. "I'll get back to you," I said and wandered back to my office.

I decided it would be a wasted effort to question Craig at this point. The guy was obviously freaked and I needed to figure out how to approach him about his connection to Girard without scaring him off.

As I pondered this my phone rang. It was Bobby. "The DNA results on Tamra's baby are in," he said without preamble.

"And?"

Bobby blew out a soft breath of air. "And your instincts were right. Rhineholt wasn't the father."

Oh boy.

Chapter Thirteen

"It's not enough to build an entire case around, but it's looking more and more like Rhineholt killed his wife because she was having an affair," Bobby told me.

Something didn't sit right. "Bobby, how did the cops get Jeff to agree to a DNA test in the first place? I mean if he thought Tamra was cheating on him, he had to figure there'd be a chance the baby wouldn't be his. Especially if Jeff was using condoms. And if it turned out that it *wasn't* his kid, it would just serve as another motive for killing her."

"I don't know," Bobby said. "Maybe he felt like he didn't have a choice so he went along with it and hoped for the best. They've got someone watching his house in case he gets an idea to bolt."

My "call waiting" began to beep. "Hang on a sec." I checked Caller I.D. but didn't recognize the number. "I've gotta get this," I told Bobby. "I'll call you back."

I clicked over to the other line. "Brandy Alexander," I said.

The voice on the other end sounded nervous. "Uh, hi. This is Danny Lang. Joe Allen over at Dante's Garden said you wanted to talk to me."

It took me a second for my brain to kick in. The "no sleep" thing was starting to affect my recall. "Oh, hi, Danny," I said, reaching for a pen and paper. "Thanks for getting in touch with me. I assume Joe filled you in on what I wanted to talk to you about."

"He said something about that girl, Laura, who was murdered around four years ago."

"Right. Joe mentioned she was a regular at Dante's Garden and that she was a big fan of yours. I was hoping you might remember something about her that the police may have overlooked."

Danny breathed softly into the phone. It was quick and shallow. "I don't know what I can tell you," he said finally. "I mean it's not like I really knew her all that well. It was a long time ago and whenever we got together we didn't do all that much talking." He emitted an embarrassed laugh. "Hell, she never even told me her real name. She always wanted me to call her by some cutesy nickname."

"Look," I told him, "This girl's murder case is about to be reopened," which was a slight exaggeration (okay, a big fat lie, but I needed some leverage here). "Now, if you tell me what you know, maybe we can avoid the cops getting involved."

"Jesus! The *cops* know about me and Laura?" His voice took on a slightly hysterical note. "Oh man, they don't suspect me of killing her, do they?"

Drawing on my ability to quote entire scenes from old episodes of Law and Order, I managed to bullshit Lang into thinking I was the only thing standing between him and death by lethal injection.

His panic was palpable. "I think I should call my lawyer."

Oh crap. I may have gone a tad too far. "No, no. That's not necessary. Look, to tell you the truth, your name hasn't even come up. Danny, I just need an hour of your time. I promise you, anything you say will be off the record."

Lang agreed to meet me at DiVinci's for a late lunch, which was good, seeing as somebody had eaten my hoagie. Nobody fessed up, but Art said he was sure it was an honest mistake—whoever it was.

DiVinci's was packed, so we sat at the bar and waited for a booth to open up. I ordered a coke and sprung for a Newcastle for Danny. Judging by his former occupation, I'd half-expected Richard Gere from American Gigolo to walk through the door, but Danny turned out to be a nice guy. He looked vaguely familiar although I was sure we'd never met. I would have remembered someone who takes his clothes off for a living.

"I started working at Dante's Garden because I needed money for college," Danny confided, settling in with his beer. "The tips were great and the work was easy. That is until Laura started coming around."

"What do you mean?" I asked, taking a sip of my coke.

"Well, when I first began to notice her at the club, I thought she was just a cute college kid out for a good time. I did think it was kind of weird that she always showed up alone. You know, with places like that the women usually come in packs to celebrate birthdays or bachelorette parties. Anyway, Joe told me he thought she was hot for me and I've got to admit it made me feel good. I even thought about asking her out. She was a little young for me, but I figured she was old enough. I mean she wasn't underage or anything."

"So what changed your mind?"

He looked over at me. "You don't have any recording devices or anything on you, do you? I mean you did say this is all off the record."

I made the sign of the cross on my chest. "I give you my word, Danny. I'm not here to make trouble for you. I'm just trying to piece together what really happened to this girl."

Danny took a long slug of beer. "It's funny. I've never told anyone this shit. But for some reason I want to tell you." After he was through, I almost wished he hadn't.

According to Lang, Laura came up to him one night after the club closed and asked him if he wanted to take her home. He was more than happy to accommodate her and they ended up in bed. "Everything was fine at first, but then things got weird."

"In what way?" I had to choke out the words because truthfully, I didn't want to know. I'm not comfortable with my own sexual exploits, let alone someone else's.

"That girl was hardcore. I mean like borderline S&M. To tell you the truth, I was freaked out by some of the things she wanted me to do to her." He paused, lost in thought. "Look, I'm not saying I didn't enjoy it, but afterwards I always felt kind of disgusted with myself."

"Well, if she made you feel that way, why did you keep seeing her?"

"She paid me to," he mumbled.

"Oh," I said, as non-judgmentally as possible, but it still came out as "eewww."

"Look," he said, and his voice got really quiet. "If I had to do it over again I wouldn't. I was really sorry to hear about what happened to her, but honestly, I wasn't surprised. The last time we—uh—you know—she went nuts and I finally stopped seeing her."

"Why? What did she do?"

"She tried to kill me."

"On purpose?" Okay, that sounded really lame. "What I meant was maybe she just got caught up in the throes of passion and—"

Danny cut me off, shaking his head. "No. This was too calculated. She knew exactly what she was doing that night. Laura liked to play fantasy games," he explained. "Usually she'd set it up so that I'd start out being the aggressor and then she'd turn the tables on me. I'd go along with it because the money was good and I guess it was kind of exciting. But this particular night was different. She tied me spread eagle to her bedpost and she came after me with a butcher knife. It wasn't the first time she played out this little scenario, but it was the first time she used a real knife. I'm telling you, I thought that was it."

"Wow. So what happened?"

"I managed to untie myself before she did any major damage. But I swear she would've cut off my balls if I hadn't gotten out of there."

"Jesus, Danny," I said. "Who knows how many guys she's done this to, or how far she'd actually take it. Why didn't you tell the police?"

Danny blushed. "I was too embarrassed to tell anyone. I'm only telling you now because of what you told me about that Harmon dude. I'd just always figured he was guilty."

A deep and abiding chill came over me. What kind of torment must this girl have endured to end up such a psychotic wreck?

A booth opened up and we grabbed it. I guess all that sadomasochistic sex talk really revved up the old appetite. I ordered a large pizza with everything on it. I'm sure a shrink would say I was suppressing my anxiety with food, but I had to suppress it with something, so why not pepperoni and extra cheese?

Just as our pizza arrived, the door opened and in walked Tina Delvechione and her "girls," as she used to refer to the twin peaks sticking out from under her shirt. She was laughing and hanging on to some guy's leather jacketed arm. I thought I'd be friendly and wave hello when I realized the guy she was hanging onto was DiCarlo.

"Quick, slide over!" I instructed Danny. I got up and scooted in next to him in the booth. "Pretend you like me!"

Danny shot me a quizzical look. "Pretend I *what?*"

I glanced over at Bobby and Tina. They were headed our way.

"Shh. Never mind, just follow my lead."

"Uh, it's kind of hard to eat with you sitting on top of me like this," Danny said.

"Oh. Sorry." Reluctantly I returned to my side of the booth.

By the time Bobby and Tina reached our table, I had worked myself into a righteous snit. Tina was leaning against him like a cat in heat, brushing her boobs along the side of his arm. *Well of all the nerve! The bitch is practically dry humping him in front of me!*

217

Not to be one upped, I cast Danny a flirty little smile and stretched my arm out across the table to hold his hand. Then Danny stretched out his arm too, only he slid past mine and grabbed a slice of pizza instead. So then I had to make like I was only reaching for the pizza too, which is why I should never try to act sexy. I just can't pull it off.

"Yo," Bobby said, a smile playing on his lips. *Nothing gets by that guy. Damn it.*

"Sorry to interrupt your meal, but could I see you outside for a minute?"

I excused myself from the table, which wasn't really necessary seeing as Danny didn't even notice I'd gotten up. He was too busy offering Tina my lunch.

The wind had picked up, causing the temperature to drop about ten degrees. I should have grabbed my coat. I was freezing. "So when did you and Delvechione become an item?" I asked through chattering teeth.

Bobby flashed me a smug grin. I wanted to smack it right off his stupid face. "Jealous?" he asked, unzipping his jacket and handing it to me. I slipped it on, wrapping myself in the lingering warmth of his body heat.

"Dream on, DiCarlo. I just never thought you'd go for the airhead type, that's all."

"You sure you want to call her an airhead?" he asked me.

Alright, so Tina had a 4.0 average all through college and graduated with honors, but that doesn't prove anything. "Look, I'm in the middle of …something with that guy in there, so what did you want to talk to me about?"

Bobby sighed, his tone growing serious. "The police picked up Meyers for questioning this morning, but it doesn't look like they're going to be able to hold him."

"Why not?" I began shaking again, but this time it wasn't from the cold.

DiCarlo pulled me to him and wrapped his arms around me. "I'm sorry, Bran. They just didn't have enough to book him on."

"But Heather identified him as the guy she saw coming out from under my car." My eyes were filling up and I pressed my face into Bobby's chest to keep from crying.

"Look, sweetheart," he murmured, stroking my cheek, "I know you're scared. And I'll do whatever I can to keep you safe. But you can't keep putting yourself at risk."

I was too tired to argue. And anyway, I knew he was right.

"Thanks for filling me in about Meyers," I said, disengaging myself from his arms. "I guess you'd better get back to Tina."

Bobby peered through the window. "I don't think there's a big rush with that. It looks like Tina and your date have hit it off."

I took a peek in too. She was sitting on his side of the booth and he wasn't complaining. "Yeah, well, for the record, he's not my date. I was just interviewing him for a story. Nothing too exciting," I added, figuring now probably wouldn't be the best time to bring up my investigation into Laura's sordid past.

"Listen," Bobby said. "You wanna split a pizza? My treat."

Before I could give him an answer my phone rang. I checked the readout. It was Nick. "Yeah, pizza sounds good," I said. "Why don't you grab a table and I'll be with you in a minute?"

It must've been cop instinct that made Bobby reach out and pull the phone from my hand. Either that or the way my face went neon red when I saw who was calling. "Santiago," Bobby said coolly, reading Nick's name off the Caller I.D. He tossed the phone back to me.

"You could've just asked me," I said, flipping open the phone.

Bobby shrugged. "More fun this way."

I knew he was mad, but if he was going to act like an ass I wasn't going to worry about it. I turned my back to him and said hello into the phone.

"Hello, angel." I felt my cheeks go red again. Good thing I'd turned around.

"I just got off the phone with Anthony Mitchell's sister, LaShawna," Nick said. "She's agreed to talk to you about her brother."

"Nick, that's great. Does she know how I can get in touch with Anthony?"

"It would be a neat trick if she did. Mitchell's dead."

"Dead? Is she sure?"

"She's sure. She flew down to Miami last month to identify the body. Official cause of death is listed as a heroin overdose. LaShawna doesn't buy it. She works a 3-11 shift at some convenience store down on Patterson, but she said to meet her at her place tomorrow night after she gets off."

"Tomorrow night?" I quickly scanned my brain to see if I had anything else going on. Well, there *was* that "Facts of Life" marathon on TV Land, but I guessed I could tape it. "Where does she live?" I asked.

"Ninth and Indiana."

I gulped hard. "The Badlands?" The Badlands is a local term for a good chunk of the southern part of North

Philadelphia. It has the distinction of being one of the worst drug-infested and dangerous areas of the city.

From behind me, DiCarlo let out a steady stream of curse words. Jeez, I'd forgotten he was there. "I'll call you back," I said to Nick and disconnected.

I turned back to Bobby. "So," I said brightly, "how about that pizza?"

He pulled me by the lapels of his leather jacket until we were flush against each other. I could hear his heart beating at twice its regular pace. It sounded pissed off. "Tell me you're not serious about going there," he said.

"Okay, here's the thing," I said into his chest. "I've got a really good lead on this witness in the Harmon case and—"

"I'll go with you."

I couldn't possibly have heard him right. "What did you say?"

Bobby did a big "put upon" sigh. "I said if you're so hell bent on going there, I'll go with you."

"Look, it's nice of you to offer and all, but you know as well as I do nobody's going to talk to me with a cop trailing after me."

"Then I guess you're out of luck because you're not going alone."

"I never said I was."

"Santiago's going with you?" I gave a brief nod. Bobby held his hands up in a gesture of surrender and stepped back. "Well, that's just fucking fine by me."

I yanked off his jacket and handed it back to him. "Y'know what? I'm not hungry anymore," I told him, which was a humongous lie. I was freakin' starving. "I'll see you later."

I left him standing on the sidewalk and marched back into DiVinci's to retrieve my coat. Tina and Danny were just leaving. They had the leftovers in a box. "Oh, uh, thanks for the pizza," Danny said. At least he had the decency to look embarrassed.

Now that I had officially skipped lunch I had a lot more time on my hands, so I sat in the parking lot ruminating about what would trigger the kind of behavior Danny Lang had described. I had a strong feeling I already knew, but I needed to hear it from an expert. I took out my cell and called information for Dr. Levi's office. She was in between patients and graciously allowed me to run it by her.

"Well," she said after I'd filled her in, "I wouldn't normally diagnose someone over the phone, but from what you've told me, my guess is the young woman had been sexually molested as a child, quite possibly over an extended period of time, so as an adult she tried to fix it."

"Fix it? How?"

"By replaying the scene over and over, but changing the outcome so that she would have the power she lacked as a little girl. As I said, without ever having met her, this is only a guess."

"Dr. Levi, I read somewhere that this kind of thing is often perpetrated by someone the victim knows and trusts. Like a babysitter or a family member."

"That's true, which makes it all the more tragic."

I thanked Dr. Levi for her time and hung up. Something Danny Lang had said was bugging me. I hadn't picked up on it before, but now it was foremost in my mind. I punched in his number.

"It's Brandy," I said when he picked up. "Listen, when I spoke to you on the phone earlier today, you said Laura never told you her real name."

"That's right."

"And that she made you call her by some cutesy nickname. Do you happen to remember what it was?"

"Yeah," he said. "She told me to call her 'Kitten.'"

Oh my God.

I called Bobby on my way back to the office. "Sorry," I said when he picked up. "You were being really nice to me and I acted like a jerk."

DiCarlo gave a long whistle. "Wow. I didn't see that coming. Thanks."

"Yeah, well, I just thought I'd tell ya." What I didn't tell him was that Sophia was the luckiest kid in the world to have a dad who would love and protect her instead of a father like Laura's. Ethan's words reverberated in my ears. *"Laura was the light of his life. He used to call her Kitten."* How could he do that to his own kid?

"I know a way you could make it up to me," DiCarlo said and I could hear the smile in his voice.

"Yeah? How's that?" I didn't say I *would* make it up to him but I had to admit I was curious about what he had in mind.

Before he could give me the details, his call waiting beeped. "Damn, it's the station. Hang on a second." He was back in a flash. "Gang killing on Snyder. Looks like you're off the hook for now." Rationally, I was relieved. Hormonally, it was a different story. "Oh, and *for the record*," Bobby said, "I just ran into Tina outside of DiVinci's. It wasn't like we were on a date or anything."

223

"Oh? I really hadn't given it any thought."

"Sure," Bobby laughed and hung up.

It was almost 4:30 p.m. and I hadn't eaten anything since my early morning encounter with the powdered jelly doughnuts. I decided to call it a day and go home. There was a turkey pot pie in the freezer and some Rolling Rock in the fridge. What more could a girl ask for.

My mom called on the drive back to my house. "Brandy, honey, is that you?" *She called my cell phone, who did she think it would be?*

"Yeah, mom, it's me." I swallowed the Tastykake I bought at the Seven-Eleven to tide me over until I got home and asked why she was calling.

"We're invited to Aunt Henna's tonight for dinner. She's really hoping you can join us." Aunt Henna is my mother's aunt. Her real name is Silvia, but she's been Aunt Henna ever since the 1960's when she gave herself a Henna rinse and all her hair fell out. It had since grown back and is now in the process of falling out again. The last time she was in Carla's salon, she insisted on hair extensions. Aunt Henna is a hundred and eight.

"Mom, I'd love to, only I'm swamped with work. You guys go and enjoy yourselves. I'll see you when you get home."

Half an hour later I pulled up in front of the house, took out my stun gun, checked for stalkers and sprinted up the steps. Adrian greeted me as I walked through the door. I went into the kitchen to nuke the pot pie. My parents had already left for Aunt Henna's. My mom had left some brisket in Adrian's food bowl. It was untouched. I guess he'd learned a little something from the meatball incident.

I'd only been home alone for an hour but I was already starting to regret my decision not to go to my great-aunt's. I didn't like being alone. And worse, I hated that I didn't like it. I called John and invited him over.

"I thought we could put on my mom's old Richard Simmons' exercise tape, "Sweatin' to the Oldies" and sit in front of the TV and eat ice cream sundaes while we're watching it."

"Sorry, doll face," he told me. "I've got a date."

"Oh."

I guess he could hear the disappointment in my voice because he asked me if I wanted to come along. "We're going to the art museum. They're having a 'by invitation only' viewing of 'Japanese Literati Culture in the Edo Period,' but I could probably scrounge up an extra ticket."

"No, that's alright. I've already seen it."

John choked back a laugh. I don't know what he thought was so funny. I *could've* seen it. "Well, if you change your mind, let me know."

I decided to give Mike Mahoe a call and give him a chance to redeem himself for ratting me out to Bobby. Mike was still at work, he informed me, and was very busy. Way too busy to talk.

"Oh, that's too bad," I said. "I've got an extra ticket to the hockey game tonight."

"Really?" he said, perking up. "Oh, hey, as it turns out, this report I'm typing up isn't due until next Thursday, so I'm free as a bird."

"Uh huh," I said.

Mike sighed. "There are no hockey tickets, are there?"

"Come on Mike. Just one little favor. I would've asked Bobby, but he's out investigating a gang murder. Honest, it's not going to get you in trouble."

All I wanted was an update on the status of Jeff Rhineholt. I sort've felt responsible for him, seeing as I was the one who'd sent the Jersey cops sniffing in his direction in the first place. "Do this for me please, Mike?"

"I can't believe I ever liked you," Mike grumbled. "You're a pain in the rear."

I took that as a yes and waited for him to call me back.

Thirty minutes later the phone rang. "Are you sitting down?"

"I am now. What's up?"

"You know that guy Richard you kept going on about?"

"What about him?"

"He turned up. Claimed to be the father of Tamra's unborn child. He made a statement this afternoon. He said Tamra was planning to leave her husband for him... I really shouldn't be telling you all this."

"Just tell me one more thing. How bad does it look for Rhineholt?"

"On a scale of one to ten, he's off the charts."

Jeff Rhineholt answered the phone on the ninth ring. His voice was boozy and his words accusatory, but there was no real rancor behind them. All things considered, he was fairly mellow... or semi-conscious. I think he'd had a lot to drink.

"I can't believe you've got the nerve to call me," he said when I identified myself. "Haven't you done enough damage?"

I couldn't believe I had the nerve to call him either. "Look," I said getting right to it, "I don't think you killed Tamra."

"Is that right? Well, you're the only one who doesn't. They're going to arrest me any day now. There's an unmarked car sitting in the front of my house in case I try to make a break for it. As if I had anywhere to go. My own family is afraid of me. I've been put on mandatory leave from work." A sob caught in his throat. "You want to know what's funny?" he said.

"What's that?" I asked softly.

"They think I killed my wife, but with Tamra gone I've got nothing left to live for."

I got a sick feeling in the pit of my stomach which I chose to ignore. "Jeff, I really want to help you. But you need to be straight with me. The last night you spent with Tamra you said you were arguing about work. What were you really fighting about?"

"You wanna know what we really fought about? I'll tell you. Hold on." I waited while he blew his nose. Rhineholt was starting to slur his words and I was wondered if booze wasn't the only thing he was self-medicating with.

I heard him swallow something and then he got back on the phone. "My lawyer doesn't want me talking to anyone." He emitted a short bitter laugh. "What the fuck does he know? Nobody wants to talk to me. Only you and your reporter buddies."

And the cops who are probably tapping your line.

"Jeff, about that night," I prodded.

"Tamra wanted a baby. I didn't. She'd been pregnant twice before. They both ended in miscarriage. I never thought she'd get over it. I—I didn't want her to go through that again."

"So that's what the fight was about?" I asked. "She told you she was pregnant?"

"No," he said, crying openly now. "I found out that night that she had been pricking holes in my condoms. I didn't know she was pregnant until the autopsy report."

"Did it ever occur to you that you may not have been the father?"

"No. Stupid, huh? I agreed to a paternity test because Tamra swore to me she wasn't having an affair and I needed to believe that. I loved her."

"Jeff, are you alone now?" He didn't sound right and I'd had enough experience in high school with wayward friends to know when someone was in trouble. "Jeff?"

Shit.

"…and then I called 911 and told them I thought he had overdosed, and the cop that was sitting in front of his house went in there and called the paramedics."

My first impulse was to call the station with an exclusive, but I just couldn't bring myself to do it, so I called Janine instead. I knew the news would get out eventually, but Jeff had enough trouble without me adding to it. Guess I'll have to work on my "killer instincts" if I'm going to make it in the news business. My conscience is always getting in the way. *Stupid conscience.*

"So did you find a date for Paul's bar mitzvah?" Janine's not one to dwell on the negative. God bless her.

"I'm working on it," I told her and hung up.

My parents came home at 11:00. My dad had his arm around my mother's waist, guiding her through the front door. She was giggling. It's not often I hear my mom giggle. It was a kind of disconcerting.

"Your mother's a little tipsy," my dad informed me. "She was hitting the vino pretty hard."

"I had to do *something* to choke down that meal," my mom told me. She leaned into me, summoning up her best stage whisper. "Your aunt is a *terrible* cook."

My parents headed upstairs to bed, while I stayed up to watch The Daily Show and fantasize about what it would be like to be married to Jon Stewart. I imagined I would laugh a lot.

At around one a.m. I put Adrian on his leash and shoved him out the front door to pee. I didn't want him wandering off, but I was too chicken to walk him. He could only go as far as Mrs. Gentile's side of the porch, which was where he chose to take a mini dump. I kicked it off the porch figuring it would fertilize her azaleas.

Before I went in, I took a surreptitious glance down the block. Halfway down, parked three cars past the street lamp was Craig's Toyota. *Okay, enough was enough.* I was all set to march up to his car, drag him out of there and force him to tell me what was going on, when someone beat me to the punch. A hooded figure emerged from the shadows and approached Craig's car.

I could barely make out a thing from my position on the porch, so I grabbed Adrian and ran back inside the house, taking the stairs two steps at a time. When I reached my bedroom, I pulled out the binoculars and parted the curtains ever so slightly.

Craig was walking around to the passenger side of the car. Actually, it looked more like he was being escorted. Craig climbed in and then the person in the hooded parka jogged around to the other side and climbed in behind the wheel. Before the rational part of my brain had a chance to kick in, I bounded down the steps, grabbed my bag and my cell phone and dashed out the door.

I jumped into my car and turned on the ignition leaving the headlights off. Craig's car had already turned the corner so I drove slowly, waiting until they got a ways down the block before turning the corner after them. The streets were practically empty, which made it difficult to go unnoticed. I decided to do a front tail, something I'd read about in a James Bond book once. I stepped on the gas and passed in front of Craig's car. Then I moved to the right, staying several car lengths ahead.

They turned North on Broad Street which made it easier. Traffic was denser now. I flipped on my headlights and hung back again, scooting in behind a large van. At a red light I picked up the cell and punched in Nick's number.

"Are you okay, angel?" Nick asked, upon answering. If he'd been asleep—or worse yet, entertaining, he gave no indication of it.

Only now did I stop to think about what I had done. *I'm driving around unarmed in the middle of the night, following potential murderers. Oh God. I must be as crazy as everyone thinks I am!*

"Nick, I'm sorry. I know it's late. I just didn't think I should call the police. At least not yet." I was babbling but I couldn't seem to stop myself.

Nick cut in, his voice low and reassuring. "It's okay, darlin'. Just tell me what's going on."

The light changed and I moved ahead, careful to keep a healthy distance between the two cars. "Craig was parked in front of my house again. And then some guy showed up and it seemed like he was hassling Craig, but I couldn't be sure. They took off in Craig's car, so I jumped in mine and followed them. They just made a right onto Washington and it looks like they're heading toward the river."

"I'm not far from there. Stay on the line with me and if you're spotted, turn around and drive to the nearest police station."

I felt tons better now that I was in contact with Nick. I kept my eyes on the car ahead as it traveled North on Delaware Avenue. We were parallel to the river now. I could see the big naval ships floating in the harbor. During the day this area is bustling with activity, but at night it's just plain spooky.

A big deserted parking lot loomed ahead. The Toyota began to slow down, pulling into the lot and cruising to a stop next to an upscale riverfront restaurant. It was closed for the winter. I cut my lights and parked behind a dumpster, about a hundred yards away from the Toyota.

"I'm at Clancy's Steakhouse," I told Nick.

"Got it." He said something else but it was lost in a garble of static. My phone was cutting out on me.

"I can't hear you," I shouted, but the connection was lost. I tried to punch in his number again but I must have been in a dead zone. I truly hoped that wasn't an omen.

I took out the binoculars and scrunched down in my seat. From my vantage point I could see the hooded stranger exiting the car. Craig got out too—reluctantly, from the looks of things. He was hanging onto the door frame when the other guy yanked his arm away from it and began prodding him toward the river. Craig didn't need much prodding, as his companion was holding a gun.

"Oh shit," I said, breaking out into a huge, clammy sweat. I tried the phone again, this time to call the cops, but I couldn't get it to work. My sense of self preservation kicked into high gear and screamed at me to *get the hell out of there in a hurry*. Unfortunately, the rest of me couldn't leave Craig alone and helpless to fend for himself.

They were standing alongside the guard rails now. I could see ice patches floating on the water. The wind had picked up, driving the mini icebergs upstream. Craig was gesturing with his hands, the way little kids do when they get excited. The guy in the hooded jacket tucked his gun into his pocket. "Well, that's a good sign," I thought. "Maybe he just wants to talk to Craig," when without warning he raised his arm and smacked Craig hard across the mouth. Craig's hands flew up to his face, trying to protect himself from another assault.

Nick, where the hell are you?

The man hit him again. I watched in horror as tears mixed with blood streamed down Craig's swollen face. Now the guy was pummeling him in earnest. Craig tried to ward off the blows, but he was no match for the larger man, who began shoving Craig toward the break in the railing leading to a docking ladder. Reaching inside his pocket, he pulled out the gun and held it to Craig's head.

Without thinking I gunned the engine and tromped on the gas, flying across the open parking lot toward the two men. I hit the high beams and the horn simultaneously, momentarily distracting them both. Craig was the first to recover. He reached up and knocked the guy's hand away from his head and took off running. But in one swift movement, the other guy raised his gun and shot Craig in the back. Craig stumbled and fell backwards through the opening in the railing, disappearing into the freezing water below.

I screamed and immediately a bullet pierced the windshield. Overcome by rage and exhaustion I floored it straight for the shooter. Trapped between the railing and the oncoming car, he tried to vault over the guardrail.

At the last possible moment, my common sense prevailed. Premeditated murder would not look good on a resume, no matter how justified I felt, so I slammed on the brakes, skidding into the guy and knocking him flat. He might still be alive, but he wasn't going anywhere. His leg was trapped under the right front tire.

I jumped out of the car, ran over to the guardrail and peered down into the river.

I could just barely make out Craig's motionless body, floating away on a small island of ice. I yelled out his name and thought I heard a muffled grunt in response.

I lay on my belly and stretched my arm out as far as it would go but I couldn't reach him. I stood up, frantically searching for something, *anything* to hook onto Craig and haul him back in. "What the hell do I do now?" I shouted to the universe.

"You could start with getting the goddamn car off my leg, I'm dying here," grunted a voice from behind.

I felt the blood rush to my face. Seeing as he'd just tried to shoot me, the needs of this asshole were not at the top of my list of priorities. I spun to confront him and promptly slipped on the ice, this time falling off the dock.

Crap.

I hit the freezing water head on. Completely submerged, I held my breath and flung my arms and legs about, desperately trying to right myself. When I got my head above water I gulped for air and felt a stabbing pain in my chest. My lungs were a block of ice.

As I struggled to stay afloat, the weight of my clothes kept dragging me beneath the surface. I tried to peel them off, but they were too heavy, and in my panic I only succeeded in becoming more entangled. I sucked in a mouthful of water and gagged.

I'd only been in the water for a few minutes, but it felt like eons. I was exhausted. The water was so cold it burned, but soon that sensation went away and I could no longer feel my arms or legs. I knew enough first aid to be able to recognize the early warning signs of shock. The dock was only a few feet away, but it might as well have been a mile.

Oh my God. I cannot die. It's simply unacceptable. If I die now I'll never get to hold Franny's baby, or sing at Paul's bar mitzvah or visit "Cats That Look Like Hitler.com." Dying would mean I'd never get to taste Uncle Frankie's lasagna again, or go to a Phillies' game, or laugh so hard with John I'd crack a rib.

It just wasn't a good time to die. With my last ounce of strength I pushed down on the water and tried to propel myself forward, but it was a fruitless effort. *If I die, I'll never see Nick's face again, or hear his voice or see him smile. I'll never get to tell him that I love him, not for the way he looks, but for how he makes me feel.*

I felt myself slipping under again, and in that instant I could almost hear him calling my name.

Chapter Fourteen

"How's she doing?"

My eyes flew open and I found a uniformed stranger staring back at me. I tried to focus on her face but what with the lights and sirens it was all a blur. My chest felt like a truck had rolled over it and decided to park there overnight. I was encased in heavy blankets, and someone had placed an oxygen mask over my mouth and nose. Confused and more than a little claustrophobic, I ripped off the mask and inhaled the cold night air.

"Take it easy. You're alright," the paramedic soothed, taking the mask from my hand and readjusting the blankets.

I tried to turn my head in the direction of the other voice, but it was like trying to lift an anvil.

A murky recollection of being dragged and lifted from the water rushed back at me. Suddenly I felt a warm hand on my cheek and Nick's face appeared before me. His clothes were soaked and as he knelt beside me I noticed an angry gash on the left side of his face, just under his ear.

"You're bleeding! What happened?" I croaked. My throat was unbearably dry, which was odd, considering I'd just swallowed half the Delaware River.

"Don't worry about it, angel. It's nothing a Tetanus shot and butterfly bandage can't handle." He cut me a smile, but he couldn't hide the weariness behind it.

I struggled to a sitting position and looked around. I was at an utter loss for words. Nick had saved me. Again. Somehow a hearty "thanks" just didn't seem enough.

An ambulance was closing its doors. It pulled away, sirens blaring. "Craig," he informed me. "He's unconscious but alive."

Nick had arrived a few minutes after my phone went out and witnessed most of what had transpired. "You could've just driven away when you saw the gun," he said quietly.

"No. I couldn't."

He picked up my hand and pressed it to his lips. "No, I guess you couldn't."

Someone rolled the car off of the other guy's leg and was administering first aid. He looked over my way and started yelling. "Crazy bitch. She tried to run me over."

Right on both counts.

We ended up back at the police station. A couple of detectives led Nick and me to separate offices and took our statements. They took Gun Boy over to Jefferson Hospital with a police escort. Turned out a bum leg wasn't his only problem. Seems he was missing a middle finger too.

I guess our stories checked out because after an hour Nick and I were free to go. We ran into Bobby on the way out. He'd been up all night interviewing potential

236

witnesses in the gang slaying. He looked like he could've used a couple of slugs of Red Bull.

I could tell by the look on his face that he'd already heard about my little adventure. Giving a cursory glance at Nick he turned to me. "Are you okay?"

"Yeah. I'm fine." I flashed him two thumbs up. "I just need to get out of these clothes." They had dried in the stuffy confines of the police station and were starting to give me a rash.

Bobby turned to Nick. "I can take it from here."

If Nick minded being dismissed by Bobby he didn't show it. "Bobby—" I protested.

Nick cut me off. "It's okay, angel." He hugged me to him, his mouth pressed against my ear. "The man cares about you. Cut him a little slack."

I hugged Nick back, forcing down a huge lump in my throat.

There was a longing deep inside me as I watched him walk away.

Seeing as my car was now "state's evidence," I didn't have a ride back to my house. Truth was I couldn't face going home yet anyway, so when Bobby suggested he take me back to his place to get cleaned up and pull myself together, I gratefully accepted.

"Oh, but what about Sophia?" I asked. It was four in the morning and she'd be waking up in a few hours. I didn't want to get in the way of their time together.

"I knew I'd be pulling an all-nighter," Bobby said. "She's sleeping over at Eddie's mom's."

DiCarlo didn't say much on the ride home. His night hadn't exactly been a piece of cake either. On the way out of the station I'd overheard some cops talking about the gang killing he was investigating. The unintended victim was a little ten-year-old girl.

Even though I was freezing my butt off, out of courtesy I left the window open. I didn't want to stink up his car by smelling like week old dead trout. I leaned my head against the headrest and I must have dozed off, because when I opened my eyes we were passing Gavone's Bar, and I knew we were close to his place.

Bobby's house is in the neighborhood of 11th and Wolf. The homes along this block are old, spacious and affordable. We pulled up to the curb and he climbed out. I was a little slower on the uptake. That dip in the pool had taken its toll on me. Bobby came around and opened my door, stretching a hand out to help me.

I'd never been to his house before. Oh, I'd done the obligatory "drunken drive-by" one night with Fran and Janine when I first moved back to town,--a mini stalking expedition fueled by one too many margaritas, but this was the first time I'd seen Bobby's digs up close and personal.

He let me in and closed the door behind him, tossing his keys on the end table next to a cranberry colored couch. A pile of foam rubber building blocks sat in the corner of the living room, along with a kid sized table and matching chairs. A tiny tea set adorned the table, complete with what looked like plastic cupcakes. I tested one to make sure.

I wanted to snoop around a little more, but Bobby gestured for me to follow him upstairs. "Bathroom's straight ahead," he said, detouring into what I assumed was the master bedroom. "There are fresh towels in the linen closet. If you give me your clothes I'll run them through the wash for you after you're finished in the shower." He emerged from the room carrying a long sleeved button down man's dress shirt. "You'd swim in my boxers, so this'll have to do until I can get your stuff laundered."

"Thanks," I said, getting all teary-eyed. "Listen, I don't want you to go to any trouble for me. You must be exhausted."

"Yeah, I am," he admitted. "But I'm not the one who almost died tonight." He looked like he wanted to say more, but something stopped him. He handed me the shirt, leaning over and sweeping the bangs out of my eyes the way he'd done countless times over the years. "Go take your shower."

I stood under the steaming water and scrubbed Baby-No Tears shampoo into my hair. I'd left my clothes in a discreet pile outside the bathroom door. They really stunk. Maybe Bobby would decide they weren't salvageable and burn them.

When the hot water ran out I climbed out of the shower, ran the blow dryer over it and then washed out my underwear and blew that dry too. I just couldn't parade around Bobby's house "commando." I can't even do that in my own house and I live alone! I slipped on his shirt and went to look for him.

He was stretched out on his bed, hands locked behind his head, staring up at the ceiling. The lights were off, but the curtains stood open letting in the light of the full moon. Not wanting to disturb him I turned to leave, but he sat up swinging his legs over the side of the bed.

"Don't get up," I said. "I can let myself out."

"And how do you plan to go? No car, remember?"

Good point. "I can call a cab."

"You know I'll take you home any time you want to go. But you don't have to rush off. Your stuff is still in the dryer."

It seemed easier to stay than to explain to my mother why I was arriving home at dawn with no pants on. "Okay. Thanks. Do you mind if I use your phone? I want to check on Craig."

"Already did," Bobby said. "He slipped into a coma about an hour ago. I also called the station to see what's up with the shooter. His name's Sean McCauley and he's not talking. He's got some hotshot lawyer and bail's already been posted."

"Hmm. Must have a rich uncle stashed away somewhere."

"Yeah, maybe."

Bobby followed me with his eyes as I paced around his room. Being in such close proximity to DiCarlo and a bed was making me nervous. I began fiddling with the things on his dresser. A couple of framed pictures of Sophia, his badge and wallet. A pink plastic bracelet with unicorns dangling from it.

He stood and walked over to me, taking the bracelet out of my hand. "This one's mine, but if I ask Sophia real nice, I bet she'll make one for you too."

"You've always been able talk the girls into doing your bidding," I told him, only half joking.

Bobby's mood shifted, his voice dropping to a whisper. "All the girls but you, Bran. Why did you call Santiago tonight instead of me?" The question seemed to come out of nowhere but I knew he'd been brooding about it since we left the police station.

"Bobby, you were working. And even if you hadn't been, you've got a daughter who needs you. What would you have done, run out on her in the middle of the night?"

Bobby took a step back and massaged his temples. He was making an effort to keep himself under control, but it was a struggle. "You've known this guy—what, two months? I've known you a lifetime. He's the first name on your Goddamn speed dial, for Christ sake."

"How did you—"

He shot me a disgusted look. "Lucky guess."

"Listen," I said, "maybe I should go. You're tired, I'm tired. I don't want either of us to say anything we'll regret later."

"That's right, sweetheart. Run away. After all, if we don't talk about it, the problem doesn't exist."

Yeah. Kind of. "Look, I'm not going to have this conversation about Nick. Whether you like it or not, he's been a good friend to me."

And that's when he lost it. "Is that what you think I'm upset about? *Your relationship with Santiago?*"

"But you just said—"

Bobby forced out a bitter laugh. "Santiago is just the tip of the iceberg. No, I'm not thrilled about it, but you're a big girl. You get to pick and choose your friends all by yourself. But Christ Almighty, Brandy, this goes so far beyond that, it's not even funny. It's not about your choice of companionship. It's about your constant need to do whatever the fuck you want whenever the fuck you want to do it, without any regard to how it impacts the people who love you."

"That is *not* true," I yelled, knowing full well he spoke the gospel. "But what kind of a person would I be if I

241

could help someone and I just stood back and did nothing?"

Bobby slammed both hands down hard on the dresser. I think it was to keep from throttling me. "Will you just shut up and fucking listen for a change? It was one thing when you wanted to help Tamra. She was your friend and I know you'd never walk away from that. But now you're risking your life for some bag of shit career criminal who would spit on you if you passed him on the street. You've put yourself in danger so often over the past few months, if I didn't know you so well I'd swear you had a death wish."

"A death wish! Well, that's a lousy thing to say!" I tried to stomp out of the room, but he moved in front of the door, blocking my exit.

"I said, *if I didn't know you so well.*" He reached out and pulled me roughly to him. "But I do know you, sweetheart. I know you're so scared you can't see straight. But what scares you more is giving in to the fear. So you pretend you're fine and you push on. And the worse it gets the harder you push."

Suddenly I couldn't breathe. He was right, of course. So I did what I do best. I pushed. I pushed him hard and he pushed me back. Right down onto the bed.

I popped back up but Bobby loomed over me and forced me down again, pinning my arms to my sides and wedging a leg between my knees to make sure I stayed down.

I struggled against him, my look mutinous. "Let me up," I screamed.

"Not until you admit I'm right."

"Fuck you, DiCarlo." I drew my leg up and aimed for his crotch, but he moved deftly out of the way and pinned me harder.

"Say it," he demanded.

"Tears of frustration streamed down my face. "I hate you," I sobbed.

"Say it!"

"Okay, you're right! So what do you want, a medal?"

In an instant the anger drained from his body, to be replaced by something even scarier. "You *know* what I want," he said, lowering himself on top of me.

I did know. And God help me, I wanted it too.

Bobby didn't wait for permission. He just took what he wanted, his mouth hot on mine, searching, finding, savoring the taste of each other. He let go of my arms and tore at my shirt until it fell apart in his hands. Then he reached down and unzipped his jeans and kicked them off. I grabbed at his tee shirt and lifted it over his head and then we were skin to skin, his rock hard abs pressed against the fullness of my breasts, the heat coming off us threatening to set the bed on fire.

I ran my finger along his form, tracing the body I had once known so well. He groaned at my touch and then swore and reached for a condom. I helped him slip it on and then, raising my hips and holding me tight, he thrust inside me.

We tried to take it slowly but the need was too great. I wrapped my legs around him, my heart banging wildly against my chest as the pressure in my lower belly grew, hard and fast, and it rocked us both over the edge so quickly it left us out of breath and soaked in sweat. Afterwards, we lay there in stunned silence, awed by the magnitude of what we had done.

Bobby rolled off me and collapsed onto the bed, panting. He was on his back, and as I lay next to him, watching the rise and fall of his chest as his breathing returned to normal, I had the sudden and perfect realization that what had just happened between us was inevitable. In that moment another truth became evident, and calmness washed over me.

"Bobby?"

"Yeah?"

"I love you."

"I know you do," he said without surprise. "I love you too."

"But we're not right for each other, are we? Not now, anyway."

He was quiet for a beat. "Yeah," he sighed, "I know that too."

He reached out and drew me to him and I curled up in his arms, feeling very safe and very loved.

I woke up to the distant sound of my cell phone going off. I was alone in the bed. I looked at the clock on the dresser. It said 9:20 a.m. I'd been asleep for three hours, but it felt like three minutes.

Bobby walked into the bedroom holding my phone. He was fully dressed and wearing a tie.

"You look nice," I said, feeling around under the covers for my underwear.

Bobby grinned. "So do you." He leaned over and kissed me on the forehead and then handed me the phone. "It's your mother," he said, checking the readout.

"Oh jeez, I can't talk to her now. I'm sitting naked in your bed. She's going to know that. *Mothers know these things!*" I dropped the phone and wriggled into my panties.

The phone stopped ringing and went to voicemail. "I should call her," I groaned, as my conscience kicked in. "She's probably heard about the shooting by now and she must be worried sick."

"It's okay," Bobby said. "I pulled some strings last night and managed to keep your name out of it— at least for a while. For the time being you're just an 'unidentified female.' Now as far as where you spent the night, you're on your own."

Turns out my mother was calling to ask where I kept the furniture polish. I told her I didn't have furniture polish. She uttered a horrified squeal and ran right out to correct the situation. I half expected my failing to be the lead story on the morning news. "This just in! An 'unidentified female' has admitted to using her shirt sleeve to remove dust from the tv screen. Her mother is devastated and could not be reached for comment. More on this story as it unfolds."

I got dressed and went downstairs. Bobby was in the kitchen eating breakfast. He poured me a bowl of Honey Bunches of Oats and joined me at the table. "I figured you could use the sugar rush," he told me. "You didn't get a whole lot of sleep last night."

Just as I shoved the first spoonful into my mouth, my phone rang. "Hullo?"

It was Nick. My first instinct was to tell Bobby it was a telemarketer and hang up, but we turned a corner last night in our relationship and I wanted to test out our newfound honesty. "Nick" I mouthed to him. Bobby rolled his eyes, but he didn't throw his bowl of cereal at the wall or anything, so I figured we were cool.

"Hey," I said softly into the phone, battling the shyness that always seemed to overtake me whenever I was around Nick... or heard his voice... or thought about him in passing. "Listen, I never really thanked you for what you did for me last night."

Bobby made a face and walked his bowl over to the sink. *Okay, so he's not quite ready to drink from the cup of friendship.* I put my bowl in the sink as well and walked out into the living room.

"Easy stuff darlin'," Nick told me. "So are you still up for visiting LaShawna Mitchell today?"

"Absolutely. But hey, you really have done enough for me, so I'll understand if you can't make it tonight. I should be fine alone." I don't know why I say these things. Nick learned early on it was utter bullshit.

"Actually, I've got some business to take care of over in that neighborhood, this morning, which works out well seeing as LaShawna had to move up the meeting time. I'll pick you up. How soon can you be ready?"

That all depended on how soon Bobby would be leaving the house. Even though we'd reached an understanding, it was stretching it to think he'd welcome Nick into his home with open arms. "Um, Nick, can I call you back in just a minute?"

"Not necessary, sweetheart." Bobby walked into the living room. His shoulder holster was strapped to his chest and I suspected there was another at his ankle. "Finish your conversation. I'm shoving off now." He bent down and gave me a quick, brotherly kiss on the cheek. "Shut the door when you leave and be careful."

"That's it?"

"Let me talk to Santiago for a minute."

I handed him the phone. "You hurt her, I'll kill you." He handed the phone back to me. "Yep, that's it."

"You look nervous, darlin'." It was noon and Nick and I were driving along Indiana Avenue in the heart of "the Badlands." The name conjured up images of the old west—gun slingers, saloon brawls, shoot outs at the O.K. corral—all of which seemed like good, wholesome fun compared to the city scene laid out before me.

Entire blocks of buildings were boarded up, but that didn't stop people from living in them. Junkies, boasting the purest heroin in the country hung out on street corners making open trades. Prostitutes, some as young as eleven, lined up in full force, peddling their wares in the grey, mid-winter afternoon. This was urban blight at its very worst.

Nick was at the wheel of a Mercedes truck. I didn't know how good an idea it was to drive a fancy car in this neighborhood, but he seemed unconcerned.

"Uh, Nick, you did say you had business around here, right?"

"That's right."

"Are you a drug lord, by any chance?"

He cast me a sideways smile. "No."

"Pimp?"

His grin got wider. "Why? Are you looking for representation?"

That left "gun trafficker" and I really didn't want to go there.

"So," he said, throwing a casual arm over the back seat of the truck, "how did your reunion with DiCarlo go last night?"

"My reunion?"

"You did spend the night, didn't you? I was just wondering if he's officially reclaimed the palace."

My face went beet red. "If that means what I think it means I—uh—*y'know*, that's none of your business!"

"As I recall, I was given a rather stern warning by the detective this morning. That kind of makes it my business."

"Oh. That." I was not prepared for this conversation. "Listen, do I go around asking you about every palace you've reclaimed? No, I do not." Mostly because it would depress the hell out of me to know how many there were. "And why are you laughing?"

"I'm sorry," he said.

"No, you're not. You just want to make fun of me."

"Honestly, that's not it. You just constantly surprise me, that's all."

"Oh. I don't mean to."

"I know," he said, suddenly serious. "That's what makes it all the more charming."

Well, that shut me up. I mean how can you yell at a guy who thinks you're charming?

Nick pulled up in front of an old, Catholic church and parked. Gang graffiti decorated the crumbling exterior of the building and the front doors. Four Hispanic guys, about twenty years old or so gathered in the doorway, smoking crack. They looked up when Nick cut the engine. One had a six-inch buck knife hanging off his belt. He raised his eyebrows and said something to the others. They laughed, showing an impressive amount of gold teeth.

Nick pulled an oblong package from the glove compartment and opened the driver's side door. "Wait here, I'll be right back."

I panicked. "Couldn't I come with you? I haven't been to confession in ages!"

He cut his eyes to the guys who were now openly ogling me. "Sure, but stay close."

"What's in the package?" I asked, trotting alongside him.

"Something for the collection plate." He was smiling, but his eyes never left the men blocking the doorway. He took my hand and brushed past them, giving a slight nod as they scattered to let us through. What was it about Nick that let them know without him ever raising a finger that he was the alpha male?

A priest greeted us at the door and ushered us inside. He looked to be in his late thirties, with the wide, flat nose of a boxer and soft brown eyes. "Nicholas," he said, embracing him with easy familiarity. Smiling he added, "And who is this?"

"Sal, this is Brandy Alexander. Brandy, Father Salvador Domingo, also known as The Beast of Bourbon Street."

"Those days are long gone, Nicky, but I can still beat your sorry butt. It's nice to meet you," he said, reaching out to shake my hand. There was a warm, easy-going air about the guy and I liked him immediately.

"You guys go back a long way, I take it."

"Ah, good times, eh Nick?" But the look between them was bittersweet. I filed this under "ask him later," knowing it would probably be a fruitless effort. Nick never talked about his past.

Nick handed Father Sal the package. "This should do the trick," he said.

The priest took it and stuck it between the folds of his robe. "Nicky, I don't know how to thank you. "This will help so many people." The two lapsed into Spanish after that, losing me after "gracias." I think that was the idea.

Our crack smoking pals were gone by the time we got back to the truck. I climbed in and buckled up. "Nick," I said slowly. I knew I was treading in deep water, but I had to ask. "Whatever was in that package you gave the priest—it wasn't legal, was it?"

"Does it matter, angel? The legal choice is not always the moral one." He gave me a quick smile. "But you know that." And there you had it.

LaShawna Mitchell lived in a one bedroom walk-up on Manola Avenue. She shared this space with her three young children, a large pit bull, and, from what I saw crawling out from under the stove, a shit load of cockroaches.

We were seated at the table in her kitchenette. The Pit Bull lounged at Nick's feet gazing up at him adoringly. I hoped *I* didn't look at Nick with the same love-sick expression, but I suspected I might.

With the exception of the creepy crawlers, LaShawna's home was immaculate.

"Sorry about the roaches," she apologized, reaching under the sink for a can of Raid. "I've been trying to get the damn landlord to do something about them, but he's too cheap to hire a fumigation service."

"Oh, don't worry about it," I said, as I watched a roach sashaying across my shoe. "We didn't even notice them." I discreetly shook it off and pulled my feet up under my legs. Then I took out a pad and pencil and began.

According to LaShawna, Anthony lived with her and the kids until he left the state suddenly, four years ago. He knew David Dwayne Harmon from the neighborhood.

They hung out together on occasion and had a casual friendship.

"Were you surprised when your brother testified against Harmon at the trial?" I asked.

"I was shocked. In this neighborhood, people don't get involved in other people's business. It's too risky. I asked him why he did it and he just said he had his reasons and anyway I shouldn't worry because he wasn't planning on sticking around. Said he had some travel plans."

"Did he ever indicate to you whether his testimony was true?"

"I didn't ask. I figured what was done was done." LaShawna lowered her eyes. "Anyway, I always suspected someone paid him to testify at that trial."

"Why is that?" Nick interjected softly.

"Because Anthony wouldn't have come forward on his own. Money was a powerful incentive for my brother. Right before the trial started, Anthony began bragging that he was about to come into some big bucks. I told him he was dreaming. He worked at a car wash, how was he gonna come into money. He just laughed and said he met all kinds of interesting people at his job. I told him don't hold your breath, but damn if he didn't walk in one day with a wad of cash the size of your head. He knew I was hurting financially and he wanted to help me out. I told him I wouldn't take no drug money. That's when he told me it wasn't like that. He'd met some rich guy through a friend of his, and he did him a favor, so now he was just reaping the rewards."

"I don't suppose he told you what the favor was."

"I asked, but Anthony told me it wasn't my business."

"But you think it had something to do with his testimony. Did that rich guy have a name?" I asked.

251

LaShawna shook her head.

"You said Anthony was working at a car wash during this time. Do you happen to remember the name of it?" If I was lucky, maybe someone there would still remember him and be able to shed some light on this favor he did.

"Sure do," LaShawna said. "It's the Wash N Wax on the northeast corner of Germantown and Belmont." *Which just happened to be located directly across the street from Ditto's Car Repair where Zach Meyers worked.*

"LaShawna, does the name Zach Meyers mean anything to you?"

"Yeah. He used to call here sometimes. I remember because he was one rude bastard." LaShawna put her hand to her mouth, stifling a big yawn. "I'm sorry. I was up half the night with a sick baby."

"You've been really helpful," I said. "I've just got one more question. When was the last time you spoke to your brother?"

"About four months ago. He called here asking how I was and I told him not so good. I'd had my heart set on going to nursing school, but my funding fell through and I was pretty depressed about it. About an hour later Anthony called back and said he thinks he can get me the money, but he didn't want to say any more until he knew for sure.

That was the last I heard from him, until three weeks ago when the cops called to say they'd found his body. The report said he'd been mainlining heroin and he overdosed. But if you knew my brother, you'd know he'd never do that. He was completely phobic about needles. They only found the one set of tracks on him. I tried to tell the authorities, but nobody would listen to me. That's why I'm talking to you. Maybe you can find out what really happened to him."

We stood and walked back into the living room. "Wait here a minute," LaShawna said. She disappeared into the bedroom and came out holding a framed photo in her hand. "That's me and Anthony. It was taken four years ago at the Red Lobster. He took me there for my birthday."

The family resemblance was strong. Boner had his arm around LaShawna and they were both smiling into the camera. "It's a nice picture," I told her.

She nodded, her eyes welling up. "I know what they said about Anthony out on the street and I'm not saying it wasn't true. But he was a good brother. He took care of me."

Chapter Fifteen

"You did good today, Brandy Alexander."

We were sitting at the counter at Melrose Diner, having made a pit stop on the way back from LaShawna's. I ordered the meatloaf and mashed potato platter. And some fried chicken fingers…and a slab of apple pie…I'm a stress eater. Nick contented himself with a cup of coffee and some buttered toast.

"It's just so sad, Nick. Boner may not have contributed much to the rest of the world, but LaShawna really loved him. He looked out for her, and now she's on her own with three kids to raise…are you gonna eat that toast?"

Nick laughed and slid the plate over to me. "Don't worry about LaShawna. She's a strong person and she's got goals. It may take her a while to get there, but I think she'll be okay."

"Nick," I said, after a moment's pause, "I feel really bad asking for a favor after everything you've already done for me, but I was wondering if you'd lend me the truck."

"It's yours for as long as you need it. What's up?"

"Well, LaShawna's not the only one with goals." I dug into my meal, grateful to be eating meatloaf that wasn't made by my mother. "I've decided not to heed my boss's excellent advice to lay off the wealthy and influential Stewart family. I'm gonna go have a chat with Laura's mom. I figure she must be lonely what with her pedophile husband being laid up and all."

"You sure you want to do this now? You had a pretty busy night."

The hysteria that I had so far managed to contain now began a steady climb upward. "I don't have a minute to waste, Nick. I have less than three weeks to find out who really killed Laura Stewart or an innocent man is going to die, well, maybe not so innocent, I mean Harmon is a real jerk, but as far as I know that's not a capital offense. And then talking with LaShawna today confirmed my suspicion that Boner was paid to lie at the trial, and then he goes and tries to squeeze more money out of whoever paid him to lie, so they fix it so that he'll never ask again, and if you throw in Tamra because we still don't know if her death is related, well, the body count is really starting to add up...and it's just sheer luck that they haven't killed me yet...but the night's still young!"

Nick shook his head, the corners of his mouth tilting slightly upwards. "I'm beginning to have a newfound respect for DiCarlo," he said. "Do what you've got to do, but be careful."

As I dropped Nick off at his place my cell phone rang. It was Taco, the drummer from our old garage band. We'd started performing again recently and I think we've really gotten our edge back.

Taco was calling about our latest gig. "Don't forget we have rehearsal tonight. I'm still not sure who's gonna sing lead on Hava Nagila."

That did pose a problem. The only one who knew the words was Paul and he was the bar mitzvah boy.

"Um, Taco, I'm kinda busy right now. Why don't you work it out with the rest of the guys and get back to me."

"*Alright.* If you want it to sound crappy…"

I disconnected and the phone rang again. It was Franny. "Do I look fat?"

"Fran, you're six months pregnant. You *are* fat—but in a good way," I added. Too late. Franny started to cry.

When was I going to learn? The tough, practical Franny I knew and loved had gone A.W.O.L., leaving in her place this alien creature with monster hormones. I braced myself for the mother of all mood swings.

"Eddie was right," she wailed. "I'm a cow!"

"Did he say that?"

"Not exactly."

"Well, what did he say?"

"He told me that I'm beautiful."

"What was the man thinking? He should be shot." I hung a left on Broad Street. Rush hour began earlier and earlier these days. It was only mid afternoon but traffic was already backed up. "Listen, Fran, I love you but I've gotta go. I'll come over later and you can make fun of my wardrobe. That always cheers you up."

"Okay. Wear that hideous pea coat, the one that smells like wet dog."

The phone rang for a third time. "Hey Johnny, what's up?"

"I'll get right to the point, Sunshine," John said. He sounded nervous. "I've got some good news and some bad news."

"I'm really not going to like this, am I?"

"Not so much," he said. "The good news is Lucinda took your photo out of the window."

"That's *great* news. So what's the bad?"

"She sold it."

"She what?" I yelled and nearly rear ended a trailer.

"Oops, sorry, Sunshine, the connection is breaking up."

"It is not." Jeez, he didn't even bother to make those fake static noises with his mouth.

"I'll call you later," he told me.

"Don't you hang up on me, Mister," I yelled. And then the line went dead.

I turned off my phone and tossed it back in my bag.

According to the Department of Records The Stewarts lived on Crestview Lane in Chestnut Hill. Home to the Philadelphia aristocracy, the neighborhood oozes old money and the perks that go along with it.

I pulled onto the block and stopped in front of a beautiful, turn-of-the-century house with white stone columns. The gate was unlocked, there was no sign that said, "Intruders will be shot on sight" and no snarling Rottweiler standing guard on the front steps, so I figured that was practically an invitation to come calling.

I buzzed the intercom and waited. After a minute a woman's voice called out to me.

"May I help you?" It had the boozy quality of someone who had spent the better part of the afternoon self-medicating. There was a camera located in the corner of the entryway. I looked directly into it and smiled as benignly as possible.

"Hi. I'm looking for Mrs. Stewart. My name is Brandy Alexander and I'm a reporter over at station WINN. Are you Mrs. Stewart?"

The woman who opened the door looked to be sixty going on a hundred. Years of heartache can do that to a person. She greeted me with a smile and dropped ten of those years. "I've seen your show," she said. "My husband thinks you're adorable."

Yeah, I'll just bet he does. "Listen, Mrs. Stewart, do you mind if I come in for a few minutes? I have something I wanted to discuss with you."

I would have been surprised if this woman minded anything. She was three sheets to the wind and then some. She furrowed her brow, deep in thought. "My son said something about a reporter the other day, but I can't seem to recall what it was." She stepped aside to let me in and led me though a designer decorated living room into the kitchen.

"Would you like something to drink?" she asked. She refilled her glass with ice and splashed some scotch into it.

"Um, no thank you. Listen, Mrs. Stewart, I heard about your husband's stroke and I'm very sorry. I realize this isn't a great time for you, and I don't mean to intrude any more than is absolutely necessary, but I need your help. Your son may have mentioned that I'd been to visit him."

Mrs. Stewart sat down at the table, drink in hand. "Now I remember. Ethan told me you'd been to see him. You're here to ask me about Laura and the man who killed her, aren't you?"

I nodded. "I'm afraid I wasn't very tactful and I may have upset your son." *Just a wee understatement.* "Anyway, that wasn't my intention. It's just that I have reason to believe that David Dwayne Harmon didn't murder your daughter."

Mrs. Stewart sighed deeply, gazing at me through watery eyes. "Ethan is going to be so angry with me. He warned me about reporters coming around, badgering us." He says our family has been through enough, and he's right of course...but why are you so convinced that the man is innocent?"

And there's the rub. I *wasn't* totally convinced that Harmon *hadn't* committed the murder. I just wasn't a hundred percent sure that he had. After talking to Danny Lange I was convinced that the sex between Laura and Harman had been consensual. Maybe her death was an accident. Maybe she forgot her "safe" word and things went too far.

I honestly didn't know which idea would be more horrifying to this poor woman; the thought that her daughter had been raped, or the idea that she was so emotionally damaged that the only way she could express her anger was through sado-masochistic sex play.

I figured now wouldn't be a great time to bring up the fact that her husband was a royal "perv" who had been molesting their child, so I switched subjects. "Mrs. Stewart, were you here the day Tamra Rhineholt interviewed your husband?"

"No. I was out to lunch with some friends."

"Do you remember how he reacted when you got home?"

"My husband was very upset. He even snapped at me, which was unusual. Bill is generally a very patient, loving man. When I was divorced, my son Ethan went to live with his father. But his dad was killed in a boating accident when Ethan was sixteen, so he came to live with us. I'd always had a difficult time with Ethan, but Bill was wonderful. He welcomed Ethan with open arms and was very loving toward him."

Oh my God. How blind could this woman be? He had to have been molesting Ethan too! No wonder Ethan threw me out of his office. I must have really hit a nerve. Well, that and the fact that I accused him of murder.

"Mrs. Stewart, did your husband talk to you about the nature of his conversation with Tamra Rhineholt?"

She shook her head. "Bill was uncharacteristically withdrawn. He did call Ethan. I think he wanted to spare me whatever it was that Rhineholt woman told him. But he needed to confide in someone. They were in the study when Bill had his stroke. Thank goodness Ethan was there. It was a nightmare. When I entered the room, Bill was on the floor. Ethan said he'd just collapsed and he ordered me to call the paramedics while he tried to revive Bill."

The booze was really starting to affect her balance. She could barely keep upright. "Did you know that Ethan has decided to move back here while Bill is convalescing? He wants to bring Bill home as soon as possible. He feels he'll get better sooner if he's in familiar surroundings. Ethan loves Bill very much. He's so devoted to him." She finished off her drink and wobbled over to the sink. "Frankly, uh—what did you say your name was?"

"Brandy."

"Frankly, Brandy, I'm worried about my son. I think he's taking on too much. Maybe it's his way of coping with the trial and Laura's death. He and Laura were so close."

She paused, lost in her pain. Suddenly she looked up and smiled. "Laura worshipped her big brother. There's an eight year difference in age you know. Most older brothers wouldn't bother with a pesky little sister, but not Ethan. He'd spend hours playing with her, buying her things. He really spoiled her. He used to insist on babysitting for Laura so that Bill and I could spend time alone with each other."

"Did he really?" I asked, and a gnawing feeling burned in my stomach.

"Oh yes. He was so good to Laura. He used to call her his little kitten."

"Oh, but I thought Laura's dad..." The gnawing feeling turned into a full blown nausea as the implication of her words finally hit me. *How could I have been so wrong? It wasn't Laura's father who had molested her for all those years. It was her brother! Her brother the doctor.*

My mind spun with new possibilities. *What if Harmon told Tamra the nickname Laura went by? Ethan finds out she has this information and panics. So Ethan sets me up to think it was his stepfather's pet name for her, in order to throw me off track—and Laura's dad isn't exactly in a position to argue the point at the moment. When Tamra visited Mr. Stewart, did she tell him she suspected that Ethan had been sexually abusing his sister? Could that have been what prompted his stroke?*

The front door opened and in walked Ethan. *Oh shit. Time to go.*

"Mother, where are you?" He paused in the kitchen doorway, his look of confusion quickly turning to rage at the sight of me. "I thought I made it clear you were to leave my family alone. I'm calling the police."

261

"I was invited in, Dr. Girard." I looked to Mrs. Stewart for confirmation, but she was draped haphazardly over the sink, puking up her liquid lunch.

"My mother appears to be finished talking with you. I'll walk you out," he snapped, taking my elbow.

He silently marched me through the house. It reminded me of the time in fifth grade when my teacher escorted me to the principal's office because I accidentally called him a turd. But that was only because he was one.

When we got outside, he dropped my elbow. "As you can see, Ms. Alexander, my mother is very fragile. I don't know what your game is, but I trust you won't be back here disturbing her again."

"Actually, I just came here to apologize to you, Dr. Girard. I realize I was way out of line at your office. You're obviously going through a rough time, what with all the media attention on the Harmon execution and I'm sorry if I added to that stress in any way."

"Girard's mouth twitched slightly. "Thank you. Now, if you don't mind, I'm very busy."

"Oh, of course." I turned to face him, my utter loathing for the man helping to keep my fear at bay. I wanted to expose him for the lying, disgusting, possibly murderous scumbag he was, but I didn't have it all figured out yet. So I thought I'd stir the pot a little. "By the way, a friend of yours says hello. Craig Newman?"

The mention of Craig's name seemed to render him speechless. He cleared his throat a couple of times nervously tapping his fingers along the side of his leg while he processed where I might be going with this.

"I don't know any Craig Newman," he finally settled on.

"Really? He seems to know you very well. You met at a fundraiser for Helping Hands. Pancake Breakfast...ring any bells?"

"No. I'm sorry. I'm on the board of so many organizations. Really, I need to ask you to leave now. My mother needs me."

He watched me as I made my way down the driveway and then he turned and walked back into the house. As soon as he was out of sight, I headed back up. His BMW was parked about a hundred feet from the house, so I knelt down to avoid being caught on the security camera. The license plate had caught my eye and I wanted to look at it more closely. To be specific, it wasn't the license plate itself, but the plastic frame that went around it advertising the place the car had been serviced. Ditto's Car Repair. Why was I not surprised?

After my encounter with Dr. Sleazeball I really wanted to go home and take a bath, so I could only imagine how Laura must have felt. The adrenalin that had sustained me while I was face to face with him slowly began to fade. I pulled the truck around the block and sat there waiting to feel normal again.

After a minute I realized that wasn't going to happen, so I pulled out my notepad and started the process of denying my feelings. If I worked, I didn't think about the danger. And if I didn't think about the danger, it didn't exist. Wow. Bobby was right. He really should consider a career in psychology.

I began to peruse my notes. The most frustrating part about all of this was the only person who could have shed some light on Laura's life was dead. Her therapist was gone, a casualty of what appeared to be a massive cover-up. Laura's records were gone, and Laura had no close

263

friends she confided in. I had one hope left. It was a long shot, but maybe Dr. Applebaum was highly unprofessional and went around blabbing all of her patients' secrets to her husband. One could only hope.

I put in a call to Peter Applebaum. His voicemail picked up and I left a message asking him to call me back. That done, I turned to my notebook again. It always came back to connections. How did certain people and events tie in to other people and events?

As I pondered this, it soon became clear that the one person who tied everyone together was Dr. Ethan Girard. I began to construct a plausible scenario. Ethan takes his car in to Ditto's for repair and runs across Zach Meyers. They get to talking, and Girard senses Meyers can perform other services besides car repair. Meyers is more than happy to accommodate the good doctor—for the right price. Meyers then enlists the aid of Sean McCauly and they set out to kill Tamra. Only the numbnuts confuse me with Tamra and go after the wrong girl.

I thought back to the night of the kidnapping. There was a third man there. The one with the upper crust accent. *Ethan*! No wonder he sounded so familiar when I met him at his office. We'd already met, albeit unofficially, in the trunk of his henchmen's car.

I felt like I was overlooking a big chunk of the puzzle here, but if what I was beginning to suspect was true, the last place I should be parked was half a block away from Girard's house. I started the motor and scrammed out of there.

I double parked in front of Franny's house and hopped out of the car. Although I was feeling better now that one of my would-be assassins was safely ensconced in jail, I still exercised basic safety precautions. I beeped my horn to let Fran know I'd arrived. Then I pulled out my stun gun, defense spray and rape whistle and sprinted the five feet from the curb to her front door.

Fran was on the phone with Janine. "Hang on a second, Neenie." She covered the mouthpiece and whispered, "Tony Tan break-up crisis. We may need to do an emergency Häagen-Dazs run." She turned back to the phone. "Neenie, I'm not sure that's legal....no, I didn't say we *wouldn't* help you. I'm just not sure where we can get a bucket of tar and feathers at this time of night...Home Depot? Let me ask Brandy."

"Give me the phone," I said, holding out my hand. I got on the line. "Janine, you don't even really like the guy," I told her. "Remember you said he whistles through his nose while you're having sex and he uses the word "indeed" in like every other sentence. Only British people should use that word. You're better off without him. Plus now you can go to the bar mitzvah with me." I handed the phone back to Franny.

"Is she feeling better?" asked Fran.

"I don't know. She hung up on me."

"So, you wanna go get some Häagen-Dazs?"

"Nice wheels," Fran said. We were on our way to the Acme to pick up the ice cream. "Where's the Le Sabre?"

"Funny story," I told her. "In fact, I've got a couple of funny stories to tell you."

"Wow," Fran said an hour later. We sat in the parking lot of the Acme, finishing off a pint each of rum raisin ice cream. It was as close to drinking as Fran allowed herself to get these days. "So you think this Girard guy was doin' his sister and Tamra found out about it so he arranged to have her killed?"

"It's starting to look like it. I mean think what it would do to his career if what he was doing to his own sister got out? Assuming Tamra had information to this effect, she could've ruined him. Maybe she even threatened to." I scraped the last of the ice cream out of the carton and yawned.

Franny raised her perfectly shaped eyebrows. "Bran, when was the last time you slept? I thought having your parents in town would help, but you're starting to resemble the walking dead. Hey, is that why they took you off the air?" Franny was nothing if not direct.

"Probably," I conceded. "But Eric told me I'd be "more valuable" out in the field, which, roughly translated, means the network doesn't need another discrimination lawsuit so close on the heels of the last one so they're humoring me for a bit."

Franny finished her carton and shifted uncomfortably in her seat. Even with an eight pound basketball in her belly, she was still one of the most beautiful women I knew. She was also one of the most intuitive. She fixed me with a look. "There's something else going on," she decided, startling me out of my post-rum raisin euphoria. "Something you're not telling me. I can see it in your eyes."

"Get out! You can not." I pulled the mirrored visor down and checked just to make sure. "Franny, I just spent the last hour filling you in. What could I have possibly left out?"

"The part where you slept with Bobby." Oy.

I'd *wanted* to tell Franny. *Was dying to, in fact.* But I still hadn't fully processed it myself. She'd start asking me all kinds of questions I didn't have the answers to. I'd thought I was doing a pretty good job of hiding it, but I should have known she'd sense I was keeping something from her. Franny knew me better than I knew myself.

"Unhhh," I grunted. "Am I that transparent?"

"Honey, you're an open book. But in this case, Bobby told me."

I practically shot out of my seat, banging my head on the roof of the truck. "*He did?* Well, how did *that* come up? What, were you all just sitting around having a few laughs when out of the blue he mentions, 'Oh, by the way, I slept with Brandy. Please pass the beer nuts?' I can't believe he told you!"

"Will you calm down?" Franny didn't even bother to hide her grin. "He thought you'd already told me, which, I might add, was a reasonable assumption. He just wants to make sure you're all right, that's all. So, are you?" she added, her voice softening.

I settled back down, grateful to get it all out in the open. "No. I don't know. I'm all mixed up."

"About Bobby?"

I thought about it. *No. Not about Bobby. Blame it on bad timing, or circumstance or the natural progression of things, but it's just not in the cards for us to be together right now.* I shook my head.

"Then that leaves Nick."

I sighed. "Yep. That leaves Nick."

"So where exactly does it leave him?" Franny prodded. "And remember, it's me you're talking to."

I scrunched up my face and forced the words from my lips. "I'm in love with him."

267

Franny opened her mouth to respond, but I cut her off. "Look, I already know what you're going to say. The guy is wrong for me on every level. I mean I barely know anything about him and the little I do know scares the crap out of me. Falling in love with Nick is emotional suicide."

Franny rolled her eyes. "Well, that's a ringing endorsement. Let's break out the wedding cake."

"Sarcastic response is duly noted and *not helpful*, Fran!"

"Alright. You want an honest opinion, here goes. Aside from the fact that associating with Santiago could land you in a third world prison cell, I think it's great."

"Franny, knock it off. I'm in pain here."

"No. I'm totally serious. Look, I know you're in pain. I also know that as concerned as you are about which side of the law Nick resides on, you're more bothered by who he's spending his after-hours with. But if you love him, for cripe's sake, just go for it!"

"Well excuse me for not wanting to throw myself into a no-win situation. Nick has been very up front with me about what he can—and *can't* offer me. I'd be an idiot to go down that road knowing how hurt I could get."

She put up a hand to stop me. "I'm sorry, Bran. I don't want you to get hurt, either. But at least you're finally allowing yourself to feel *something for somebody*. You've kept yourself emotionally barricaded for like the past four years. How's that been working out for ya?"

I made a face. "Not that great, actually."

"So do you want to spend the rest of your life wondering what could have been?"

I peered over at Franny. Then I reached out and gave her a tentative poke in the belly.

"Ow. What are you doing?" she yelled, swatting my hand away.

"Just checking to see if you're really Janine in a fat suit."

Chapter Sixteen

I dropped Franny off at her house and headed home. Half way there I changed my mind and made a pit stop at the hospital to see Craig. I just couldn't shake the feeling that I was partially responsible for what had happened to him. For whatever reason, he'd gotten in way over his head with some pretty creepy people, but I believed in the end he'd actually been trying to protect me.

Even if Craig was still unconscious, I thought he might enjoy some company. I stopped and picked up a cheesecake in case he woke up while I was there and needed something worth living for.

I recognized the police officer posted outside Craig's room. She was Nancy Beringer, the younger sister of Micky, a guy I'd gone to school with.

"Hey, Nancy. How's it goin'?"

"It's goin' alright, Bran. How about you?"

I shrugged. "Can't complain. Listen, Nance, that guy in there is a friend of mine. I was wondering if I could go in and sit with him for a little bit."

"Sorry, Brandy. Orders. Besides, he's in a coma."

"Yeah, I know, but—I brought cheesecake." I held it up for Nancy to inspect.

"Word down at the station is you saved his life," she said, eying the bakery box.

"Yeah, well, I can't take any credit for that. Actually, my friend Nick is the one who fished us both out of the river."

"Nicholas Santiago," she said and I swear she blushed. "I read the report."

"You know him?" I asked.

"Every cop in the tri-state area has heard about Santiago. They all seem to want a piece of him. Personally," she confided, "I think the guys I work with are just jealous. That man is seriously hot." We nodded our heads in simultaneous agreement.

"So has Craig had any visitors?" I asked. I hated to think of him all alone.

"Not that I know of. But I just came on duty a little while ago."

I was all set to offer Nancy some cheesecake when something caught my eye. Instinctively, I stepped behind her and pulled up my hood, hiding my face.

Nancy peered around at me. "What are you doing?"

"Nothing." I stared down the hall, but whatever I thought I'd seen was already gone. "Listen, Nancy, I've gotta go. Say hi to Micky for me."

I walked over to the nurse's station. "Excuse me," I said to the least harried looking nurse I could find. Nurses are among the hardest working people I know. And recently, I've gotten to know my fair share. "I thought I saw my obstetrician go by a minute ago and I wanted to say hello. Dr. Girard?"

271

"Sorry. I didn't notice. Obstetrics is on the third floor. He may be on his way there."

"Oh, so if he were visiting a patient, she wouldn't be on this floor then?"

"Not likely." She gave me a polite but dismissive smile and returned to her work.

What was the likelihood of Girard having a patient at the same hospital that Craig was in? And what was he doing skulking around Craig's floor? *He must have come by to check on Craig—a guy he professed to not even remember—and got scared off by the guard outside the room.* I wondered what would have happened if Nancy hadn't been there monitoring Craig's visitors. The thought scared the hell out of me. Then again, what didn't these days.

I decided to run my suspicions by Bobby. He'd be able to tell me if I had enough to go to the cops with. I got back to my car and punched in his number.

"Yo," he said. I heard music in the background. It sounded like something off of a Saturday morning kiddie cartoon. The music stopped and there was a round of applause.

"Where are you?"

"Big Bird on Ice. It's the hottest ticket in town for the 'under five' set. So what's up?"

"It can wait," I told him. I would not allow my problems to interfere with Bobby's evening out with his little girl. "Give Big Bird my love and I'll talk to you later."

"You sure?"

"Positive." I hung up and drove straight home.

I walked in the door and found my dad and Uncle Frankie sitting on the couch watching the 76er's game.

There was a half-eaten bucket of chicken wings on the coffee table. I kissed them both and grabbed a wing.

"How was your day, doll?" My dad passed me the Ranch dressing and a napkin. "Careful. Your mother doesn't want sauce all over her nice clean living room."

Uncle Frankie swallowed a laugh and winked at me. I did a major sigh. "Yo, midget brat," Frankie said, "I've got tickets to the Peter Manfredo fight next week. You in?"

"Absolutely," I said, feeling significantly cheered. There's nothing like watching your favorite boxer beat the crap out of someone to take your mind off your problems. "Dessert," I added, plunking the cheesecake down on the coffee table.

I walked into the kitchen. My mother and Carla were in there. They'd been baking, judging by the tray full of burnt cookies cooling on the Formica countertop. At least I thought they were cookies. I picked one up and inspected it more closely. It was an oddly shaped blue and white frosted thing with appendages. "Starfish?" I ventured.

"Jewish Stars," Carla corrected me. "Your mother thought it would be nice to add them to the party favor bags for the bar mitzvah."

"And you didn't stop her?" I whispered to Carla. I spied a pile of small plastic Cellophane bags lying on the table. They were stuffed with notepads that had Paul's name and the date of the bar mitzvah printed on them. Plus a Glitter pen. Items suitable for a nine-year-old girl's slumber party.

"Have you run this by Paul?" I asked. "He may not be totally comfortable with the whole 'party favors' thing."

"Trust me," my mother said. If I know your brother, he'll be very happy we took care of these details for him."

And if I know my brother, he'll be searching for a rock to crawl under. Paul's original idea was to invite twenty of his closest friends and relatives. My mother somehow managed to boost those numbers to a hundred and sixty-eight.

"Honey, grab some bags and start stuffing," my mother said.

Just then my cell phone rang. "Ooh, sorry, Mom, it's work," I told her, not even bothering to check Caller I.D. "I've got to take this."

I walked out of the kitchen and opened the phone.

"Brandy. It's Mike Mahoe."

I was surprised to hear from him. Mike used to like me. But now that he's gotten to know me, he avoids me as much as possible. He thinks I'm "trouble." Sheesh.

"Mike, hi. What's up?"

"I thought this might interest you. I just got word from my friend at the Pennsauken Station. They've arrested Jeff Rhineholt for his wife's murder."

I didn't get home until almost midnight. Eric had sent a photographer out to meet me and we staked out the court house and the city jail. Jeff's lawyer made the obligatory, "You've got the wrong man" statement and promised his client's full cooperation.

At this point, I didn't know what to think. I'd been so sure that Ethan had arranged for Tamra's murder, but the cops must've thought they had a pretty solid case against Rhineholt or else they wouldn't have arrested him.

I put in a call to the precinct to speak to my old pal, Detective "Bunny," but for some reason he wouldn't get on the line. *He couldn't still be mad about the Binaca, could he?*

I decided to give it a rest for the night and start fresh in the morning. I was running on empty and as much as I fought it, I *had* to try and get some sleep. I climbed the stairs up to the bathroom and splashed some water over my face, dragged the toothbrush across my teeth and got into bed.

My body was more than ready to transition from awake to comatose. However, my brain had a different idea. It wanted to stay up and think about Nick. And once my brain made that decision, my body went along for the ride.

I wonder what Nick is doing right now? Ooh, I hear Jackie Chan's going to be a guest on Letterman tonight. I'm sure he won't want to miss it. I should call him. It's not very late. I climbed out of bed and got my cell phone off the dresser.

"Hi," I said as soon as he picked up.

"What's up, angel?" And at that precise moment I knew he wasn't alone. Maybe it was the slight hesitation in his voice, or the preoccupation, or just the innate knowledge that something wasn't quite right. But I knew he was with another woman. *Oh, why couldn't I have had this psychic revelation before I picked up the phone! Unhhh!*

"Um, Jackie Chan's on Letterman," I mumbled. "Thought you might want to know—uh—what with you both being martial arts experts and all..." *oh Jeez.* I hung up the phone.

Nick called me right back. "Thank you for calling to let me know," he said, ignoring the fact that I'd just hung up on him. "I'm a big fan of Jackie Chan's."

"Yeah, me too," I said, wondering if I'd ever actually seen any of his movies.

Nick's voice receded into the background. "Just leave it over there," he whispered.

"What?"

"Oh, sorry, I was talking to someone else."

I knew it! What's her name? I hate her so much! "Listen, you've got company. Me too. I've gotta go."

Nick cut me off. "Alphonso says hi."

"Alphonso? That's your company?"

"You sound surprised. Who were you expecting?"

"Nobody."

"So who's yours?" he asked.

"Who's my what?"

"Who's your company? You said you had company too."

"Did I?"

"You sound tired, darlin'."

"Oh, no. I'm fine."

I am so far from being fine it's not even funny. "Well, Alphonso's waiting. I'd better let you get back to him."

"Alphonso left. It's just you and me."

"Really?"

"Really."

I snuggled back under the covers and let the sound of his voice wash over me. He asked me how the rest of my day went, so I told him about my visit with Mrs. Stewart and my realization that it was her son who was the giant perv of the family. I also mentioned the connection between Meyers and Girard and ended with my visit to the hospital and how I'd narrowly missed running into Ethan.

"There's another possibility, darlin'," Nick said when I'd finished. "Maybe Girard wasn't there to see Craig. Could be he followed you to the hospital."

My insides twisted into a knot. "Do you really think he followed me?"

"It's a possibility, in which case it might be a good idea for someone to keep you company for the next few days."

"Are you volunteering for the job?" *Oh crap. I hadn't meant to say that out loud. I forgot Nick doesn't have a problem calling my bluff.*

"I'd be happy to take the night shift, angel. In fact, I could start right now, but somehow I don't think Mama Alexander would appreciate that."

"No, I guess not," I said, far too reluctantly.

Some time during the course of our conversation, I drifted off to sleep. I woke up in the morning with the cell phone cradled against my ear. Wow. I'd logged six full hours and not a single scary dream. A minor miracle by my standards.

I jumped out of bed and plugged the phone into the charger. Then I grabbed some fresh jeans and a powder blue crewneck sweater and headed for the bathroom. Good thing I'd had a decent night's sleep. I needed all the strength I could muster to confront the hideous creature that lurked in the bathroom mirror.

My mom had left some eyeliner and lip stick on the counter. I picked up the eyeliner, debating whether to risk making a bad situation worse. I don't usually wear make up, mostly because it itches. Plus, I never wanted anyone waking up beside me in the morning, going, "Oh my God, is that what you really look like? I've made a horrible mistake!" I figure it's better to let guys know what they're

277

getting up front. I took another look in the mirror and forced myself to make an exception.

When I got out of the bathroom, there was a message from Peter Applebaum on my cell. I gave him a quick call and asked if I could come by and speak to him. I was intentionally vague. Informing Peter that there was a good chance his wife's "accidental" death was no accident was something best discussed in person.

Rocky was waiting for me at the foot of the stairs. She was wearing pajamas. They were red and white striped with holes cut out for her tail and other significant body parts. Adrian lounged on the couch in front of the TV in what could only be described as a smoking jacket. He looked like a mini, mutant Hugh Hefner.

My dad walked in from the kitchen balancing two cups of coffee and a bagel. Adrian scooted over and my dad sat down next to him on the couch. One of the cups was filled mostly with milk. He set that one down in front of the dog. "Heather came by," he told me. "She said thanks for the other day and she dropped off these outfits."

Adrian began lapping up the coffee-milk. "Your mother thinks they're adorable," my dad mused. "Personally, I think they look silly. I mean, why would you want to treat a dog like a human? It's a dog. Hey, watch this." He flipped Adrian a piece of the bagel. Adrian caught it in his mouth and dunked it in his coffee. "I taught him that."

"I'm impressed. I can't even get him to roll over."

My dad looked at me for a beat. "Are you shooting a segment on clowns today?"

"No, why?"

278

"Oh. I just thought…you look very…colorful," he settled on.

"Too much?" I asked. I guess I'd gone a little overboard on the blush. But that was just to make up for my deathly pallor.

My dad shrugged. "What do I know, hon? You always look beautiful to me."

"Thanks, Dad." I leaned over and kissed him, leaving a big SWAK mark on his cheek.

"So, your mother says you're not sleeping," he added, clearly uncomfortable. My dad isn't good with personal conversations. Guess the apple doesn't fall far from the tree. "Is there, uh, something you want to talk about?"

Well, let's see… Someone tried to kill me, I slept with Bobby, cracked up Paul's car, I'm in love with an outlaw and I almost killed a man…but "almost" doesn't count…

"Nah. I'm good. Hey, are there any more bagels left?"

I arrived at Peter Applebaum's at 11:00 a.m. He greeted me with a smile tinged with curiosity. Of all the tough spots I'd found myself in over the course of the week, this was one of the hardest. I was about to tell a man whose world had collapsed the day his wife died that someone had done it on purpose. Only what if it turned out not to be true? Was it fair to subject him to horrifically painful memories before I was one hundred percent sure of my facts?

I followed Peter's wheel chair into the living room and took a seat on the couch. "Thanks for agreeing to meet with me again," I told him. "I'll try not to take up too much of your time."

"It's not a problem," he said. "Although I am wondering what I can do for you. I wasn't terribly helpful the last time you were here."

"Actually, you were more helpful than you thought."

"Really? How so?"

"Well, you steered me to Dr. Levi and ironically, it was the information she *couldn't* provide that helped me put it all together. Peter, what I'm about to tell you may be difficult to accept, and to be honest I'm not even sure I'm on the right track. But—"

"Listen," Peter interrupted, "I did a little investigating of my own after you came to see me last week. From what I've read, your track record is pretty impressive, so why don't you just tell me what this is all about?"

I took a deep breath and began. I started with the night his wife's office had been burglarized and worked my way through to the day of my car accident and how it appeared that someone had tampered with my brakes. He sat rigid in his chair, absorbing the information, stopping me from time to time for clarification.

"So you believe Girard had my wife killed because he was afraid his sister had told her about the molestation."

I nodded. "Girard was an up and coming doctor. This kind of information would have ruined his career before he even got started and quite possibly landed him in prison. When Harmon went on trial, Laura's past was bound to come out. So I figure he arranged to have the files stolen and then got rid of anyone Laura may have confided in. Four years later Tamra begins a new investigation, so he gets rid of her too."

When I was finished Peter sat there with the tortured look of someone who had been though hell and hadn't quite made it back to the other side. He was shaking, tears rolling down his cheeks. "All this time I've blamed myself for Traci's death," he said.

"Peter, I'm so sorry. I knew this would be hard for you."

I waited a minute (it was probably more like thirty seconds, I have no self control) and then I continued. "Listen, I've made a lot of headway in connecting Girard to this crime, but I need something concrete to show that he had a motive for killing Tamra and your wife. If I can prove he'd been molesting his sister that should be enough to convince the cops to look into him."

"I'm sorry. I still don't see how I can help you."

"The last time I was here you told me you haven't been up to Traci's office since she died. Has anyone cleaned out that space for you?"

Peter shook his head. "Except for Dr. Levi taking the files, it's just the way Traci left it. I know it's silly," he shrugged. "I've just never been able to bring myself to do it."

"I'd like to check out the office. The people who broke in may have taken Laura's file, but there's a chance that they overlooked something. Possibly Traci took notes that hadn't made their way into the file yet. Do you mind if I have a look around?"

Peter wheeled himself over to the other side of the living room and opened up a cabinet. He took out a key and handed it to me. "I want you to nail this bastard."

Except for the layer of dust coating every surface and the dead plants perched on the window sill, Dr. Applebaum's office appeared perfectly preserved. A big mahogany desk dominated the room, the top of which was cluttered with framed photos of Peter and Traci and a beautiful Labrador Retriever, an I heart Philadelphia mug

281

and various other knick knacks. A mahogany file cabinet stood against the wall, tucked in behind the desk.

Alongside the opposite wall sat a beige corduroy couch and a matching comfy chair. It made for a cozy, comfortable place to spill one's deepest darkest secrets. I just prayed the ghosts of some of those secrets were still hanging around.

I started with the file cabinet. Predictably, it was empty. Dr. Levi must have taken the rest of the contents. I began opening up desk drawers, perusing every scrap of paper, but I couldn't find a single connection to Laura. In the bottom right hand desk drawer I found a four year old Hershey bar and a small notepad. I opened the Hershey bar. I mean it's not like anyone was going to miss it.

The notepad was filled with hurriedly scribbled, random thoughts regarding various patients. I read the first one. "A.K. appeared more withdrawn than usual today. Re-evaluate meds." I quickly flipped through the rest of the book. Dr. Levi said Dr. Applebaum only had five patients, not counting Laura. If there was something in the notepad pertaining to her it wouldn't be hard to find.

Toward the back of the pad I found an entry dated May 2nd. "L. still not talking, but journaling very effective. A real breakthrough today."

When I was a kid, one of my favorite books was Harriet the Spy. It was about this girl who went around spying on people in the neighborhood and taking notes that she kept in a journal. Her parents thought she was crazy so they took her journal away and sent her to a psychiatrist. The first thing the shrink did was give her a new journal.

My heart flipped in my chest as a wave of hope coursed through it. *Dr. Applebaum had Laura keep a journal.* She must have used it to confide all the feelings that she couldn't bring herself to verbalize. But if a journal did exist, what happened to it?

I took a bite out of the Hershey bar. It was two years past the expiration date so it tasted a little funky, but chocolate is chocolate so I ate it anyway.

"Okay," I told myself. "Think logically." *Laura had no close friends and she kept people at a distance. Deeply troubled and with no one to confide in, she decides to go for help. She begins seeing Dr. Applebaum, but she clams up when she's in the office. Dr. Applebaum encourages her to write down her feelings.* Seemed plausible so far.

Now, I assume most patients would take their journals home and use it in between therapy sessions in order to monitor their own emotions, like if they start to feel anxious or they have a revelation. However, Dr. Applebaum couldn't get Laura to talk to her, so...maybe she was using the journal as a form of communication between them...in which case she would be reading the entries...which meant she would have left the journal in the office!

I jumped up so fast I nearly choked on a hunk of chocolate. Frantically, I began ransacking the place, pulling books off the shelves, rifling through drawers.

The left hand desk drawer was locked. I rattled on it for a while and then tried to pry it open with a butter knife I found that had been doing double duty as a letter opener. Finally I gave up and began searching for the key. I scanned the room for possible hiding places and then I moved over to the windowsill and began lifting the potted plants. Under a dead cactus in the corner sat a small silver key.

I stuck the key in the lock and turned it. The drawer opened easily, exposing the contents inside. I reached in and extracted a leather bound spiral notebook. I was hoping for a sign on the front of it that said, "Laura's journal. All will be revealed!" but life is rarely that accommodating.

I turned the page and found the first entry, dated six weeks before Laura died. The handwriting was small, neat and feminine and the sentiment expressed was short and to the point. *"Sex is power."*

The next entry was dated a few days later. It was longer, but the handwriting was miniscule, as if the person who wrote it was trying to limit its power by shrinking its size. The tone was by turns angry, scared, defiant. I found one passage particularly heartbreaking in its almost childlike narration.

"Nobody knows the real me. I've tried to tell Daddy about Ethan, but he just sees what he wants to see. Laura is invisible. Sometimes even I don't think she exists."

I looked for the page marked May 2nd. Dr. Applebaum thought there had been a breakthrough that day. There were some pages torn out. I suspected Laura had removed them herself. Maybe they were so private she couldn't bring herself to keep a written record, no matter how safe the environment. Finally, I found what I'd been looking for. It was the last journal entry, disjointed and chilling, written in large, angry strokes.

"Ethan said he's coming over. Well, he's in for a surprise. I'm not his kitten anymore. The years of self-loathing…it was not my fault. IT WAS NOT MY FAULT. I will no longer allow him to ruin my life. I trusted him. My brother. My protector. My lover… God how I hate him. How could he do this to me? I was just a little girl. I'm telling him tonight. It's over."

Ethan went to see Laura on May 2nd? That was the same day she was murdered.

Nowhere in the transcripts was there mention that Ethan had visited her on the 2nd. Was he there right before Harmon came over or...Holy cow!

Chapter Seventeen

A wave of nausea hit me with such intensity I bolted toward the window and shoved it open, gulping in the brisk winter air. *It was Ethan! He killed his own sister! Jesus Christ, why didn't I see it sooner? Because the thought was so repulsive it was beyond comprehension.* And yet I knew it like I knew my own name.

Laura was going to tell him she wouldn't be with him anymore. Maybe she threatened to tell people what he'd been doing to her all these years. Or maybe he didn't like being rejected. Possibly, she went crazy on him. According to Danny, it wouldn't have been the first time. Whatever the motivation, Ethan had to be the one.

He must have seen Harmon entering her apartment on the evening of May 2nd, so he sat in his car for a while waiting for him to leave, and then he came back after Harmon left, killed her and then messed up the apartment to make it look like there had been a struggle between Laura and Harmon.

But then Ethan had to make sure that Harmon would be convicted. Enter Anthony Mitchell. Mitchell was employed at the car wash across the street from where Meyers worked. Mitchell and Harmon hung around the same circles. I'd figured that someone had paid Mitchell to say that Harmon confessed to him about killing Laura. Even though Mitchell wasn't the most credible witness, his testimony was icing on the cake.

But if Dr. Applebaum read the entry, when she heard that Laura had been murdered, why didn't she tell the police about Ethan going over there that night…unless she hadn't heard about Laura's death right away. There was only a small window of time between Laura's murder and Traci's car "accident." And even if she had heard about it, Harmon was such a despicable character it would be easy to assume he was guilty.

I began silently tallying up the death toll. How could Girard be responsible for so many shattered lives? I mean once you get the hang of killing, is it just that much easier to take another life and then another? It really did seem to be the ultimate in sick ironic humor that the guy's chosen profession was an obstetrician. *"Give a life, take a life, that's my motto!"* What a world.

I put the books back on the shelves and straightened up as best I could. Then I took Laura's journal and locked up Dr. Applebaum's office, pausing to pick up the photos on the desk.

Peter was waiting for me at the door, his wheel chair blocking the entrance. He smiled apologetically and rolled out of the way.

"I thought you might want these," I said, placing the photos in his lap.

He studied them for a moment, a sad smile flickering across his face. "Did you get what you were looking for?" he asked.

"I did," I said, holding up the journal. "We're not there yet, but we're getting there."

On the way home I put in a call to Eric. I really didn't want to go into the office and run the risk of being on the receiving end of one Lynne's snotty remarks. I'd gotten away with knocking her over once, but I wasn't sure it would fly a second time around.

Also, I was sort of wondering if I still had a job. Wendy was back full force. I'd caught her on the news this morning, sitting in as one of the judges in a local "Oprah Winfrey Look-Alike Contest." Boy, some of those people didn't even remotely look like Oprah. I think one lady had mixed her up with Weezy from The Jeffersons.

Eric was in a meeting, so I left a message for him to call me. I also called Bobby and got his voicemail, so I left a message for him too, telling him to get in touch with me ASAP. For all of our disagreements, I know Bobby trusts my instincts. I needed him on my side if I was going to present a case to the police, and I couldn't afford to make any mistakes. Lives were depending on me.

It was past lunchtime and I was starving. I hadn't eaten anything since the ice cream, half a moldy candy bar not withstanding. I cruised down South Street in Nick's truck, looking for the new Indian restaurant that had just opened up. According to Carla, the food isn't very good but they give you a lot.

I passed by Lucinda's gallery and spotted Johnny climbing out of his BMW. I double parked next to him and honked. He pretended like he didn't know I was there and kept walking, head down, as if being buffeted by high winds. I opened the passenger side window, leaned across the seat and yelled out the window.

"Yo, jerk-o. I know you see me."

John looked up, a sheepish grin plastered to his face. He walked over to the truck and leaned in through the window.

"So how's it goin'?" he asked.

I climbed out of the truck and came around to the side where John stood. I was wearing my shitkicker boots with the two inch heels so we were eye to eye. "You tell me John. Did you get my photo back?"

"Oh yeah, about that. Funny thing. Um, not yet."

Unhhh! I sat down hard on the hood of Nick's truck and jammed my fists into my pockets to keep from popping John one. "John, the one thing, *the one thing* I asked you not to do."

"I swear to God, it wasn't my fault. I wasn't there. Lucinda must've sold it by accident. I haven't seen her so I didn't get a chance to ask."

I looked beyond John into the gallery's big picture window. I could see movement in the room and the bony presence of its owner. "She's in there now. Let's go ask her who bought it and get it back."

I jumped off the hood, all set to march through the doors, but John caught me by the arm. "That's not such a good idea."

"Why not?"

"The thing is after the other night, you've sort've been banned from the gallery."

"*What?*"

"Honey, you're lucky she didn't charge you with grand theft. That photo sold for $1200.00 bucks."

"You've got to be kidding!"

John actually had the audacity to be offended. "I happen to be an artist of some renown here. Any collector would be proud to own my work."

He began waxing poetic about his pictorial achievements but I wasn't really listening. I was too busy trying not to cry. I guess John picked up on the psychic vibes, or else it was the tears of frustration that were beginning to well up and spill down my cheeks that gave me away. Whatever, he stopped talking and put his arm around me.

"Okay, Sunshine, what's this really about?"

"My life is so out of control, John," I wailed, choking back little snuffling noises.

"Yeah," he said. "I've been meaning to talk to you about that."

"You mean it shows?"

"Just a little." John reached into his coat pocket and extracted a travel packet of Kleenex. "Here," he said, handing it to me.

I took out a tissue and wiped my nose and then tried to hand him back the packet.

"That's okay, you hang on to it. Look, sweetie," he added, dropping his voice in the soothing way people do when addressing the mentally unstable, "I really am sorry about the photograph and I'll do whatever I can to get it back for you. But there's a bigger issue here."

I felt the beginnings of a "heart to heart" coming on and began to panic. "John," I told him, swiping the tears away with the back of my hand, "I just had a momentary lapse, brought on no doubt by near starvation. You really want to help me? Take me out to lunch. The 'all-you-can-eat buffet' down at Hannigan's only lasts until three, so we'd better hurry."

John shrugged his narrow shoulders in surrender. "Fine. I'll take you to lunch. But we're going to have this conversation sooner or later."

Later, Johnny. Much later.

Hannigan's is a combination Irish Pub-Nordic schmorgusborg. Even the beer tastes like herring. We took separate cars because I'd planned on heading over to the police station right after we ate.

I tried calling Bobby again, but he still didn't pick up and my anxiety level was growing exponentially with every passing minute. Somehow I doubted that a "puff piece" reporter's gut instincts would be enough to convince the cops to reopen the case.

I needed a credible witness to verify what I knew to be true. Unfortunately, anyone who fell into that category came with an obituary attached to them...all except for...

Ignoring the enormous "No left turn" sign at Broad and Walnut, I swung a u-ie and headed away from Hannigan's. At the next red light I whipped out my phone and called John. I could hear plates clattering in the background.

"Hey, where are you?" John demanded. "They're almost out of Swedish meatballs."

"Listen," I told him, "I'm gonna have to take a rain check on lunch. I think I've got a lead on this story I've been working on. Keep your fingers crossed that my hunch pans out. I could really use a break."

"This must be big," John said. "It's not like you to pass up a free lunch."

I clicked off with John and my stomach roared in protest. My digestive juices had been really looking forward to those meatballs. I punched in redial. "Can you get me some meatballs to go?" I asked. "And those little powdered cookies for dessert? I'll swing by your place later to pick them up."

The light turned green. I stepped on the gas and began slogging my way through mid-town traffic. I was headed for Hillgarden Convalescent Home, the current residence of Laura Stewart's stroke-afflicted father, Bill. With any luck, I'd have my credible witness within the hour.

The way I figured it, Bill Stewart was my best hope—and my last chance—for finding out what really happened to Laura. According to Laura's diary, she'd tried to talk to her dad about what was bothering her, but he'd refused to accept what she had to say. On some level, Stewart had to have known what was going on between Ethan and Laura, but until she flat-out told him, he could go on denying the truth. But what if Tamra confirmed his suspicions the day she visited the house? Mrs. Stewart said Bill was very agitated after Tamra's visit, but he wouldn't discuss it with his wife. He did however, talk to Ethan.

Ethan had blamed Tamra for Mr. Stewart's stroke. But Bill was alive and kicking after Tamara left, which was more than one could say after his conversation with his stepson. Maybe he'd put two and two together and realized that Laura's murderer wasn't some random stranger, but her own half brother.

Mrs. Stewart was so grateful that Ethan was there when Bill went down for the count. But there had been no one around to dispute Ethan's version of what had taken place that night. What if Bill had confronted Ethan with his suspicions? Did the realization that his biggest nightmare was true cause Bill's stroke? If that were the case, Ethan would have a vested interest in seeing that his stepfather keep those suspicions to himself. For all anyone knew, Bill could have been unconscious for several life-threatening minutes before Ethan called the paramedics. *Would he have even made that call to 911, had his mother not walked into the den and discovered her husband lying half- dead on the floor?*

I pulled up in front of Hillgarden Convalescent Home and jumped out of the truck. My grandmother had spent a fair amount of time at Hillgarden before she died so I knew my way around. There was a reception area on the first floor, with the patients' rooms laid out in a square overlooking a garden.

My first order of business was to find out if anyone was in the room with Mr. Stewart, before I marched in demanding he rat out his stepson in the literal blink of an eye. This was going to be difficult enough without having to explain my presence there, should his wife be keeping a bedside vigil. I mean, what would I say? *"Nice to see you again, Mrs. Stewart. I just dropped by to collect incriminating evidence from your dying husband about your son, who, I'm pretty sure murdered your daughter…is this a good time?"*

I began walking toward the reception area when I saw a man emerge from a room at the far end of the hallway. He was pushing a guy in a wheel chair, along with one of those portable stands that had an I.V. bag hanging from it. The rig got stuck in the door and I was about to run over and offer my assistance, when I recognized the man pushing the chair. It was Ethan and he was headed in my direction. Oy.

Since I didn't have time to whip out the Groucho glasses and fake mustache, I yanked up my hood and turned my back to them, finding a sudden interest in the abstract paintings hanging on the wall. As they shuffled past me I stole a glance at the two of them. Bill Stewart was strapped into his chair like the guest of honor at an electrocution. He was bundled in blankets up to his neck, his jaw muscles slack against his chest. The only sign of life was in his eyes, which were darting around in his head like a human pinball machine.

As they reached the visitors' desk, Stewart raised his head to the receptionist and emitted a series of garbled sounds, his neck muscles straining from the effort. She smiled kindly at him. "I'm sorry, Mr. Stewart, I can't understand you."

I gave myself points for not vaulting over the desk and shouting, "He clearly said, 'Ethan's trying to kill me,' you moron," and hunkered back against the wall.

"Claudia, I'm taking my stepfather out to the garden for a while," Ethan cut in. "He seems a bit sluggish today. I think a change of scenery and some fresh air will do him good." The poor guy didn't seem sluggish to me. He seemed freakin' terrified.

Stewart's head began to rock back and forth, the noises emanating from his throat gaining momentum. Claudia praised his efforts like a proud mother. "Oh, Mr. Stewart, you've made so much progress over the past few days. You keep this up and you'll be speaking again in no time."

Ethan blanched under the fluorescent lighting. With Stewart starting to regain his speech, it would be only a matter of time before he'd be able to tell people what Ethan had done. That was the good news. It was also the bad news, since Ethan knew that and wasn't shy about saving his own neck at the expense of someone else's.

I didn't think he would try anything with visitors and nursing home staff cruising around. I figured I'd wait until he left for the day and then go back in and talk to Bill.

I inched my way out the front door, ran back to the truck and hopped in. From this vantage point I could see both the courtyard and the front door of the convalescent home.

I was cold and hungry and I really had to pee. I popped open Nick's glove compartment on the off chance he had a bag of M&M's or a Snicker's bar stashed away somewhere. All I could find was a box of raisins and they weren't even chocolate coated. They were the regular kind and a little on the stale side. I poured out a handful and stuffed them into my mouth. Then I got out a pair of mini binoculars from my pocketbook, settled back in the seat and trained my eyes on the courtyard.

I don't think I could make a career out of being a spy. Surveillance work isn't really my thing. There's too much waiting around for stuff to happen. I'm more of an "instant gratification" kind of gal. I put the binoculars back in my bag and waited some more.

To pass the time I drummed out Christmas carols on the dashboard and played a couple of games of Five Card Draw on my cell phone. That ate up about ten minutes. I was about to start making my birthday wish-list when the phone rang. I checked the readout and smiled.

"Hey," I said.

"Hello, angel." Nick's voice was rich and warm as hot fudge, and a rush of heat spread throughout my body. "Where are you?" he asked.

"I'm sitting in your truck, outside Hillgarden Convalescent Home. Girard's in there with his stepfather. I'm waiting for him to leave so that I can talk to Stewart."

"Oh? What's the occasion?"

"I found Laura's journal. Ethan killed his sister, Nick. After reading her last entry, I'm sure of it and I think Stewart knows it too. I just need him to confirm it for me."

Nick hesitated a beat and when he spoke again there was an uncharacteristic quality in his tone. Something that bordered on worried.

"Does DiCarlo know where you are?"

"No. Why?"

"No reason. Just be careful, darlin'. This guy is desperate, and desperate people do desperate things."

After we hung up, I rooted through the glove compartment some more and found a book on tape, which would have passed the time quite nicely *had it been in English*, but, as luck would have it, was in Russian. *Oh jeez, as if I don't feel inadequate enough around Nick. I mean how many languages does this guy know? Note to self: Stop pretending that speaking Pig Latin makes me bilingual and learn a real second language.*

I picked up the binoculars again in time to catch Ethan wheel his stepdad back inside through the garden side entrance. Fifteen minutes later he emerged alone and headed toward the parking lot. I waited until he pulled into traffic and then hopped out of the car and made a beeline back to the building.

To keep things uncomplicated I decided to circumvent the front desk and sneak in through the service entrance. That put me directly in front of Mr. Stewart's room. The door was made of metal, with a small, rectangular, wire mesh window that hit almost eye level to me. I stood on tiptoe and peered in.

He was propped up in a semi-sitting position on the bed, the covers drawn to just under his chin. I could see the soft rise and fall of his chest as he lie there, eyes closed, his head resting against the pillows. According to Eric, Bill Stewart was a powerful man, but there was no indication of that now. I knocked softly so as not to startle him and entered and approached the bed. His eyelids fluttered open and he stared at me blankly.

I figured I might as well plunge right in. The guy wasn't exactly in a position to throw me out. "Mr. Stewart, my name is Brandy Alexander and I'm a reporter with WINN news. I'm very sorry to intrude on you like this but it's imperative that I speak with you. I need to ask you some questions about your daughter and your stepson."

Stewart opened his mouth and emitted a barrage of noise akin to a seal pup in distress. It took me a minute to realize he was saying, "Laura." His eyes filled with tears and instantly I felt ashamed of myself. *Oh God, I've made him cry. I'm a terrible person.*

I grabbed a tissue off the bed stand and wiped his eyes for him. "Look, Mr. Stewart, I realize you don't know me, so you have absolutely no reason to trust me. But I think you may be in danger and I want to help you. Only you have to work with me here. Do you understand what I'm saying to you?"

Stewart blinked two watery eyes at me.

"Good." I took a deep breath. "You know something about the night Laura was killed, don't you? Something to do with Ethan."

The muscles in his jaw began to twitch and he gave an excruciatingly slow and painful nod of his head.

I tried to sound as non-judgmental as possible. *As if there were any way to make an accusation about incest and sorocide appear like polite bedside chit chat. "Mr. Stewart, would you prefer lime Jell-O with those lamb chops or did you want to go with the sorbet? And, oh, by the way, I think your stepson boffed and offed your daughter and if you could just confirm that for me, that'd be great."*

"Um, here's what I think, Mr. Stewart. I think Ethan was molesting Laura and when she threatened to tell people about it, he killed her." I took the waterworks that sprang from his eyes as a "yes" and moved on.

"You confronted Ethan about this on the day you had your stroke, didn't you?" Another head nod, accompanied by a huge, strangled sob. "And then he left you there to die." I had no more questions. The look of anguish in his eyes said it all.

"Mr. Stewart. I don't mean to scare you, but I'm pretty sure Ethan sees your recovery as a liability. You've got to make a statement to the police before he comes back to finish the job. Would you be willing to do that?"

He nodded his head again, and I swear I saw relief in that semi-frozen face.

"Listen," I said, walking toward the door, "I'm just going to get one of the hospital staff in here so they can verify what you indicated to me. And then I'll call the police and have them come down here to help you. Okay?" I didn't wait for an answer.

I began to pull open the door, but something stopped me. Through the wire mesh window I spied a man dressed in a white hospital attendant's uniform slip out of the service entrance and head straight for Bill Stewart's room. Only I got the distinct feeling he wasn't there to aid and comfort.

My heart pounding in my ears, I backed away from the door and dove toward the bathroom, issuing a directive along the way to the paralyzed man in the bed. "Ethan's coming. Act natural!"

I had barely wedged myself behind the bathroom door when Ethan entered the room, carefully shutting the main door behind him. He stopped at the foot of the bed, gazing with chilling impassivity at the motionless figure lying prone in front of him.

Stewart stared back at him, eyes unblinking, willing himself to see past the man standing before him to the boy he loved like his own son. A moment passed and once again the tears flowed freely, only this time they were Ethan's.

Wiping his eyes with the back of his hand, he shook his head, emitting a short, embarrassed cough. Then he walked around to the side of the bed, his back to the bathroom. I closed one eye, straining to see through the crack in the door and praying he didn't get a sudden urge to take a leak before finishing off the old man.

Ethan fumbled in his pocket for a moment and extracted a hypodermic needle. *Maybe he came back to give him a B12 shot. I hear that does wonders for your energy level. Oh shit, probably not.*

Bill Stewart lay helpless in the bed, his eyes never straying from Ethan's. Ethan began to speak again, his voice soft and apologetic, a direct contrast to the unthinkable act he was about to commit.

"I don't want to do this, Bill. I really don't. You've been good to me, but you've left me no choice...none of them did. I see how you look at me now, like I'm some kind of a monster. But I never forced her. It wasn't that

299

way between Laura and me. I gave her what she wanted, what she needed. I loved her, dad, you know I did."

He held the needle to the light, gently flicking out the bubbles. "You'll have to trust me though; this is really for the best. You wouldn't want to live like this anyway. Look, don't worry. You won't feel a thing."

Mr. Stewart's jaw dropped open and he began an assault of mind-numbing sounds which I'm sure, roughly translated to "For the love of God, Alexander, do something!"

I dropped to my knees and slowly opened the bathroom door. If Stewart could just keep up his dolphin-speak long enough to distract his step son...

I belly crawled along the floor, barely breathing, inching my way toward Ethan with stealth-like precision. He was hyper focused on Stewart, quietly imploring him to shut the hell up. I was almost there. Just a few more feet and—my cell phone went off.

I froze, mid crawl, listening to the absurdly tinny sound of Green Day's Good Riddance, an eerily fitting choice under the circumstances. I looked wildly around to see where I'd left my phone. And then I spied it, sitting on the floor in the corner of the room. It must have fallen out of my bag when I first came in.

I watched in horror as Ethan strode over and picked it up. He examined it for a beat, flipped it open and waited.

Even with his ear pressed against the receiver, my mother's dulcet tones permeated the room.

"Hello? Brandy, is that you? *Helloooo.*" *Oh, crap.*

I scrambled under the bed, which was really stupid, considering all Ethan had to do was look down to see me trapped there like a beached whale. The sudden movement must have caught his eye because the next thing I knew we were eyeball to eyeball.

He reached out and grabbed for me, catching me by my coat collar. I began to scream and he tightened his grip, yanking me forward by the lapels. His look murderous, he stood and dragged me to my feet. "You never learn, do you?" he hissed in my ear.

I whipped around, balled up my fist and punched him square in the face. Blood spurted from his perfect nose. He cursed and reeled back and I kicked him hard in the shin, catching him off balance.

Ethan toppled over, pulling me down with him. I struggled free of his grip and stumbled toward the door. He crawled to his knees and lunged for me, catching me around the middle. I screamed again and was clawing desperately at his arms, when in a flash, the door flung open and Nick appeared in the entry, a colt forty-five gripped tightly in his hand. It was trained at Ethan's head.

Ethan snaked his arm around my neck and dragged me up alongside him, the hypodermic needle still clutched in his hand. Now he raised it and pressed it firmly against my jugular vein. If I gulped I was a goner.

"Drop the gun or she's dead," Ethan warned.

Drop the gun, Nick. I don't want to be dead. Drop the gun!

"I can't do that," Nick said calmly.

Shit. Why not?

As if he could read my thoughts, Nick locked eyes with me, silently asking me to trust him. "Because this scumbag is going to use you as a human shield until he's safe and then he's going to kill you anyway, darlin'. Isn't that right, Girard?"

Ethan didn't bother to deny it. Nudging me forward, our heads less than an inch apart, he began a slow shuffle toward the door. Suddenly, I had trouble breathing. My skin felt clammy and black spots swam before my eyes. "Nick," I implored, and in that instant I heard the crack of the gun as it blew a bullet past my head and imbedded itself into the front of Ethan's skull.

Chapter Eighteen

"...and then he pulled the trigger."

"Just like that?"

"Yeah, just like that."

"Wow."

Seated on my couch, Carla curled her feet beneath her and passed around a pitcher of margaritas. We all took deep slugs including my mother, not bothering with glasses. Franny eyed the pitcher longingly and rubbed her stomach.

"Do you think you can manage to stay out of trouble long enough for me to give birth?" she asked. "It's not fair that you almost died and I have to deal with it sober."

"I definitely should have taken that into consideration. I'll try to time my escapades better in the future," I told her.

Bobby had called everyone from the police station to fill them in on what happened. I was grateful that he'd given them a heads-up. I didn't have the energy to relive the ordeal without major liquid fortification.

"So how did Nick know you were in trouble?" Janine wanted to know, taking the pitcher out of my mom's hands. "They're stronger than they taste, Mrs. Alexander."

"Nonsense," my mother told her and promptly passed out on the floor.

My dad wandered in from the kitchen. "What happened to your mother?"

"A little too much celebrating," I said.

"I'm *fine*," my mom mumbled from the rug. *So that's where I get it from.*

"Sure you are, Lorraine." My dad helped her to her feet and led her up the stairs.

I turned to Janine and held out my hands for the pitcher. "Nick just knows things," I said. I took a large gulp and continued my saga.

Fortunately for Nick, there was a witness—one that wasn't in love with him and could give the cops an unbiased account of what had transpired. An ancient security guard employed by the nursing home to keep gang bangers from tagging the side of the building was standing in front of the reception area when Nick came in looking for Bill Stewart's room. They were halfway down the hall when they heard me scream. The guard was more than happy to let Nick take care of Ethan, seeing as the only weapon he was packing was a rape whistle.

When the police arrived he verified that Nick had shot Ethan in order to save my life. Ethan had died instantly. Afterwards, Nick and I didn't have much of a chance to chat. I was too busy throwing up. Must have been all that stale candy I ate.

"So how are you holding up, there, sunshine? John asked.

"Great," I told him. "Couldn't be better." The doorbell rang and I jumped a mile.

"Uh huh," he said, opening the front door to Paul and Uncle Frankie.

"H-how's mom?" Paul asked, after hugging the stuffing out of me.

"She's feeling no pain at the moment. And before you ask, Paulie, I'm okay. Really."

"She's not," John mouthed behind my back.

"I *saw* that."

"*Fine.* I wasn't trying to hide it from you. She's not." he said aloud. "She's drowning her troubles in tequila. At least try the wine I brought. It's more civilized."

DiCarlo showed up ten minutes later and I went into the kitchen to get more glasses. He followed me in. "Craig Newman pulled out of his coma tonight," he told me.

"You're kidding." A half a day sooner and it would have saved me a crap load of trouble.

"You were right about everything," Bobby said, taking the glasses down from the cabinet. "Craig met Girard at a fundraiser. Girard befriended him and then managed to convince the poor guy to spy on Tamra. He told Craig she was in way over her head with this investigation and if Harmon got out of prison he'd go after her next. By the time Craig figured out that he'd been duped, it was too late. He'd inadvertently given Girard a copy of the key to the Rhineholt's house and now Ethan was threatening to expose him as Tamra's killer. And if that wasn't enough motivation to keep his mouth shut, Girard threatened to kill you." Well, that explained Craig's nightly vigils parked in front of my house.

There was something else on Bobby's mind. I could tell by the little vein on the side of his temple. "Bobby, it's all over," I reassured him. "This is good news."

"Yeah, it is."

"So then what's wrong?"

DiCarlo sighed. "Santiago saved your life tonight."

"Well, jeez, you don't have to sound so disappointed about it."

"That's not what I meant, Bran. It's just that—he was there for you. I wasn't."

I walked over to Bobby and slipped my arms around him. "If you had known, you would have been. There's no doubt in my mind." We hugged, grateful to be in each other's lives. "So what happens to Harmon now?" I asked, after a beat.

"Long story short, he'll be released, which is a damn shame when you think about it. The guy may not have been responsible for killing Laura Stewart but society's still better off with that bastard in jail." Having met the man, I really couldn't argue the point.

I woke up at five a.m., fully dressed and face down on my bed. We'd run out of margarita mix sometime after midnight but luckily there was still plenty of tequila left. At one point Carla started singing "Wind Beneath My Wings" and caused a mass exodus. Having passed out somewhere between the tequila shooters and the Jello shots I was spared her rendition of "The Rose."

I lifted my head and found John to the left of me. Turning back the other way, Janine was on the right. They were dead to the world. I climbed over Johnny and made my way to the bathroom. Ten minutes later I was showered, dressed in fresh jeans and an El Duderino tee shirt and on my way downstairs.

I turned on the television and caught the first wave of local news. Unhhh! There I was front and center as a recap of last night's events paraded before me. I started to

leave the room, but then the camera panned to the right
and Nick appeared on screen. I stopped in my tracks and
I'm pretty sure my heart stopped too. Resisting the urge
to French kiss the television set, I stood there staring into
the face of the man I loved.

An attack of the crazies hit me like an All Points
Bulletin. *Oh my God. I have to go to him. Right now. It's—
what—five thirty? He must be up by now. I mean how long can a
person sleep? I'll just drop in for a quick hello. After all, the man
saved my life for like the third time this week and I never even
showed my appreciation. I know! I'll take along a tray of my
mom's lasagna. After all, nothing says thank you like home baked
shoe leather.*

In my sleep deprived, hangover-altered mind, I knew
two things for sure. One, I *had* to tell Nick I loved him.
And two, if I gave myself any time to think about it I
would chicken out. I ran to the kitchen, grabbed the
lasagna and headed out the door.

It was still dark when I pulled into the loading zone.
An early morning jogger was just coming out of the
building and I squeezed on through the open security gate,
flashing him an apologetic, "I forgot my key" smile.

The elevator descended from the fourth floor. As I
waited for it to arrive I got the vague feeling that maybe I
should have called first, or better yet, stayed in bed and
waited for John and Janine to wake up so that they could
talk me out of coming altogether. But having little to no
impulse control it really wouldn't have made much
difference.

The elevator door opened and a woman stepped out.
She was about my age and very beautiful. That vague
feeling became a boulder in my chest, but I was on a

307

mission and denial is my constant companion. I got into the elevator and pressed number four.

Nick opened the door on my first knock. "Did you forget something?" he asked. "Oh," he said, smiling. "Hello angel, you're up early."

"I…um…uh…" *Oh jeez. He's naked.*

"Come on in," he said, thoroughly unselfconscious. *Well, why not? He was perfect.* "I've got to run in a minute. I have a meeting in Camden. But make yourself comfortable." Nick disappeared into the bedroom.

"No, no. That's alright," I babbled, clutching the lasagna to my chest. "You weren't expecting me. I—I should have called first."

This cannot be happening. That woman I saw obviously just left here. What nerve! He saves my life and then goes home and has sex with someone else? If he was going to have sex with anyone after shooting Ethan, it should have been me!" The boulder slipped down into my stomach and stayed there.

"Listen," I shouted, entering the living room, "I'm just going to leave the lasagna here. My mother wanted you to have it while it was still fresh." I was having a little trouble talking, what with battling hysteria and all.

I was almost back across the room when Nick returned. He had put on a pair of faded jeans and a long sleeved black tee shirt. I was dressed in a huge winter coat and shaking uncontrollably. "Are you cold?" he asked.

"No…yes…a little bit…I saw a woman coming out the elevator," I blurted out. "Did she spend the night with you?" *Oh crap, I did NOT just say that.* "I'm sorry. It is *so* not my business."

"Are you sure you're okay, angel?"

"Absolutely. I—I've got to get home. Bobby's waiting for me." *I don't know why I made that up. It was stupid, really.*

"So," he said, "you and DiCarlo are back together then?"

"Yep," I told him, digging a nice deep hole for myself. "We sure are. We're really in love." *Gaaah! I'm stealing dialogue straight from the Disney channel!* "Listen, I just came here to thank you. I really have to go."

Nick looked at me with a mixture of concern and—*fuck all*—pity. "Not just yet."

I tried to bolt but he stood in front of the door blocking my exit.

"What?"

"You're not in love with DiCarlo, Brandy."

"And how the hell would you know that?"

"Because you're in love with me," he said simply and without a shred of arrogance.

I froze. "No I'm not."

"Yes, darlin', you are."

"Nick," I groaned, too tired to deny it. "Could we just not talk about this? Could we just—not?"

He leaned in to me, cupping my chin in his hands. "Look at me, Brandy."

I shut my eyes tight, in the hopes that he'd get bored and leave.

"C'mon darlin', look at me."

I sighed and opened my eyes again.

His voice gentled. "I don't want to hurt you, angel. The truth is you're one of the few people in the world I'd call my friend. But you want me to love you and that's not going to happen. I enjoy women. I don't get attached to them. It's not in my make-up."

I nodded as the full force of his words sunk in. *Nick doesn't love me.*

When I was a little girl whenever I felt sad or hurt I'd try to fool everyone into thinking I was okay by flashing what my mom referred to as my "brave smile." I really thought that I was fooling everyone, but my mom said it was, in fact, heartbreaking. I've perfected it since then. I was sure of it. To prove this, I flashed him one now.

"It's no big deal, Nick, really. I'm fine. Just a little tired is all. Listen, I'm gonna go now. I'll make sure you get the truck back this afternoon. Thanks for the loan—and— um, I'll see you around." And with that stellar speech I burst into tears.

"Just—tired—is—all," I reiterated, feeling like a complete idiot. I pulled a wad of tissue out of my coat pocket and blew my nose.

He stood there, staring at me for what seemed like an eternity, then he checked his watch and sighed deeply. "Angel, I hate to do this to you, but I've really got to run. Stay here for as long as you need to." He pulled me to him and kissed me on the forehead. "Take care of yourself, Brandy Alexander." And he was gone.

Humiliation and a deep sense of loss washed over me and I cried myself silly. I missed him already and he was only officially out of my life for a minute and a half.

After another round of tears, I went in search of more tissue. There was probably some in the bathroom, but Nick's bedroom was the more compelling choice. I opened the door slowly, in case there was another woman in his bed that he'd forgotten to mention. It was empty. Thank God for small favors.

The early morning light cast dim shadows on the wall. The bed was rumpled and without thinking, I picked up his pillow and held it to my cheek. It smelled like Nick. *Just Nick.*

Moments passed as I stood there taking everything in, committing it all to memory. Because I knew I wouldn't be back. *Nick doesn't love me. I'm his friend, but he doesn't love me.*

I stared at the bed until snot began to drip down toward my upper lip, reminding me of why I'd come into the room in the first place. Tissue. Right. I opened the nightstand drawer and my heart lurched. Nestled between the Buddhist Bible and a nine mm Glock was a photograph. John's photograph. Of me. *Oh—My— God…*

Epilogue

"Bran, we need to talk," John said, looking serious.

It was the day after my brother officially "became a man" and John had offered to take me to lunch. We were seated at a corner table, upstairs at Ralph's Italian Restaurant, a South Philly institution. I'd ordered the Giambotte and mussels. And a side salad. And dessert. I was really hungry.

"Huh…" I said. "I'm not going to like this, am I?"

"Probably not. It's chock full of sentimental overtones."

"Oh, man," I sulked. *I should've known there was no such thing as a free lunch.* "Well, let's get it over with."

John reached across the table and took my hand. "Look, kiddo, remember when we were fifteen and I tried to tell you who I am? I was really struggling to find the words and you rescued me. You said, 'I know who you are, and I love who you are.'"

"I said that?"

"Yeah. I wrote it in my diary."

"You're such a girl," I told him and punched him in the arm with my free hand.

John sighed. "The point is you saved my life that day and I owe you the truth. Sunshine, you're a mess. You can't do this on your own and I can't help you." He tucked a folded piece of paper into my hand. "Here's the number for a very good therapist. Call her. Do it for me. Because I love who you are and I want you back."

The events of the past few months had taken such a toll on me I could barely recognize myself anymore. I wanted me back too.

I looked up at Johnny and smiled. "Okay," I said. "I'll give her a call."

CPSIA information can be obtained at www.ICGtesting.com
Printed in the USA
LVOW06s1528110913

352006LV00001B/126/P